FINAL
TARGET

Eve Seymour is the author of nine novels and has had a number of short stories broadcast on BBC Radio Devon. Educated in Malvern at a girls' boarding school, which she detested, she spectacularly underachieved. Sixth form in Cheltenham proved a lot more interesting, enjoyable and productive.

After a short and successful career in PR in London and Birmingham, she married and disappeared to Devon. Five children later, she returned and began to write seriously. In a bid to make her work as authentic as possible, she has bent the ears of numerous police officers, firearms officers, scenes of crime, the odd lawyer and United Nations personnel. She also works by day as a freelance editorial consultant, specialising in crime fiction.

Eve lives with her second husband and often has a houseful of offspring, sons-in-law, partners, and a growing tribe of little ones. Nomadic by nature, she is planning another move very soon.

🐦 @EveSeymour
www.evseymour.co.uk

D0241525

Also by E. V. Seymour

A Deadly Trade
House of Lies

FINAL TARGET

A JOSH THANE THRILLER

E. V. SEYMOUR

KILLER
READS

A division of HarperCollins*Publishers*
www.harpercollins.co.uk

Killer Reads
An imprint of HarperCollins*Publishers*
1 London Bridge Street
London SE1 9GF

www.harpercollins.co.uk

This paperback edition 2018
2

First published in Great Britain by Cutting Edge Press 2014

A catalogue record for this book is
available from the British Library

ISBN: 978-0-00-827172-5

Set in Minion by Palimpsest Book Production Limited, Falkirk, Stirlingshire

Printed and bound by CPI Group (UK) Ltd, Croydon, CR0 4YY

CHAPTER ONE

As soon as the lights went out I knew I was in trouble. Power cut, blown fuse, act of God – happens to honest folk. My dirty past ensured a different scenario. I was a cigarette paper away from a hole in the head.

Streetlight ghosting through the window made my body a perfect target. I stepped away from the door and dropped down onto the floor, belly-low. Unarmed, fear stuck like a chisel in my chest. At any second I expected the stutter of gunfire, the shatter of glass, the room stitched with metal. Game over.

Black seconds thudded past.

Killer-calm, I went through the moves. My prospective tenant hadn't yet shown. Booked through an agent, the elusive Miss Armstrong could only view my rental property after work. The lady was, allegedly, hardworking and couldn't spare time during the working day. From my new perspective on the floor, it seemed that she was the bait for someone out to get me, and there were dozens of possibilities. Odds-on my attacker was a hired assassin, someone who'd filled the void I'd left behind and, if he didn't shoot within the next five seconds, he was on his way in. I'd always preferred to get up close and personal. It was a fair bet that he was cast in the same mould.

Eyes adjusting to the darkness, I used my elbows for traction and scooted across the carpet to the kitchen. A knife offered little protection against a gun, but it made me feel more secure. It was also possible that I'd strike lucky. I didn't intend to die without a fight.

Cracking the door open, I slid inside. Windowless, the room pooled with dark, shifting shadows and that gave me an advantage. In one swift movement, I stood up, reached out, swiped the biggest knife from the block and stepped behind the door. Mute, breath sucked in, I waited.

'Hex, is that you?'

I froze, peered dead ahead, exploring the darkness. The mention of my soubriquet, known only to a favoured few, sounded at once intimate and incongruous.

'McCallen?'

'Apologies for the subterfuge.'

I don't like surprises. One moment I believe death is about to wave me through its checkpoint, the next the only woman who has ever truly fascinated me rocks up and wants to play games. Displeasure gave a cutting edge to my voice. 'Is this your idea of a joke?'

'I pretended to be your new tenant because I didn't think you'd agree to see me.'

'What about the light trick?' I hissed.

'Nothing to do with me.' The air around me parted. Citrus and sandalwood and hints of tobacco, then McCallen's breath on my face, her lips brushing my ear, then my mouth. If she'd come to kill me, I was a dead man, but at least I'd die happy. I kissed her back, long and slow. Sure, she'd rattled me, but then McCallen always did.

'Must be a power cut,' she murmured.

'You think?'

No sooner had the words left my lips than we were flooded with light. McCallen took several paces back and we blinked at

2

each other.

She looked even better in the flesh than I remembered and, if I were honest, I'd thought about her a lot in the intervening twelve months. I took a moment to appreciate her full lips, neat nose and her voluptuous figure. Her copper-coloured hair was longer. It suited her.

'Are you going to put that down?' The amusement in her green eyes implied that I'd overreacted. It wasn't as if the location was some rural backwater where power surges and consequent electricity cuts are commonplace. This was Cheltenham, big population, home of GCHQ and high tech. As far as I was concerned, the jury was still out. I don't do coincidence. What I could be certain of was that today was not my time to go.

'Old habits.' I replaced the knife in the block.

'You're looking good. More rested.'

Not one for small talk, I cut to the chase. 'How the hell did you get in?' It wasn't the most obvious question, but it was the one that sprang to my lips first.

'I'm a spook. How do you think I got in?'

'Even you can't travel through walls.'

Her mouth creased into a smile. 'You know what? I've missed you.'

Inside, I was delighted. Outside, I was Mr Cool. The rational side of my brain told me that McCallen had blagged her way back into my life for one reason only, to use me. 'And how did you track me down?'

'Joe Nathan, as you now like to be called, is not much of a stretch from Joshua Thane.'

This worried me. If McCallen had seen through it, so could others. She let out an earthy laugh. 'Honestly, Hex, you must be losing your touch. Remember the false passport you had in Barcelona?'

I sighed. My last gig. Mystery solved.

'So how's life now that you've gone respectable?'

Boring, mundane and banal. 'Terrific.'

'Managing to stay out of trouble?'

Nice try. 'Fancy a drink?' I smiled.

She smiled back. 'Why not?'

On the way out I checked the fuse box in the communal hall. No switches thrown. No evidence of trouble. Didn't mean a damn thing. If anyone had messed with the box, he'd have worn gloves.

Surrounded by chi-chi shops, the flat was off Montpellier Street and we could take our pick of bars. Finding one that wasn't rammed, even in January, required more effort. We finally commandeered a table in the window of the Montpellier Wine Bar, a popular, if expensive, hangout for Cheltenham's upwardly mobile and fashion-conscious.

McCallen took a seat and asked me to get her a vodka, 'straight with ice and a slice of lime'. In spite of her upbeat manner, I thought I caught a trace of something haunted in her eyes, and wondered how the hell I was going to disappoint her without causing offence. Whatever she'd come to ask, my answer had to be no. I'd spent too long trying to rehabilitate myself to get involved in something that might force me to cross a line again. Nice as the kiss was, I didn't believe she was after a date.

I pushed my way through to the bar, ordered a pint of lager and a double Russian Standard for McCallen, and mused on why exactly she was here with me and my newly adopted persona. Coming up empty, I paid for the drinks and returned. We chinked glasses like old friends and I settled in for the warm-up before the main act.

'Why Cheltenham?' she asked.

I'd come back home, but I didn't wish to reveal this to her, or anybody for that matter. 'As good a place as any,' I shrugged. 'Classy, friendly, full of wealthy people, not too nosey, and the architecture's impressive.'

'Of course, you're in property now.'

It sounded as though I was a major entrepreneur. I was involved to the extent that I'd bought several houses, done them up and let them out. The rise in demand for affordable rental accommodation chimed with my plans for an honest life. I was making a respectable rather than lucrative living, my blood money already given away to charities and good causes. 'Not much career opportunity for an out-of-work contract killer,' I said with a flat smile.

She shot me a stern, reproving look. 'Don't do yourself down. You redeemed yourself.'

I wished I had her certainty. Truth was, I was like an alcoholic on the 'Twelve Steps Programme'. I thanked a higher deity each day for not having to get up in the morning and kill to order. The thought of what I'd done for almost fifteen years made me feel physically sick. It mattered not that my targets were bad men, men who'd tortured and who had also employed people like me to stay on top of their criminal and grubby piles, but I'd be a liar if I said that I didn't miss the trappings of my old existence: the buzz, the lick of danger at my heels, the variety, the international travel and the feeling of power. For the past three hundred and eighty-nine days I had stayed in one place and let life haul me, one twenty-four hour set at a time. I no longer carried a gun. I'd dispensed with anything that could be reasonably called a weapon. I had walked away from the company I kept. I avoided old haunts. I wanted to tell McCallen that I'd embraced my new life with a wholehearted sense of wonder and gratitude. I couldn't quite do that yet. Yes, I had good days, but the bad 'I don't know what the fuck I'm doing' days outnumbered them. I guess it was character building and good for what passed for my sorry soul.

'You must be wondering why I've tracked you down.'

'I take it MI5 haven't sent you in an official capacity?'

She hooked me with one of her big smiles. That was the thing about McCallen – she didn't just smile with her lips, she smiled with her eyes. 'Strictly off-the-books.'

And that spelt trouble. Having lusted for McCallen for so long, I didn't like the effect she was having on my sense of purpose.

One look and she could derail me.

'I have a proposition,' she said.

'Unless it's connected to a business opportunity, I'm not interested.'

She lowered her voice. 'It doesn't involve violence.'

'What does it involve?'

'Knowledge.'

Against my best intentions, I must have conveyed curiosity. McCallen went on to explain. 'I'd like you to take a look at a set of photographs.'

I grinned, took a slug of my pint. 'Are they dirty?'

McCallen elevated an eyebrow that suggested she thought me base.

'What sort of photographs?' I was an expert in asking the obvious.

'Crime scene shots.' She reached for her bag. I stayed her arm, looked deeply into her eyes.

'No.'

'Why not?'

'Slippery slope and all that.'

'Where's the harm?'

'You wouldn't understand.'

She sat back up, sipped her vodka. In spite of the noise from the bar, we were enveloped in our own silent bubble. I'm an infinitely patient man so I can live without conversation. I can do quiet. McCallen is different.

'I'm providing you with an opportunity to do good,' she insisted.

'Nice pitch.'

'Won't you reconsider?' She turned those big green eyes on me. I wondered if I could get her beyond kissing. A steamy image of us both on a bridge in London flashed through my mind.

'Why me? You have plenty of other means at your disposal.'

'Because it's private.'

'Private or personal?'

Colour invaded her cheeks. She said nothing. The first 'tell'.

I took another drink. 'Are the police involved?'

'Yes.'

'Then let them do their job.'

'It's not that simple.'

It never was where McCallen was concerned. Ambitious, looking to the main chance, her career was as important to her as my survival was to me.

'Look, it involves three innocent people.'

'Really?' The cynicism rang clear in my voice.

'All were shot dead in the same place by the same person.'

I blinked slowly and clenched my jaw. 'Wasn't me.'

'I appreciate it wasn't you.'

Glad we'd cleared that up, I took another drink.

'You must have read about it in the news.'

'I make a point of not reading the news.' Another part of the 'weaning off' process.

At this, she broke into a wide smile. 'Even better. I was afraid you might have a preconceived view.'

'Can I ask you a question?' I realised then that I'd caved in.

'Afterwards.'

She wanted to reel me in first.

'I don't need to tell you that the identities and lifestyles of the victims will reveal far more than the crime scene,' I said.

'But the crime scene paints an interesting picture to a man of your particular talents.'

My particular talents? If only McCallen knew the whole, unvarnished truth – that I'd learnt from the very best, that my mentor had been a man who worked for Mossad, that I'd loved him as a son loves a father and that the tang of his betrayal was still sharp and bitter in my mouth. I shook my head, but my eyes failed to conceal my interest. Like a rat in for the kill, McCallen could spot weakness at fifty paces. She stood up, whisked a large brown envelope out of her bag and placed it on the table in front of me. 'I'm going to get some air. I'd appreciate it if you'd take a look and give me your honest opinion.'

'About what?'

'Anything that leaps out of the picture.'

What she meant was the sequence of events, location, and the type of individual responsible, amateur or professional.

'You're not expecting me to be able to identify the killer, are you?'

'Be good if you could, but my expectations aren't that high.'

'Thanks for the vote of confidence.'

At this, she pursed her lips and blew me a kiss.

I glanced around. I'd chosen a relatively private spot in amongst a horde of serious drinkers. Everyone seemed too intent on having a good time to bother with a guy like me. It didn't stop me from checking or watching for the sidelong look followed by the suddenly averted gaze.

'Pretend they're holiday snaps,' McCallen said, disappearing out into the night.

CHAPTER TWO

The envelope stared at me like the bad fairy at the wedding feast. I stared back, belligerent. Draining my glass, I thought about having another drink and changed my mind. I didn't know for how long McCallen intended to take the night air, but I wasn't taking risks. Scooping up the envelope, I slipped it inside my jacket and left the bar. My intention was to walk around the block and return, the envelope unopened. My subconscious had other ideas.

Letting myself back into the rental apartment only metres away, I switched on the light, poured myself a glass of water and sat down. The paper crinkled as I moved, the envelope a sharp-edged rock digging into my heart. Only photographs, the devil in my brain told me. Where's the harm? Do you really want to put yourself in temptation's way, the other part of me said, aren't you supposed to be walking away from all that? *I'm providing you with an opportunity to do good*, McCallen said. What she really meant was that I was giving her a chance to solve part of a puzzle. For some unspoken reason, she couldn't ask anyone else. I was flattered. And for reasons I hadn't yet nailed, I was more than tempted.

The devil won out.

I opened the envelope, slid out three black and whites, three identical in colour, and three close-up shots, again in colour. I laid them out in front of me like a croupier placing cards on the table, and took out my phone to capture the images. Next, using the MagniLink facility, I studied each in detail.

The first photograph provided an aerial shot of a two-lane road running through a section of dense woodland. Studying the leaves on the trees, which were oak, ash, chestnut and beech, I guessed it was taken around May or June. From the angle of the sun and hint of dew on the ground, it must have been early morning. Clearings revealed signs of human activity, animals and horse tracks, and beyond these, a criss-cross of paths and narrow roads, undoubtedly a tourist trail. As killing places went, it was an ideal location. No CCTV. With quick road access, the killer could get in and out within seconds and had plenty of cover for a speedy getaway.

On the road, a sleek-looking vehicle, a Jaguar, was positioned almost at right-angles as if the driver had changed his mind about the direction in which he was driving and had decided to turn around. Metres down the road from the Jag, most likely travelling from the opposite direction, an overturned mountain bike, top spec and only used by a serious cyclist. One body lay on the road almost underneath the bicycle. Another body hung out of the open door on the passenger side of the Jaguar. Spent cartridges littered the scene. Untidy. I'd come back to these later.

I moved on to a close-up of the Jaguar. Rounds of gunfire had extensively damaged the front and offside of the vehicle. Standard procedure: windscreen smashed, metal perforated by so many rounds that it looked like the car had been sliced open by a king-size can opener. This meant the weapon's magazine capacity was at least thirty rounds and probably fired at a rate of 700 rounds per minute, maybe more. I looked closely at the measurement of individual holes. The problem with this is that when a bullet leaves a weapon, impact changes both it and the surface with which it comes into contact. Without the actual bullet in my hand, it was difficult to estimate calibre. Clearly fired from an automatic, I reckoned it could be 9 x 19mm Parabellum, but I couldn't be exact.

The passenger door was open, the driver's door closed. Rubber marks on the road suggested that the car had moved at speed, tyres biting the asphalt in the driver's desperate bid to get out of trouble and make a fast getaway. I closed my eyes and pictured the scene: driver responds to the threat by stopping, takes fire but not enough to kill, reverses and then is felled by another round of automatic fire.

A close-up revealed the driver: her face twisted to one side, most of the top of the head removed, body slumped over the wheel, blood and brain matter decorating the expensive leather interior. Left arm extended, her hand stretched out as if trying to make contact with her male passenger one final time. Meant the relationship was close. Death conceals age to a degree, but I guessed she could have been anything between thirty-five and forty-five years of age.

Close-up of the passenger revealed that he had made some effort to flee but, caught in the spray, his upper torso was a mess of gunshot wounds. I estimated his age around the same as mine. Either way, I reckon he'd hit his thirty-third birthday. To my professional eye, the driver was first on the killer's playlist, the passenger of secondary importance.

Next up, the crime scene with the unfortunate male cyclist. The bike, keeled over on the road, trapped the cyclist's right leg. This indicated that the cyclist was facing the motorist and stationary when shot. Close examination revealed that, unlike the occupants of the car, he had been shot, at most, three times. He'd taken a bullet to the chest and one at point-blank range to the head. I suspected that this was the third in the sequence. The actual choreography would go something like this: one in the head, one in the chest, and a follow-up shot for good measure. A pathologist might state otherwise but, either way, he had been dispatched in a clinical fashion. He wasn't riddled with bullets. I imagined the cyclist's attention being attracted; maybe someone flags him down and asks for help – directions possibly – he stops to think and, before he knows it, death beckons.

I took another look at the overall shot. There were no visible tyre tracks on the verge, but the pattern of fallen cartridges told its own little tale. I frowned. My observations were so blindingly obvious; McCallen didn't need my help at all.

My mobile phone rang. It was McCallen. 'Where are you?'

'Back at the flat.'

'I'll come round.'

I let her in and she sat down opposite and let her beautiful eyes meet mine. 'Thank you.'

'For what?'

'For doing something you didn't want to do.'

I fixed her with a cool stare. 'It was pretty much a pointless exercise.'

'Why do you say that?'

'None of my observations are rocket science. Any interested amateur would draw the same conclusions.'

'Which are?'

I shook my head. 'No trade until you answer my questions.'

'Fire away.'

'Who are the couple?'

'India Griffiths-Jones and her toy boy lover Dylan Woodgate.'

'Their occupation?'

'Griffiths-Jones was a banker, Woodgate a city trader.'

'Have you followed the money trail?'

'It's clean.' She unexpectedly dropped her gaze. Meant she was lying.

I arched an eyebrow. McCallen glanced up at me with a cold

look, lips zippered. Planning to return to this point later, I pressed on.

'Where are the deceased from?'

'Griffiths-Jones, born O'Malley, is originally from Newry, Northern Ireland. Woodgate from Kent. Both worked in the City.'

'Political motivation?'

'Police considered a possible connection to the Real IRA in the early part of the investigation, but it's been discounted.'

'The relationship between the two – illicit or otherwise?'

'Smart of you.'

'That's what you expect from me, isn't it?'

She smiled. 'Illicit. Griffiths-Jones's husband had no idea about her extracurricular activities until his wife's untimely death.'

I gave my eyebrow another workout. Giving an order to kill one's spouse on account of an affair was an obvious motive for murder. I'd never got involved in domestics, but I knew men who would and did.

'He checks out,' McCallen said, attempting to head off that particular line of enquiry.

'As in, he has an alibi?' Which meant damn all in my previous line of work. Those who gave the orders were nowhere near the crime scenes and they always ensured their alibis were watertight.

'As in, he didn't do it.'

'So they simply happened to be in the wrong place at the wrong time?' I said.

'Why do you say that?'

'Because the cyclist was the target.'

'That's not what the police believe.'

'Well they're wrong. He was killed first.'

'How do you know?'

I wondered whether McCallen was really dumb or acting

dumb. Had to be the latter. 'His death was played out in a distinctly different fashion. Whereas the occupants of the car had been treated to a spray and pray approach, the cyclist was coldly and surgically removed.'

'Two killers?'

'One killer who panicked when he had company.'

'Amateur?'

I paused because I couldn't be certain. 'A professional, new to the job.'

'Does he have a signature?'

I paused for a second time. I'd always favoured a three-shot approach. One in the head, one in the body, one to finish off. Sounded gruesome now, as if it had nothing to do with me. The tops of my cheekbones flushed hot to the bone in shame. 'He didn't favour a pistol, which is highly unusual for a hit. My guess is that he used one weapon, an automatic primed to fire single shot for the original kill, then he switched to multiple fire when he ran into trouble.'

She frowned. 'Sub-machine guns are cumbersome.'

I shrugged. It depended on the weapon. The Heckler & Koch MP5K short version could easily be concealed under clothing or fired from a specially modified suitcase or bag. It had been one of my favourite methods for jobs where the target employed bodyguards. I didn't tell her this.

'There was nothing random about the hit. The killer had prior information about the cyclist's movements. Odds on, he knew that the cyclist was touring the New Forest.'

McCallen's eyes danced with interest. 'What makes you say the New Forest?'

'Ponies and donkeys.'

She didn't say yes or no, just tilted her chin.

I explained my theory, then said, 'The pattern of shell casings provides the clincher. The killer thought he'd done the business and then Mrs Banker and her lover show up. No witnesses

14

equals no loose ends.'

'Collateral damage?'

'Rules of the game. If you're good at the job you shouldn't need to indulge in it.'

'What about you?' A sudden frosty note etched her voice.

'I was good at the job.' We'd hit rocky ground so I decided to change direction. 'Who was he?'

'A German tourist.'

'Does he have a name?'

'Lars Pallenberg.'

'So what's his story?'

'He was a tourist who happened to be an artist.'

'An artist, or asset?' My expression was neutral. McCallen's answer might explain why she'd come to me and nobody else. Her kissable lips parted very slightly. Only someone familiar with her could divine that McCallen's first instinct to lie was rapidly substituted by the truth.

'Both. I was his handler.'

'Tough for you.' No intelligence officer liked having an asset bumped off. Unfortunately, it was an occupational hazard. Recruit, use and let go, Reuben my mentor, once told me. 'But there's nothing you can do about it. You simply disavow, pretend he never existed and walk away.'

'He was also a friend.'

The warmth in her eyes made me feel as if I had something cold and wet and slippery crawling through my intestines. I didn't ask the obvious question.

CHAPTER THREE

'It's not what you think.'

'You have no idea what I think.' How could she possibly know? 'Your relationships are nothing to do with me.'

She paused, cleared her throat. 'What I mean –'

'You allowed yourself to be compromised.'

She fixed me with a blizzard of green. 'The association was finished before you and I met.'

'Makes no difference to me.' For a woman who'd once implied that there could never be anything between us, I thought she was labouring a point. But then that was a woman's prerogative. 'But you're going to have to help me out. Why are you discounting the obvious? Lars got made and paid the ultimate price.'

'Maybe.'

From McCallen's monosyllabic answers, I got the impression that she was holding back. I looked at her hard. If she wanted me to help her, she'd have to trust me and tell me what the hell was going on. 'Was he vetted?'

'No.'

'You kept him secret from MI5?' I was fairly incredulous.

'Uh-huh.'

'Why?'

'I don't know.'

'I love the way you lie.'

She flinched, but didn't elaborate.

'Were you careful? Could you have been seen?' I'd always thought McCallen crazy, but there usually seemed to be an internal logic to her actions. Mixing business with pleasure, if that's what she'd done, was as dumb as it gets. She'd exposed him to danger and herself to blackmail with all types of criminal permutations in between.

'Possible, but unlikely.'

I thought about it. As an intelligence officer, McCallen could be on any number of bad guys' radar. That meant whoever was seen with her was also at potential risk. But then she already knew the score in that regard. She was the expert. I was merely an educated outsider.

'Are the police doing their job properly?'

'Yes.'

'Examining relationships and connections?'

'Uh-huh.' Her eyes met mine once more.

'Which could lead straight back to you.' And when the truth was out, her job would be on the line. Now I got it.

'Precisely.'

'Presumably you covered your tracks, gave Lars assumed code name.'

She swallowed and nodded. 'The police are concentrating their efforts on the couple, which buys me a little time.'

'Why the focus on the couple?'

'Griffiths-Jones had a large sum of money that can't be accounted for deposited in a private Swiss bank account.'

Hence her lie regarding the money trail. 'Fiddling the books?'

'That's my take.'

'White noise,' I said. 'Tell me about Lars.'

'A German national who split his time between London and Berlin.'

'So not a tourist at all.' I was surprised how easy it was to catch McCallen in another lie. Signalled she was under considerable pressure. Typically, she went all pedantic on me. 'He was touring the New Forest at the time of his death.'

'Why recruit him?' An artist didn't strike me as typical spy material. It had to be down to a connection, the company he kept. I didn't expect her to reveal operational details and, true to form, she chose her words with care. 'Let's say that the UK has seen a rise in right-wing militants. A certain group has energetic links with neo-Nazis in Germany. The latest breed are drawn from all sorts of disparate cliques: the disillusioned and unemployed, flat-earthers, anti-Muslim, anti-capitalist, anti-nuclear, anti-globalisation, animal rights activists, most without clear political aims.'

'Rent-a-mob,' I pitched in.

'We're talking the extreme end of the spectrum.'

'And Lars, where does he fit?'

'Thanks to an old art school friend, he had an in to a particular group of anarchists in Berlin who have heavy connections here.'

'Then look no further. There's your answer. He was bumped off because he got rumbled, either by his contacts in the UK or those in Germany.'

McCallen shook her head. 'Lars had bailed months before. There was no reason to kill him.'

I didn't like to point out that I'd killed men for weaker reasons. When a seriously bad guy got an idea in his head that someone was for the chop, there wasn't much that could be done to dissuade him.

'You said the association was over and that he'd extracted himself from his buddies, so what was Lars doing in Hampshire eight months ago?'

She viewed me with instant suspicion. 'How the hell do you know the timing?'

'Don't be so damn suspicious.' I indicated the aerial shot. 'I'm good with trees. If you want a nature lesson, I'm happy to give it,' I said, arch. Actually, the countryside had never done it for me, but my grandfather ensured that my Gloucestershire roots were not wasted. In later life, it had proved useful.

She looked at me a second longer than was comfortable. I'd often thought that talking to McCallen was like throwing jelly at the wall and seeing if it would stick. 'I genuinely don't know why he was in the New Forest,' she said. She looked quite unhappy. However, this time, I reckoned she was being straight with me.

'When did you last see him?'

'End of January, and once briefly two months before his death.'

'Any particular reason?'

'No,' she said, slow-eyed.

'No subsequent contact?'

'A couple of phone calls.'

'When?'

'March.'

'What did you talk about?'

'The weather.' She looked ticked off.

'Fine, don't tell me.'

Her expression told me that on this we were in agreement. 'Nothing you need to know,' she added.

'Maybe Lars wasn't what he seemed.'

'That's what I'm beginning to think.'

The penny didn't drop; two-pound coins rained down on my head. 'No,' I said. 'If you've allowed yourself to be compromised, that's your lookout. No way in hell am I going to get involved, investigate, or anything else.'

'I can't go to Berlin, but you could.'

'Which bit of my answer don't you understand? And aren't you forgetting something? One step outside the United Kingdom and a Mossad hit team will be snapping at my heels.' The shout lines of my last job boxed my ears. With McCallen's help, I'd foiled a plot to sell an ethnically specific biological weapon to an extreme fundamental terrorist group, and had killed one of my old clients, Billy Squeeze, in the process. During the fallout, it had emerged that Mossad was out to get me for an unspecified crime. I'd never properly worked it out. I might have jeopardised one of their operations by taking out a player. I might have unwittingly killed one of their informers. Whatever the detail, they'd only called their dogs off because I'd removed Billy, a man on their hit list, but I knew that it was only a temporary reprieve.

McCallen responded by doing what she does best – she threw me a curve ball. 'What if Pallenberg was killed to get to me?'

I blinked. Was this the part of the story she hadn't told me? I knew that there had to be another reason and my curiosity and lust for excitement meant that I was a millimetre from being dragged into her web. 'Why would you think that?'

'Threats.'

This was my cue to ask her to spill all. If she did, then I'd be done for. She threw me a look that could best be described as ravishingly doomed. My jaw clicked because all I really wanted to do was sweep her into my arms and tell her that I'd help in any way I could.

'Not my problem,' I said.

She stood up. 'You know how to get hold of me if you change your mind.'

'I'm not going to change my mind.'

She gave a knowing smile and left.

CHAPTER FOUR

The next morning I passed on the gym, stayed in bed longer than usual and wondered if the activities of the night before had been a dream. McCallen's anarchic reappearance had awoken long-dead emotions and knocked me off balance. Made me consider what the German had that I didn't. I let out a sigh and pressed my head deeper into the pillows in a futile effort to evade the simple truth. Lars Pallenberg had not spent fifteen years of his sorry existence knocking people off.

She had nerve, I was forced to give her that. And she knew how to get to me, the 'personal threat' argument a blinder.

I finally dislodged myself from my cosy pity, got up, showered and shaved and stared at my reflection. *You're looking good. More rested*, McCallen had remarked. My normally cropped dark hair could do with a cut. The rest of me appeared much the same: blue eyes, wide nose, high Slavic cheekbones, but I got what she meant. I'd lost the hunted look.

I dressed in a pair of jeans, open-neck shirt and sweater, black loafers. Standing in the kitchen, eating a solitary piece of toast, I looked around me. I hadn't really got the hang of homemaking. I had all the right kit, furniture in the rooms, plantation shutters on the windows, yet the deliberate absence of personal touches, anything that could betray my true identity, gave it a slightly sterile air. Occasionally I'd buy flowers – freesias, my mother's favourite – but that was about as far as my interior design went.

I gazed out of the window at a grey, wet January day that was already dark before it got going. Miserable summed it up and it reflected my mood. I might have committed to a home and car and gainful employment, but I had nobody with whom to share my life because I could never reveal my past. McCallen was the only woman who knew me well, understood the way I ticked, and McCallen was off-limits and unattainable. I was the equivalent of a city after a bomb has been dropped on it – ruined and empty.

With no particular place to be that morning, I pulled on a leather jacket and let myself out onto a street of terraced houses. Collar up, I walked with a brisk step past the watchmaker's, nodding good morning to the guy inside, and round the corner to a short row of shops, my destination the newsagents. Perhaps McCallen had a point, I reasoned, as I picked up copies of the local newspaper and a couple of broadsheets with my standard pint of milk. I couldn't keep running away from the world now that I'd made a conscious decision to reclaim it. With a particular eye for any development opportunities, I did a quick browse of the window of an estate agent. Nothing grabbing me, I went back home and soon had a mug of fresh coffee and newspapers spread out at the breakfast bar like recently received gifts.

Confronted by the usual suspects: war, economic woes, the Eurozone crisis and failures in various institutions, little seemed to have changed since I'd tuned in last. Marginally bored and about to flick to the business section, a face suddenly stared out that made me skid to attention.

Smoothing out the page, I looked into the dark, heartless eyes of the man I'd known as The Surgeon, the soubriquet

22

earned because Chester Phipps was as physically strong as an orthopaedic surgeon and as skilled at exploring human anatomy in spite of his skinny physique. It was a good picture, one of which he'd have been proud had he been alive to see it. Taken a couple of years ago, it showed him wearing an elegant navy pin-striped suit, shirt loosely open at the neck. He was seated, cigarette rakishly held between his thin fingers, legs louchely crossed, his grizzled, moustachioed features gathered tightly beneath a mane of long grey hair. Staring directly at the camera, thin and intense, he could have been an art connoisseur rather than a crime lord whose interests included, to quote the man himself, 'cocaine, crack and cunts'. A headline accompanied the photograph: 'New Killing as Turf War Escalates'.

Phipps had exited the way most bosses meet their maker, his death part of the unseemly scrabble for power in the wake of the vacuum left by Billy Squeeze, a man who once retained a formidable hold on the drugs trade, a man whose ambitions had extended to genocide, a man who had done his best to stitch me up. While alive, Billy's vicious reputation ensured that nobody dared to piss on his patch or cross him, making the ensuing jockeying for power and subsequent all-out war inevitable. I'd witnessed the destructive power of fear at close quarters. Uncertainty spawns violence. Loose associations, once tolerated, shatter into a maelstrom of killing until a new natural order is established. But The Surgeon's death had me troubled for two reasons: I'd killed Billy, and Phipps had pointed me in the right direction to enable me to carry it out.

The phone saved me from further brooding. I looked at the number and groaned.

'Yes,' I said.

'Is that Joe?'

I scratched my head. 'Yes, Dan, it's Joe.'

'We've got a problem. The toilet's blocked.'

'Again?'

'The toilet's blocked.'

'No, you dope, I meant *not again*.'

'Erm ... yeah. We've tried to sort it, but –'

'Don't touch anything. I'll be round in ten.'

I took my shit-busting kit from the garden shed and walked out of the rear gate to where I parked my Z4. Having never owned a vehicle before – cars were a perk that usually wound up crushed or destroyed – it represented one of the pleasurable upsides of going straight. Opening the boot, I threw in a beast of a plunger, a drain snake, thick rubber gloves and a pair of waterproof trousers and Wellingtons. I couldn't help but grimly observe that clearing up other people's shit, of one kind or another, was a constant refrain in my life.

My student let was in St Paul's, close to the university. As this was my third visit in as many months, I was beginning to realise that renting out property to three young men was a ridiculous idea. They had no sense of hygiene, cleanliness or financial responsibility. Without a parent in tow, they reverted to the behaviour of toddlers. Both species were messy and had a habit of staying up half the night, Dan, the eldest of the trio, being a typical specimen. Likeable, smart and easy-going, he was also an accomplished liar. The rent money was never quite available or where it should be – in my bank account – and yet he always had an entirely plausible reason for delay. I'd once facetiously suggested to him that he would make a good addition to the security services.

As soon as Dan opened the door, I was assailed by the heavy aroma of curry and body odour. Upstairs had its own peculiarly vile tang.

'It's a bit of a mess,' Dan said, as I squeezed into the narrow hall and manoeuvred my paraphernalia past a bike with a puncture in the rear wheel, a skateboard and a full-size supermarket shopping trolley. The open door to the lounge revealed upended furniture. I gingerly peeked inside and saw that one curtain was seemingly held in place by fresh air, the other lying in an exhausted heap on the floor. Carpet and every available surface lay coated in empty cans of lager, cheap cider and overflowing ashtrays. I grunted disapproval and made the mistake of walking into the kitchen.

'Jesus, when did you last wash up?'

Dan peered through a curtain of dark hair and stroked a fledgling attempt at a beard. 'I was about to start on it.'

'And the rubbish?' I stared out of the window onto a vista of bulging and split bin liners. 'We have fortnightly bin collections,' I added, piercing Dan with a look that used to reduce grown men to tears.

Dan beamed and idly scratched his rear in the region where the top of his boxers conspired with his jeans. 'No stress, Joe. Take a chill pill. Jack and Gonzo are loading all the shit up and taking it to Kingsditch later.' Kingsditch was the recycling centre.

'How? On the bus?'

'Gonzo's mum is driving down for a few days. She'll do it.'

I didn't bother to ask whether or not Gonzo's mother had been warned of the treat that lay in store on her arrival. I had a feeling that this was another product of Dan's ripe imagination. Last time they'd vacated for the holidays, I'd removed twenty-four bags of rubbish from the yard and six from an upstairs bedroom. Students.

Dan loped upstairs behind me and hovered on the landing as I pulled on my shit-clearing gear. 'It's been a bit iffy for a couple of days,' he said. 'Then it overflowed.'

I said nothing. I was busy trying to prevent my gag reflex from going into overdrive. The bathroom floor was covered with filthy water, loo roll and stools the size of elephant shit. *Iffy for a couple of days* was code for a week. It also told me something else. Nobody could have taken a bath or shower in that time.

'Where's Gonzo and Jack?' I snapped as I waded in.

'In bed.'

'Get them up.'

The note of warning in my voice had the required effect. Startled, Dan disappeared as I pushed a plunger into the toilet bowl and created a seal. Working it gently up and down to start with, I then tried a more vigorous approach, pushing the plunger and letting it suck back up in a monumental effort to dislodge whatever was causing the obstruction.

Two sets of sleepy eyes appeared at the doorway, a general fug of unwashed youth melding with the odour of faeces. Nice.

'Man,' Jack said, lazily scratching an armpit. Gonzo didn't say a word, just stood slack-jawed, as though an alien had appeared in his midst.

'Go to the kitchen,' I said. 'Fill up a bucket of hot water and put two parts disinfectant in it. Bring it back with a mop. Either of you own a pair of flip-flops?' Of course they did. Teenage boys spent their entire lives in them even when it was snowing.

'Yeah. And?'

Gonzo's upward inflexion and dismissive delivery suggested that he thought me cracked. I fixed him with a particularly menacing expression from my repertoire. 'Get them.'

Both lads gawped at each other and shambled off. I continued working the plunger. Nothing budged. Time for the snake.

Dan had reappeared at the doorway and I asked him to pass me the drain snake, a wire coil with a corkscrew tip. On a previous occasion, I'd used a wire coat hanger and dislodged a hairbrush. If the snake failed, I'd have to remove the toilet, not something I was keen to do.

Feeding the snake into the opening, I wiggled it around the S-bend, the place where most blockages occur. Sure enough, and with a sense of eureka, I bumped up against something spongy, like a cushion or piece of foam rubber. Twisting the coil, I drilled in, gained purchase and yanked, the accompanying sound of water draining assuring me I'd literally hit pay dirt.

A plunge bra with enough padding to guarantee the appearance of a 38DD clung to the end of the snake. 'Yours?' I said, looking at all three youths.

'Fuck,' Dan said, clearly lost for a more articulate response.

'Must be Mandy's,' Gonzo said.

'Yeah, but how did it get there?' Jack laughed, the others joining in, doubled up and helpless.

I didn't see the funny side. 'Perhaps you'd like to tell her that real tits are nicer than fake.' With this, I sloshed out of the bathroom. 'Over to you, big man,' I told Gonzo as I pulled off my boots. 'In there with the mop and bucket.'

'Aw shit, man.'

Resisting the temptation to come back with a laconic response, I threw my next order at Dan and Jack. 'And you two needn't stand around pissing yourselves. You're on washing-up duty.'

It took them the best part of two and a half hours, and only because Gonzo's mother turned up and helped. Wondering about what my life had become, I drove back home feeling grim and flat, like a puppet with its strings cut. In an attempt to bat off a fresh wave of utter pointlessness, I took another shower, cracked open a cheeky beer, and resumed reading. Big mistake. Everything about Chester Phipps's death bothered me.

In common with most 'big men', Phipps was into security. He had a couple of bodyguards with him at all times. He rarely drove, preferring a trusted driver. His food was checked. He never went anywhere without having the location swept for listening devices, weapons or explosives. A man rarely alone, the only exception was when he was screwing, which Phipps, again in common with the breed, did quite a lot. He oozed a rare, potent mix of sexuality and intelligence that women found bewitching. The fact he was also extremely dangerous added to the allure. Notwithstanding this, he always had a man posted outside the door of every place where he hung his hat. So how come he'd wound up alone in his car with a bullet in his temple? Surely, in the wake of Billy's demise, a guy like Phipps would take special measures? The more I thought about it, the less sense it made. In the old days, I'd have asked around, but that time was past and I couldn't afford to take a risk. And that was the problem with my life. Deprived of danger, I ceased to be.

I made myself a sandwich and ate it while reading the business section. I washed up the plate, set it on the drainer and considered any number of tasks that could gainfully engage my time. Maybe I'd go for a walk, catch a film, prop up any one of a number of bars and play anonymous.

I did none of these things.

I picked up the phone and punched in McCallen's number.

CHAPTER FIVE

'Are you in trouble?'

'Part of the job description.' Her flippant response did not answer my question. If she wanted me to play ball, she'd have to do better.

'I can't help if I don't know what I'm dealing with exactly.'

Nothing gave. Maybe she was thinking. Maybe she was asleep. I tried again.

'You implied that Lars was threatened. Like to explain?'

She paused, as if weighing up how much to divulge before taking the plunge. 'He thought he was being followed and believed that his phone was tapped. Someone broke into his house in London.'

'Little things.' I hoped to get a lot more out of her now that we were safely separated by a telephone line.

'I reckoned he was paranoid. It happens sometimes when assets lose their bottle.'

'But he wasn't.'

'No,' she said quietly.

'Anything else you'd like to tell me?' Confess to, admit to, and tell the truth about, I thought.

'Someone tried to push him underneath a train on the

Underground.'

Breath ripped out of my lungs. I wanted to ask her to repeat what she'd said, but I didn't need to. I'd heard it right the first time. The train trick was the same method I'd used to kill Billy Squeeze. McCallen knew this. I thought she might openly say so. She didn't. Was someone imitating my methods? Was I seeing patterns and connections that didn't exist?

'Did he see who it was?'

'It happened too quickly. A commuter grabbed him and undoubtedly saved his life. It really put the wind up him.'

And me. This piece of news demanded a step change in my thinking. I wondered whether to tell McCallen about Chester Phipps. McCallen was still speaking.

'Afterwards I couldn't shake Lars off. He was becoming a liability.'

Hardly the odd phone call, I thought, remembering our previous conversation. 'Remind me of the timeline again.'

'From the end of January until a few days before he died.' Which wasn't what she'd originally told me. I almost missed what she said next because I was too wrapped up in the Billy death scenario. 'We spoke often on the phone. I met him in person twice.'

'Where?'

'Remote locations. He insisted on it.'

'You should have cut off all contact.' Basic procedure.

'Fortunately for me I did, which was why I didn't keep the appointment.'

Something snagged inside me. 'You were supposed to meet him on the day he died?'

'Yes.'

'In the New Forest?'

'Uh-huh.'

'Have you considered the possibility that Lars could have been faking it? You had no independent evidence that the threats to him were real.'

'Correct.'

'Can I ask you something?'

'Sure.'

'The post-mortem on Lars Pallenberg.'

'What about it?'

'Was there any reference to the amount of adrenalin in his system?'

'No.'

Had there been, it would suggest that Lars had known his killer and knew what was about to take place. It indicated to me that Lars had no clue that he was about to be killed. It was all over and done with in moments, which was as it should be with a professional hit. There was an alternative scenario. A distant yet familiar sound, like the echo of ancient gunfire, rattled through my brain.

'Do you think he deliberately set out to trap you?'

'I don't know. Maybe. Either way, he was clearly deemed expendable.'

'It explains why the killer took a heavy-duty weapon with him instead of a simple handgun.'

'Because Lars was meant to be eliminated after I'd been taken care of.'

This meant McCallen was on someone's death list, that her interest in her asset's killer was of secondary importance. Her real concern stemmed from the danger to herself.

'Do you have a file on Pallenberg – background, family ties, friends and so on?'

'Yes.'

'Can I see it?'

'Depends.'

Caught in the grind, I'd spoken before I'd had a proper chance to think through the full implications. 'Can you get me a false passport?'

'I can even arrange the flights.'

CHAPTER SIX

I flew to Berlin four days later.

After landing at Tempelhof I took a cab ride, courtesy of a Turkish driver who ran red lights and had a death wish, and booked into a modest hotel in Friedrichstrasse, close to Unter Den Linden. I'd changed my appearance by bleaching my dark hair blond and wearing a pair of fashionably oversized glasses with clear lenses. I wore a navy suit, shirt, no tie, and a wool blend overcoat with velvet revere collar favoured by bankers and high-end estate agents. Playing by Moscow Rules, the highest level of tradecraft, I checked the lobby to make sure that nobody struck a discordant note. It was just me and two receptionists – one male, one female.

The Israelis are the best in the business but I believed that, even if they cottoned on to my new whereabouts, I'd be long gone before they got a bead on me. At least that's what I hoped. To be safe, once I'd entered my room, I checked it for listening devices and explosives, starting at the door, including the lock, and making a close examination of the carpet, ceiling, window and, Mossad's speciality, the telephone. I did the same in the bathroom. Afterwards, I measured the distance from the second floor to the ground below and mapped out an escape route. If I ran into trouble on this excursion, there would be no help from Messrs Heckler & Koch. I was flying solo.

Satisfied with the room, I took out the file and recommitted to memory what passed for an obituary on Lars Pallenberg. I freely admit that he was not what I expected. For a start, he had blond hair and looked more like an economics lecturer than an artist. Fine-boned, he had blue eyes, even features and a reflective expression suggesting that he was a man of intelligence and given to introspection. I guessed he was a sensitive soul. Is this what had turned McCallen on? If so, it put me out of the running. Probably my height, around five eleven, Pallenberg did not look particularly fit or like the kind of guy who worked out. Standing still and lifting a paintbrush is not the same as moving fast and lifting a semi-automatic.

McCallen had also thoughtfully provided me with a rundown of Dieter Benz, Pallenberg's old art school friend and right-wing agitator. Sleepy-eyed, with the dissolute appearance of a habitual drug user, his expression concealed ruthless intelligence. He'd been arrested countless times for racial abuse and incitement to violence against foreigners. This was the peripheral stuff. Security services suspected that he was plotting a campaign of terror, targets and locations unspecified. Reading his profile, it seemed to me that Benz had retro leanings, harking back to the 1970s and 'golden age' of the Baader-Meinhof group. I could see how men like him drew parallels. Replace the opposition to the war in Vietnam with the war in Afghanistan; disgust with rampant capitalism, evidenced by a number of spectacular bank raids at the time, with the current crisis in the banking system. Hatred of Jews was also on his agenda, but added to his hate-list were immigrants of any persuasion, and Muslims. Germany had done its fair share to offer sanctuary to others. It hadn't always gone as smoothly as it might. The average German was sick of propping up sick European states so, for Benz, part of his pitch was an easy play to a disgruntled German electorate.

Once I'd got everything straight in my mind, I called Pallenberg's grieving family. A woman, who I assumed was Gisela Pallenberg – Lars's mother – answered the phone in German. I started off by asking whether she spoke English.

'*Ja*, a little.'

'My name is Stephen Porter. I knew Lars well.'

'An English friend?' Surprise, then hope, flared in her voice.

'I've been travelling through Russia for the past few months and have only recently heard the news of his death.'

'We are so terribly shocked. We still don't really know what happened.'

'Would it be possible for me to come and visit?'

'You are here in Berlin?'

'For a few days, yes.'

'Then you must come. Can you visit tomorrow?'

'Of course, what time?'

'Wait one moment.'

I listened to a muffled exchange that grew in sound and clarity. A man came on the line, Werner Pallenberg, I guessed, his delivery gruff and final. 'Mr Porter?'

'Yes.'

'My wife is mistaken. We have no wish to see you.'

'But –'

'That's all we have to say. Goodbye.'

I don't easily do 'no'. Had Mrs Pallenberg opened her heart to me, I'd have respected the woman's sensibilities and taken the next flight back. But she hadn't. She'd been overruled.

The next morning I took breakfast in the hotel dining room and around ten o'clock stepped out onto the street and headed towards Unter den Linden under a chilly, two-tone sky. Like a greyhound released from its trap, I buzzed with excitement. It was good to be out and about in a city that was foreign, yet familiar to me, and I quickly made my way down what was arguably the most famous street in Berlin. Here, statues stared down from the tops of buildings like Roman gods watching over the mortals below. Heading east, I crossed over where the River Spree intersects and passed the Marienkirche, a lonely church overshadowed by its near neighbour, the Fernsehturm, or Television Tower, on my right.

Most of Berlin is clean and free from litter but there are odd pockets of resistance. Karl-Liebnecht-Strasse is a busy road flanked by large, unattractive grey buildings, like old containers rusting away, covered in graffiti and in the process of demolition. Whether it was the grim reminder of a city torn in two by checkpoints, Cold War politics and casual brutality, or the fact that the air temperature had dipped, I felt a sudden stutter of unease.

Stopping suddenly, as if I'd forgotten something, I twisted around, taking a long look back. A group of Chinese students, with a guide in tow, headed my way. Beyond, male and female pedestrians, young and old. Nobody looked shifty or out of place, or interested in me. No one had a suspect comma, or listening device in their ear, or talked into their cuff, or muttered to themselves or others. A glance at the road revealed nothing I didn't already know. I could have put my anxiety down to a sudden attack of nerves. I'd been out of the game for over a year. I no longer carried. I was out of my comfort zone. But my instincts are strong and, for reasons I didn't like to consider, my foe-detector was on high alert. Rattled, I headed straight to the nearest café.

It was dark, ratty and mostly empty. I took a table right at the back, near a fire exit, and with a good view of the door. In true Germanic fashion, a jolly, dark-haired waiter with a round face and excellent English appeared. I ordered coffee and cake and, under the guise of studying the menu, watched for anyone entering the premises. Apart from a young mother pushing a child in a buggy who came in a few moments later, the only customers were me and another guy finishing a meal. I started to chill and my order arrived.

'There you go, sir. Are you visiting for the first time?'

'No.'

'You have business here?'

I glanced up, met the young waiter's eye, and cast him the type of look that would silence a comedian on amphetamines. He got the message and scurried off.

The coffee was good – strong and bitter – the cake, which came in the form of a doughnut, less so. I ate, drank and thought about what had happened. Except, nothing had happened. I'd got spooked, that was all. My mind switched to McCallen. What exactly had she got me into?

It's almost impossible to know a person completely. People are strange by definition. I knew bits about her, maybe more than some, her spy status making her remote and maddeningly unreachable. But one thing I knew for sure, McCallen always had a hidden agenda. She'd be looking at you one way with those big green eyes while her feet pointed in another direction. Had she been foolish enough to mention my leave of absence to someone she shouldn't? Was she in cahoots with Mossad? If she saw a way to advance her career, she'd have no hesitation in shopping me.

I paid and, glancing both ways, set off. The two-tone sky had decided to snow and I rolled up the collar of my jacket.

Pallenberg's grieving family lived in Prenzlauer Berg, a recently gentrified area of Berlin short on accommodation and big on bars and cafés. Artists and writers had once monopolised the area, but in the wake of redevelopment, the hard core had fled to other areas like Friedrichshain and the Turkish enclave of Kreuzberg. In recent years, Prenzlauer Berg had become a magnet for young professionals seduced by wide-open green spaces and contemporary architecture. Conversely, it had also been the target for a spate of arson attacks, a case of the 'have-nots' rising up against the 'haves', the latter eager to dance to a man like Dieter Benz's anti-immigrant, racist tune.

My destination was a renovated factory divided into apartments. Crossing a park and threading my way through a couple of squares, I appreciated the appeal of the area. Wide streets, galleries and cafés gave the location an arty, open vibe, the odd building waiting patiently to be restored like a rotten tooth in a set of perfectly maintained molars.

Snow gusting around me, I hurried towards a glass-fronted building with loft-style architecture, including a community rooftop terrace and traditional Berlin balconies with granite windowsills. I imagined an interior of light oak parquet flooring, and white and chrome state of the art sanitary ware.

Inside the main entrance, I took an elevator to the third floor. I was hoping to get lucky and catch Mrs Pallenberg at home while her husband was at work. Stepping out, I almost collided with a young woman.

'Sorry.' With a heavy German accent, she spoke in English, which immediately got my attention. Small, petite, with big eyes the colour of tannin and a sweetly dimpled chin, she appraised me with a smile, as if she knew me. Did I have a label plastered on my forehead?

'Should I know you?' I said.

She flashed another smile. 'You're Stephen, aren't you? Stephen Porter?'

'Lars's friend, yes.' My mind teemed with possibilities, McCallen setting me up the clear favourite. Was it possible that this small creature in her pixie boots, layered clothing and suspiciously easy smile was about to take me out?

'Mathilde Brommer,' she said. 'I'd hoped you'd show.'

I can usually cover my feelings well, but my guard was down. Call it stranger in a strange land syndrome. Mathilde glanced over her shoulder. 'You'll never get in. Werner is very protective of his wife. They've had a bad time with the press, you see.'

'I understand, and Mr Pallenberg, is he at home now?'

'Ja.'

'Right,' I said. Inside, I was uncertain. Outside, I maintained eye contact.

Mathilde tilted her head. Her shoulder-length wavy hair fell to one side, her exotic scent circling me like smoke around a fire. 'I don't remember Lars talking about you.'

'We met in London.'

'You're an artist?'

'I sell art. I'm a dealer.'

'Then you must know Lorna Spencer, his agent.'

'Of course.' Lorna Spencer was the name assumed by McCallen. 'Are you an artist too?'

The smile faded a little. 'Yes, didn't Lars tell you?'

'I have a terrible memory,' I said, apologetically. 'I don't remember him mentioning you.'

Pain invaded her pixie features. 'We were engaged.' She flushed deeply. 'Didn't you know he dumped me so that he could marry Lorna Spencer?'

CHAPTER SEVEN

'Do you have time for lunch?' It was the best I could come up with in the circumstances. Underneath, I was furious. McCallen had put my life at risk so that I could investigate her dead lover. Marriage, for Chrissakes. A huge part of me wanted to knock this business on the head and catch the next flight back.

'Sure,' she said.

Mathilde took me to a bar off Kollwitzplatz. Dark and cavernous, with orange and brown furnishings, it was populated by an eclectic crowd of students noisily playing ping-pong on an old table, 'arty' types and, as Mathilde described them, 'anarcho-punks'. I must have been the oldest there. Techno music popped out of the speakers, not enough to deafen, just enough to annoy, but the beer on tap was good and I badly needed a drink. Mathilde ordered Augustiner, a beer brewed in Munich, and plates of garlic sausage with fried potatoes.

'How long were you with Lars?' I said.

'We met when I was twenty. Love at first sight, or so I thought.' She frowned and her eyes darkened.

'Don't let the break-up trash your memories.'

She flicked a sad, grateful little smile. 'We moved in together after three months and for the next ten years were inseparable.'

'Until his move to London?'

'*Ja.*'

'Which was?'

'Three years ago. In the beginning, I'd fly back and forth, but he became evasive and secretive, which wasn't like him at all. He was always so honest and open. I put it down to his increasing success and new circle of friends.'

'He was hanging out with …' I broke off, as if searching for the right description.

'A lot of wealthy types with ambitious plans for him,' Mathilde stepped in. 'I knew straightaway that something was wrong.'

'Because it was out of character?'

'Totally. Lars has always been so grounded. He had nothing in common with those people.'

'What about his friendship with Dieter Benz?'

Mathilde's eyes widened in surprise. 'What friendship? Lars told you about Dieter?' She stared at me as if I'd suddenly found the ability to speak fluent German.

'You knew him?'

'Everyone knows him. Dieter was and always will be a creep.'

'And a revolutionary, according to Lars.'

Mathilde's face screwed up in disgust. 'Dieter casts himself as a romantic freedom fighter, a nationalist. It is easy, is it not, in these uncertain times, to assume such roles?'

'So why was Lars involved with Dieter?'

'He wasn't,' she said, suddenly angry. 'Lars loathed Dieter. He thought he was cunning and untrustworthy.'

'Lars shared his radical ideas.' I was running on fumes with this.

'That's crap. Lars didn't have a political bone in his body.'

'Are you sure about that?'

Mathilde looked at me with a mixture of suspicion and derision. 'How long did you know him?'

I shrugged. It was a fair point. Silence opened up between

us. It gave me time to think. I'd pushed her hard because this woman had known Lars well. She knew his beliefs and what he stood for. Lars would have to be highly motivated to take the type of risks McCallen demanded of him. Penetrating a right-wing group prone to violence led by someone like Benz required nerve and skill, and Lars didn't sound the type or up to the mark. I wondered in fairly graphic detail what McCallen had done to corrupt and charm Lars into doing her dirty work.

Mathilde took a long drink of beer. Her hand shook and the bangles on her wrist rattled. She looked away then looked back, as if gathering herself.

The food arrived. Mathilde picked up a fork and speared a piece of sausage. 'Gisela mentioned that you were in Russia when Lars was killed.'

I took a mouthful, chewed and swallowed. 'I travel often to St Petersburg. I'm principally interested in iconic art, although I have a number of artists with whom I do business who paint other forms. They get a better price through me,' I explained. 'What type of art do you do?'

'Conceptual.' To me, this meant a pile of bricks, stuffed fish and dirty knickers. Mathilde rummaged through her bag and rooted out a typically arty business card and handed it to me. I made a play of studying it. 'Different from Lars, then.' I'd checked him out. He'd specialised in exquisite figurative work, women in all shapes and sizes, beautiful, some exotic, each oozing sexuality, stuff I could get my head around and wouldn't mind hanging on my walls. I briefly wondered whether McCallen had posed for him.

A fleeting smile touched Mathilde's lips. 'He was extremely talented.'

I pocketed the card, left another pause, hoping that she would reveal a detail that would help clear the fog in my head. She didn't. I continued to eat. The dish was flavoursome and earthy, like McCallen's laugh. Hell, was I going to corner her when I got back.

Eventually, I rolled the conversation on once more. 'You remain close to the Pallenbergs?'

'I do.' Her voice trailed. I could see that she remained deeply hurt by what had happened to her.

'I'm sorry.' And I genuinely was.

She shot me an angry glance. 'You know the damn woman never even made it to his funeral?' She meant McCallen.

'I didn't know that.' It sounded thin. I knew it. She knew it. The smiley exterior slipped.

'How well do you know Miss Spencer?'

'I know her professionally, nothing more. She'd passed on several of Lars's paintings to me. It's how I originally met him.'

'Which pieces of work?' There was a suspicious light in her eyes. And she wasn't buying Lars's 'caught in crossfire' death any more than the rest of us. She wasn't buying me either. I reeled off the titles itemised in the file.

'She is who she says she is?' Mathilde threw me a fierce look.

I blinked and remained impassive. 'Who?'

'Lorna Spencer.'

'I don't understand.' My fork was poised mid-air as I gave my best impression of confusion. To be honest, it wasn't much of a stretch.

'She looks good on paper, but that's it,' Mathilde said with venom. 'The art world is small. Nobody I know has ever heard of her.'

I forced a smile. 'I assure you, her credentials are sound.'

Her eyes met mine. She didn't say it but I knew what she was thinking: *How good are yours?* I leant towards her.

'What do you think really happened to Lars?'

'She bewitched him.'

I understood. I'd been fairly bewitched myself and that was dangerous. Emotions kill.

Mathilde looked around the bar, dropped her voice a note.

'She got him involved in something, something that led to his murder,' she hissed.

I put down my knife and fork. 'That's a fairly heavy statement.'

She smiled without warmth. 'How else do you explain his death?'

'He got unlucky. The banker was the prime target, I understand.'

She cast me a look that was cool and bitter. 'Did you know that Lars was afraid for his life?'

'No.'

'*Ach*, of course, you were away.'

In spite of her German intonation, I detected sarcasm. 'He spoke to you about it?'

She nodded. 'None of it made sense. He claimed that someone had stolen stuff from his studio in Berlin and that he was being followed.'

'Here?'

'In London.'

'Did he say who by?'

'It was more a feeling he had.' She pushed her plate away. She'd hardly touched the food. 'One night he phoned and told me that someone had tried to kill him on the Underground. I wondered if he'd been smoking too much weed.'

So Lars wasn't lying. I floated my next question as though it was an interesting hypothesis. 'Do you think Benz is connected to his death?'

Shock flashed across her face. 'Why must you persist with this ...' She broke off, searching for the word, '... this absurdity? You have an English saying, "thinking outside the box". Lars was a man who thought creatively. Lars had no interest in politics. He found it a distraction. Art was everything to him. At least, it used to be,' she said, with a sigh of unhappiness.

I finished my plate of food, drained my drink. 'Do you know where I can find Dieter Benz?'

She flicked the fingers in a gesture of frustration.

'Please, Mathilde, I'd like to help you.'

'Help me do what?'

'Find Lars's killer.'

She leant across the table. 'What's it to you?'

'Call it justice, a British sense of fair play. The police are looking in the wrong direction.'

'I agree.' She eyed me carefully for a moment then picked up the fork and idly pushed the congealed remains around the plate.

'You can meet Dieter in person,' she said with an empty smile. 'He is holding a rally tomorrow morning in Alexanderplatz.'

CHAPTER EIGHT

Benz had dreads and looked older in the flesh than his thirty-four years, even from a distance.

Bone-cold, I'd followed a procession of around four hundred people – young, middle-aged and old – from Alexanderplatz to the Brandenburg Gate. You didn't have to speak German to understand what they were chanting. Many held 'Pro-Deutschland' banners, and anti-Muslim slogans with 'Stop Islamiserung!' One guy brandished what looked like a red traffic sign with a symbol of a mosque on it, crossed out in black. He had a big belly, white hair and venom in his eyes. I didn't like these people. It seemed I was in good company. Most passers-by spurned offers of leaflets by screwing them up and dumping them on the road.

I clapped my gloved hands together and narrowed my gaze against a fine film of sleet. Up ahead a small platform had been erected and Benz, with a group of shaven-headed heavies in front of him, blasted away through a megaphone. To my British ears, he sounded unhinged, but the assembled seemed to like him – lots of grunts of approval, knowing nods and the odd cheer. This was no French affair, with water cannon and riot police and flying fists. Despite the verbal trash and racist views on offer, everyone was polite and well behaved, maybe because of the chill wind factor and a sky sheeting snow, or because cops in khaki lined the route. Having a deep-seated aversion to the law, I burrowed deeper into the crowd. I wasn't happy. If anything kicked off, I'd be caught in the crush.

I was just mapping how I could creep closer to the action when I became acutely aware that the mood music had suddenly changed. Familiar with trouble, I knew how to read the signs. Benz's diatribe had increased in volume. The cops, with their watchful eyes and neutral expressions, stirred as one. Mounted police and guys in black with white helmets and visors – the riot police – emerged out of nowhere. Police dogs, not in evidence before, barked with the type of intensity that says *I am going to rip your head off.* The crowd, which had been largely dormant, collectively woke up. It was positively tribal. I craned my neck. Other voices, other faces and bodies flooded in from Strasse des 17 Juni, ironically named after a bloody uprising, as a counter-demonstration of Turks and others took to the street. Fuck.

Riots have a peculiar kinetic energy all their own. Scuffles will often break out on the fringes of a big crowd and large groups will sheer off and clash head-on with others. But at its core, a big bunch of people throbs with accumulated heat and violence. In that dark second, I felt as if my life was in imminent danger.

In mindless confusion, we moved as one. The lucky ones got knocked and jostled; those who weren't were done for. Staying upright was my main preoccupation as the baying crowd surged forward, funnelling in one ugly direction amid screams and shouts and the clatter of horses' hooves, policeman shouting, helicopters circling.

Something hit me hard on the back of my head. My teeth rattled. Warm blood trickled down into my collar. A huge man with wide, terrified eyes gripped my elbow for balance, almost knocking me to the ground. Trapped, I needed to escape and escape quickly, but I could hardly breathe for people, moving human flesh and the collective body odour of fear. Any attempt to push my way through, to catch the slipstream, seemed doomed. Instead, I bowled along, letting the flow take me, like an uprooted tree caught in a river torrent.

People went down. Other people trampled them, their hand-bags and footwear scattered like unspent grenades. I grabbed a young guy who'd lost his footing, set him straight and kept him moving, one fluid motion. The noise was deafening. Terror stalked the streets, ugly and loud.

I estimated that at any moment now CS gas would make an entrance. Bang on cue, my eyes burned with stinging heat. I was breathing in tight bursts, wheezing and coughing as an acrid cloud of tear gas burst above our heads. By some miracle, I kept in motion, with no idea where I was heading. It was like being trapped in a smoke-filled room with all your bearings gone.

Snow fell in big heavy flakes. It was treacherous under foot. The looks on people's faces reminded me of one of those weird paintings of chaos by Bosch or Blake. I couldn't work out how this would end, only that there would be a heavy price to pay in blood and injury. I didn't know whether German police had adopted the very British habit of 'kettling'. I didn't know if there was method in the madness. All I knew was that I was not in control, and for a man accustomed to calling the shots – no pun intended – this was bad news.

Looking up, I caught sight of the pentagonal-shaped exterior of the Philharmonic and Chamber Music Hall. We were moving west, towards Potsdamer Platz. Then, without warning, the depth of people abruptly thinned, and I and another guy made a break for it, popping to the surface after being caught in the deep. It felt good. I felt loose and free. As I looked about me, a thin malicious whistle of cold air passed by my left ear, followed by a dull thud.

I glanced down. Red so bright that it hurt my eyes stained

the fallen snow. The guy next to me was on the ground, sprawled in a way I instantly recognised. Eyes open. Body twisted. Blood spreading out and pooled around his head from where a bullet had passed through the base of his skull.

A bullet meant for me.

Fear briefly stammered in my chest. Fear is good. It proves you're not stupid. Screams and shouts sliced through the cold. The cute move would mean another gunman up ahead, the same way a bomber sets off a secondary device to catch those fleeing the first blast. I didn't waste time searching for the shooter. I didn't wait for the cops. I didn't even pause to breathe.

I ran.

CHAPTER NINE

I didn't return to the hotel. It took me two hours to fight my way through a lockdown of the city centre and bribe a taxi driver to drive with all speed to the airport. He could run as many red lights as he wished.

Lady Luck on my side, I caught the next flight to Bristol. I'd have gladly flown to anywhere in the British Isles. As certain of the intentions of my fellow passengers as I could be, I settled back in my seat, a large gin and tonic to hand, my brain hissing with numerous possibilities.

These were: McCallen had tipped off Mossad; McCallen, through her connections, had unwittingly turned the spotlight on me; McCallen, for reasons best known to her, had me targeted deliberately; Mathilde had been got at, either by Benz or persons unknown, or someone from my past had taken an opportunistic pot shot.

I took a deep drink, savoured the bite of gin at the back of my throat and swallowed. Mossad didn't stack up for one blindingly good reason. They don't miss. Added to this, the technique was crass. They'd never take such a risk in a public place, with the possibility of innocent casualties. If they wanted me removed, it would be my body lying in the dirt, thanks to a poisoned hypodermic, or another less high-vis method.

This did not let McCallen off the hook. She'd got me into this imbroglio in the same way she'd entangled Lars Pallenberg. Whether or not she'd deliberately set me up I didn't know. Trust was in short supply where I came from. My pathological distrust of others had saved my life on more than one occasion. I wanted to believe McCallen for all the obvious reasons, but I couldn't swear on my heart that she was worthy of it, and I was still angry with her for deceiving me about her relationship with Pallenberg. A guy doesn't propose to a woman with whom he hasn't had a close and intimate relationship, especially when he's ditching the girl he was supposed to marry. Neither does he set her up to be killed, I had to concede.

Unless it was part of a double-cross.

I took another huge gulp of gin. Someone could have seen me with Mathilde, perhaps at the restaurant, and made the connection. The thought of her being threatened clawed at my gut. I supposed it was possible she could have stage-managed my removal, but she'd had little time to make the necessary arrangements and her exact motivation eluded me.

I stared out of the window at the grey light, its impenetrability mirroring the opaque nature of McCallen's agenda. Unable to break through, I set it aside and, out of professional interest, concentrated on the method of the most recent attempted hit on me.

On the surface, it appeared opportunistic – reckless even – but it could have also been a carefully planned operation, the chaos of the demonstration a cover for cold-blooded murder. Clearly, the killer had estimated his chances and thought he could pull it off. Killing in a crowd wasn't a method I favoured, the one exception a nightclub hit, but the weapon for me was always a ring-gun. It meant you had to get up close and personal, preferably with your ring finger placed hard against the base of the skull of the intended target. It meant there was no room for error.

It meant you did not jeopardise the lives of others. A shot from a gun would never figure as an option, the possibility of hitting the wrong individual – as had happened in Berlin – too great.

Or, at least, that's what I believed had happened.

In a more relaxed frame of mind, I had to admit that the guy standing next to me could have been the intended victim. Maybe he had a dirty past, links to a criminal network, had failed to pay a debt, crossed someone up … the list was endless.

Who was I kidding?

All roads led back to McCallen. She featured in three of my five possibilities, however outlandish those possibilities were. Whether she was guilty or not, she knew an awful lot more than she had been willing to tell me. As soon as I got back to safety, I intended to find out precisely what that was.

* * *

Customs waved me through without a hitch and I picked up the car and travelled back to the place I now called home. It was dark and I was tired, the perfect set of circumstances to get you slotted. To be on the safe side, I checked before entry and on entry. I double-checked the downstairs basement room that doubled as an office and spare room for stores and laundry, the mid-floor sitting room cum dining room and the kitchen and the upper storey bedrooms, two mid-size, one large enough to imprison an unwelcome guest. Next, I showered, fixed myself something to eat and caught News 24. It emerged that the German national killed in Berlin was a train driver. The Germans were keeping schtum, but the investigation, for obvious reasons, was heading in a political, right wing, nationalist direction. Which suited me. It also suited the killer.

Within minutes, my mobile phone rang. It was McCallen.

'Are you all right?'

'Never better.'

'The guy shot in Berlin –'

'What of it?'

'Were you there?'

'Why would you think that?'

'Shootings in broad daylight on a Berlin street are rare.'

'You think I'm responsible?'

'No,' she said, steely. 'I simply thought you might be following up the Benz connection.'

McCallen never 'simply' thought anything. 'Did you now?'

'Why are you so pissed off?'

'I was an inch from having a hole blasted through my brain, and it's your fault that I came here in the first place.' I wasn't going to tell her that I was sitting at home on my comfortable leather sofa, feet up, with a beer. If she were as good at her job as I knew her to be, she'd already have checked the airport manifests.

'You can't think I set you up.'

'I can think what I like.'

'Hex, for God's sake. Look, where are you exactly?'

'You think I'm stupid as well as reckless?'

She let her voice drop to a sexy growl. 'I have never thought you stupid.'

Wise woman. I remained impervious to her flattery.

'Can we meet?' she said.

'I think we should.'

'When?'

'Tomorrow morning in Cheltenham.'

She was silent a moment, obviously working out how I could so confidently announce that I'd be happy to see her so soon in the UK.

'The Queen's, for coffee?' she said.

One of the oldest and swankiest establishments in town, it overlooked Imperial Gardens and the Promenade and had recently undergone a makeover. Seemed an odd choice to me.

She must have picked up on my reluctance. She attempted to persuade me.

'All spies meet in hotels.'

I visualised her arching a teasing eyebrow. 'I'm not a spy.' I didn't care for the hotel idea. In the serene splendour of the Queen's, it would be impossible to raise my voice, threaten, get down and dirty or extract the kind of answers I was looking for. I'd probably break fine china. 'St Mary and Matthew's church, town centre, ten o'clock.' Before she could respond, I cut the call and switched off my phone.

CHAPTER TEN

Winter fog like liquid nitrogen engulfed the streets. I offered a silent prayer to St Barbara, patron saint for 'the protection against harm' and glided across town, safe in the knowledge that if I couldn't see more than a metre ahead, neither could I be seen.

St Mary and Matthew's can be approached from three separate directions. In the middle of a more downmarket side of town and a thoroughfare for occasional shoppers and those en route to work, its location always struck me as unusual. I liked it because of its stillness. I'd chosen it because it was a good place to have the type of conversation I had in mind.

I arrived early. I did not do the obvious and wait in the porch. I did not skulk among the graves. I walked around to a set of steps that led down to the padlocked door of what I believed was a crypt. It was sheltered, out of the way and private. I waited, my back against wood, hands deep in my pockets. Mist embraced my cheeks. McCallen arrived a few minutes later and peered over the railings.

'What are you doing down there?'

'Care to join me?'

She let out a big indulgent sigh and stomped down the stone steps and into the confined space. I moved aside so that she could stand underneath an arched entrance that provided her with about a half-brick's worth of shelter. This being nothing more than a ruse to get her where I wanted her, I pounced, my gloved hands flat against the door on either side of her shoulders, my body pinning hers – no escape. She let out gasp of alarm when she saw the cold expression in my eyes.

'Back off,' she hissed.

'Not until you tell me what the fuck is going on.'

When McCallen is on the spot she makes a sound: tsk.

'Did you tip off Mossad?' Mossad was not involved, but I wanted to see how McCallen would react.

'Don't be ridiculous.'

'How do you explain what happened in Berlin?'

'I don't know what happened.'

'Yes, you do. Someone tried to kill me and missed.'

'You can't know that.'

'Unless you can tell me that the guy who took a bullet had a criminal past, or was one of yours, I can.'

She didn't say a word, just stared at me.

'He was clean, wasn't he?' I said.

'It's early days, but there's nothing to suggest he had dodgy connections.'

'So, again, why would someone take such a risk?' From left field, it occurred to me, and not for the first time, that the hit man was a beginner, making mistakes while learning his craft. Good. Errors cost lives, starting with his.

She raised her eyes heavenwards as if I were being particularly dim. 'Isn't it obvious?'

'Not to me.'

She stamped one foot. 'There are any number of people who'd like to see you dead.'

True. 'Are you one of them?'

'No.'

'So who did you tip off?'

She threw me an empty smile. 'I didn't.'

'Are you sure?'

'Why would I?'

'To further your career.'

Her eyes turned a deadly venomous green. 'You think that of me?'

'I do.'

She emitted a breath of cold air. Colour spotted her cheeks. She was angry, all right.

'I came to you with one purpose in mind, to find out who threatened and killed Lars.'

'You cynically risked my neck because you cut corners and your boyfriend got offed.'

'He was not my boyfriend and that's not true.'

'You didn't risk my neck, or he's not your boyfriend?' I glowered. 'I met Mathilde Brommer, McCallen. I know exactly how close you got to Lars. He was going to marry you.' I had not intended to say this. Her eyes widened. She seemed genuinely shaken. 'Well?' I said.

Recovering herself with speed, she threw me a look as fierce as a Russian babushka from Siberia. 'I never promised to marry Lars. He was not my boyfriend.'

'So you keep saying, but you did seduce him, right?'

'Not in the way you mean.'

I bit back a dark smile. 'Is there another way?'

'It's not –'

'You stole him from a girl he'd loved for more than a decade.'

'Not like you to be romantic. Come to think of it, why are you so bothered?'

'Because what you did stinks.'

McCallen gave a dry laugh. 'Pretty rich coming from a contract killer.'

'A former contract killer,' I reminded her.

She pursed her lips as though it made no difference. So much for her vote of confidence about my powers of redemption.

'He was a grown-up,' she said. 'Lars could make up his own mind.'

'So you don't deny it?'

'I'm not answerable to you.' Her eyes locked with mine.

'Do you use every man you meet?'

She wriggled free and punched me hard in the chest. The blow would have rocked most men. It didn't work but it did succeed in making me even angrier than I already was. My life had been trundling along quite nicely, if a little uneventfully, until McCallen showed up.

'All in the line of duty, was it?' In the absence of a reply, I launched another accusation. 'You're a damn liar.'

'It's what I'm paid for.' She stared at me with a *get over it* expression.

'So what's the real story?'

A pulse ticked in her neck. 'Someone is out to get me.'

'You already said.'

'And out to get you.'

'Old news.'

'After Lars was killed I received a phone call at my home address.'

This got my attention. 'From whom?'

'The voice was distorted.'

'And?'

'He said that Lars had been killed as payback.'

'Payback for what?'

'Billy Squeeze.' My mind flashed to Chester Phipps.

'You said "He".'

'Yes.' She shook her head, as though I simply wasn't getting it. 'Billy Squeeze made the call.'

I let out a dry, cynical laugh. 'Ridiculous. Billy's dead. I killed him.'

'Are you certain?'

CHAPTER ELEVEN

'If you have to lie, at least make it a good one,' I said.

'I'm not lying.'

'So all the stuff about Lars and his right-wing connections was an elaborate smokescreen?'

'Not at all.' She looked most put out.

When I spoke next my voice was clipped. 'Lars had no interest in Benz. In fact he loathed the man. Lars stood about as much chance of penetrating his outfit as me running for Parliament.'

'I know,' she said. 'Which was why I finally decided he'd be no good for the job.'

'Was that after you'd slept with him or before?'

She issued another cold, sullen look. No way was she getting away with silence. I'd drag it out of her if I had to. 'No matter,' I said. 'And next you dispensed with his services?'

'Correct.'

'But by then he was in love with you.'

'It happens.'

'Really?'

She ignored my question.

'Whatever you asked the poor guy to do, he did because of you.' The irony that I'd also risked exposure for McCallen did not escape me. 'If anyone got him killed, you did.'

She glanced down, chewed her lip. The fabric of her jacket shivered. 'His death,' she said, clearing her throat, 'the fact that Lars had begged to meet me on the day he died made me less certain about him. I wondered if I'd missed something. I thought he might have been compromised, or that I'd read him wrong.'

'Which was why you dragged me into it – to find out.'

'Yes.'

Except I had discovered nothing new. In truth, I hadn't been in Berlin long enough to check Lars out, let alone Benz. 'You rinsed me.'

'I did not.'

'And now you're switching your story.'

'I am not switching my story.'

'Of course not, you've just dragged Billy back from the dead for a little local colour.'

'For God's sake, I –'

'Why didn't you mention Billy before?'

'Isn't it obvious?'

'Not to me.'

'Because first I needed to be sure about Lars.'

'It didn't occur to you that you were putting me in danger?'

'You're a big boy who can take care of himself.' She flashed a smile in a vain attempt to lighten the mood. I wasn't buying into it.

'This is what I think.' I poked her hard in the chest. 'You're feeding me titbits to see how much I swallow.'

The spots of colour on her cheek flamed crimson. I straightened up. 'You know what? I don't trust you. I don't believe you and you can go to hell.'

She shouted something after me, but I was already up the steps, crossing the graveyard, back towards Henrietta Street. There was no use denying it. Like a fond greeting wrapped in barbed wire, McCallen was lethal to my physical and mental health and well-being. What angered me most was that I'd fallen for it.

Fact: by the time Billy Squeeze was exposed as a genocidal maniac, he had not a single friend left to defend him, nobody from whom to call in favours, no one who would give him sanctuary. Many rejoiced when he fell from grace, his reign of terror over, his 'manor' already carved up by others on the make. Nobody would seek revenge on his behalf now. Not the wife who knew nothing of his extraneous activities, not his three daughters, all of whom were in their mid-teens.

As for surviving the 'accident', I'd witnessed the fear in his eyes, the trapped scream in his voice, watched him tumble onto the tracks, his bones crushed beneath a train.

Billy Squeeze was dead. No doubt about it. Only one question remained: who had tried to kill me?

CHAPTER TWELVE

In a strange mood, I headed out that evening. I wanted booze. I wanted excitement.

I didn't enjoy being shot at, but my brief flirtation with danger had definitely whetted my appetite for adventure. It put me in a fix.

Seeing the evil of my ways, I'd done as much as I could to reinstate my old identity, the one I'd had before my life went bad. I was still struggling, feeling my way. I wasn't really certain who I was, but I'd been making progress. I now felt like a drunk who's fallen off the wagon.

After trawling a couple of bars in Montpellier, I made my way down the Promenade and into Cheltenham central. My destination was Coco's Beach Bar in Cambray Place where they made the meanest cocktail in town.

The interior is like a ghost train ride meets Malibu. Sand and thatched huts made from straw at the entrance and, inside, double leather seats in near darkness. Behind the illuminated bar, a full-size screen of beautiful girls on white-sand beaches playing volleyball and surfing waves. There are guys too, but they didn't interest me.

I took a high stool at the corner of the bar and ordered a

Manhattan from a young guy who had a degree in marine biology and passion for bourbon. I watched in fascination as, with expert skill, he poured and crushed, sliced and shook, and presented me with my chosen poison with all the flair of an illusionist. Ten pounds' worth of luxury and it tasted terrific. We exchanged a couple of remarks, nothing personal, and he moved off to weave his magic on the next customer. I took up my favourite occupation – people watching.

The clientele was varied: young professionals, older groups having a sharpener before dinner, guys who'd got paid and wanted to spend, businessmen hoping to pick up a slice of glamour. A group of girls wandered in and ordered a couple of rounds of Cosmopolitans, stoking up before hitting the nightlife. Me, I sat and sipped and kept my eye on the entrance. If someone had taken a pop at me they could attempt the same thing again.

As I was about to order another drink, a woman with lustrous long black hair and dark exotic features, hinting at either Spanish or maybe Jewish blood, sashayed in. She looked like a model or an actress. Like a collective call of the wild, every red-blooded male was instantly transfixed and I was one of them. Luckily for me, she took the only available bar stool – next to mine.

She spoke softly to the barman. 'I'd like a classic champagne cocktail.'

I listened hard, caught the strong French accent. The guy next to her, sleazy-looking with pouched skin, spiked gelled hair and a seasoned boozer's complexion, instantly rolled out a wad of notes and offered to pay for her drink.

'That's so kind, thank you, but no,' she said with a cool smile.

'Maybe you'd like to share mine,' Mr Lonely and Loaded insisted. 'Two straws, please,' he told the bartender.

'I don't wish to be rude,' she said, 'but I don't accept drinks from strangers.'

With a big sweep of her slender shoulders, she turned towards me. I smiled. She smiled back. Mesmerising. It was hard not to be captivated by the curve of her eyebrows, sculpted cheekbones, espresso-coloured eyes and skin the colour of warm treacle. As she crossed her long legs, her coat fell open, revealing a short crimson dress with ruched sleeves, nipped in at the waist with a leather belt. Breasts high and firm. Her shoes were velvet, strapped around the ankles, with peep-toes and deep crimson-painted nails to match. Her perfume, which I guessed was Hermès, was floral with underlying notes of musk, amber and cypress. Everything about her shrieked class and wealth. Had she been a brand of cigarette she'd have been Sobranie. I wondered who she was and what she did. Could have been a lawyer. Could have been a high-end escort. Could have been a whore. Somehow, I didn't think so. Wasn't sure I even cared.

I took a drink. She did the same. When her knee brushed mine I did not move away. As I smoothed an imaginary crease from my trousers, she ran her long ring-less fingers over the satin of her dress. I ordered another Manhattan. She ordered another champagne cocktail. When I drained my drink, she finished hers. Not a word passed between us. As I stood up to leave she slipped off the bar stool, looked me dead in the eye, arched an eyebrow, and flashed the most seductive and inviting smile. There was enough electricity generated between us to power the grid.

I followed her out, slipped into step beside her, walking close, matching her long strides with my own as she headed right then left. It flashed through my mind that she was an elaborate form of honey trap. She could be a killer or an accomplice. It was time for a reality check. She was not luring me to a dark alley, away from human heat. We were at the epicentre of town with cops, clubbers, kids out to have a good time and revellers, and we were one of them. It didn't negate the possibility of danger. I remembered the crowd in Berlin. At that moment I was willing to take the risk. I wanted it and needed it.

We hit Regent Street and a club that I'd never been to before. I paid the entrance fee, handed over our coats, and let her take me by the hand and lead me to the second floor. Within seconds, we were enveloped by the noise of pulsating music and by dozens of people dancing. It felt as if my ears might bleed.

Arms raised, snake hips twisting, her fabulous hair shimmering under the lights, my girl danced like a professional, the pace frantic and feverish. I'm not bad, but next to her, I made a clumsy dancing partner. Not that I cared. I couldn't take my eyes off her. And I wasn't the only one. It had been a long time since I'd been in a public place where half the men lusted after the woman I was with.

Wordlessly, after an hour or so, we made for the bar, ordered water and more alcohol, and danced some more. Later, we broke out onto the street. At around two-thirty in the morning, there were not so many people about, but enough cops and paddy wagons to ensure my personal security. We crossed a square flanked by shops and silent cafés. I didn't know whether we were heading to her place, whether I should take her to the empty apartment intended for the fictitious Miss Armstrong, aka McCallen, or what exactly my girl for the night had in mind. I could only hope. Silence was like static. At any moment it could charge and burst into flame.

Impulsively, she grabbed my arm, pulled me into the entrance of a big department store and pushed me up against the closed double doors. Most would surrender there and then. I caught both her wrists in one hand, forced them down, negating any possibility that she might try something nasty. A pure gasp of pleasure broke from her open mouth. She moved in close, breasts swollen against my chest. It would be fair to say that she fell upon me. What happened next was a blur of bruised limbs, torn clothing, my fingers in her hair, in her cunt, her lips on my mouth and then my cock.

I knew we should stop. At any moment someone could see us. I wasn't even sure whether what she was doing classed as an act of public indecency. It felt raw and dirty at the same time as highly sensuous. I couldn't take my eyes off her bobbing mane of long black hair, the smell of her perfume, the way in which this wonderfully sophisticated and glamorous woman got my rocks off. Scary as hell, it was like keeping a foot hard down on the accelerator of a Lamborghini as it reached two hundred miles an hour. Jesus.

We broke away, panting, a fine film of perspiration coating our skin. I loved every feral moment. The next I knew, she was walking away with long strides. I called after her.

'I don't even know your name.'

'In your pocket.'

Baffled, I slipped my hand into my coat and felt something the size of a credit card inside. Pulling it out, it said: 'Simone Fabron at Bagatelle'. Underneath was an image of the board game of the same name and a telephone number.

Fuck, I'd had a free blowjob from a high-class hooker. Foolish, for sure, but I needed her and knew I had to see her again.

CHAPTER THIRTEEN

I slept the sleep of the satiated and woke around ten. Checking my phone, I had a missed call from McCallen. Tough. McCallen and her problems were like a bad, distant memory.

I went to my local leisure centre, spent an hour working up a sweat in the gym followed by a shower and fifty lengths' front crawl in the two-thirds Olympic-size pool. In spite of my best efforts, my savage night on the town had left me needing more. I couldn't stop thinking about Simone. She was in my hair and on my skin. I had taken what was on offer and I wanted her.

After a meeting with Greg, a builder I regularly used, to discuss a house I was renovating, I took out the card and called her. I didn't tell her my name. I cut straight to the chase.

'Where are you?'

'At my office.'

Busy woman. Working by day, pleasuring by night. Something in the back of my brain dinged a warning. 'That's a pity. I'd love to see you.'

'No problem. Drop in.'

'Where?'

She gave the name of a café I knew well in the Suffolks. A

popular hangout for poets and arty types, it served great coffee but without the high price tag.

It took me eight minutes to walk there. Simone sat facing the window, laptop open and latte at the ready. She glanced up as I walked in, her lips curling, kittenish with pleasure. I kissed her once on the cheek and sat down. Wearing a black roll-neck sweater, soft tan leather trousers and boots, and little make-up, she looked more demure than the night before, yet still retained a sexy aura of mystery. Automatically, my brain flashed to her going down on me in a public place.

'Do you want a top-up?' I said, obliterating the thought.

'That would be good, thank you.'

'Same again?'

'Whatever you are having.'

I ordered a two-shot Americano with hot milk for me and another for Simone and paid.

'What are you doing?' I glanced over her shoulder as I squeezed past and sat down.

'Checking on the details of a party I'm organising.'

'Right,' I said, unenlightened.

'I'm a party planner,' she explained with another cute smile. 'Among other things.'

I met her eye and returned the smile, a moment of conspiracy between us. She stretched across and pressed an index finger to my lips. 'Not as you think.'

'No?' I held her gaze.

'I also get paid for life coaching, fashion and make-up advice.'

'Online?'

'It's where I exist.' She looked around her. 'This is my office.'

I scratched my head. It was a different world to me. 'You come here every day?'

'Non, I have many offices, many homes. Everything I have I can pack into a suitcase.'

Something we once shared in common, I realised to my surprise. 'You have to be the first woman I've ever met with such a minimalist approach to life.'

At this she smiled, displaying a perfect row of even teeth. 'I rent a room where I store a limited amount of possessions,' she confessed. 'But, yes, I like travelling light. I like being able to move around at a moment's notice. Cheltenham today – London, Rome or New York tomorrow.'

'Not Paris?'

'*And* Paris.'

I imagined gatherings of wealthy playboy types, live bands, exotic food and expensive alcohol. So that's how she'd learnt to dance so expertly. Bagatelle, I thought. It was all falling into place.

'And what do you do when you're not travelling and working?'

'Have fun.' She issued another knock-'em-dead smile. 'I ski when I can. I enjoy tennis and polo.'

'Watching or taking part?'

She leant towards me, ran a fingernail lightly over my hand. 'Playing tennis, watching polo.' She looked at me so seductively I was in danger of dragging her across the table and doing her there.

'And you,' she said, drawing away a little. 'Tell me who you are and what you do.'

I kept it simple. Told her my new name, my new line of work and nothing of my past. As far as Simone was concerned, I was Joe Nathan, local boy made good. Not keen to dwell on this, I changed the subject.

'So this party, who is it for?'

'No one and everyone.' She smiled, definitely playing with me.

I scratched my chin. 'Is Bagatelle a brand name, or what?'

She waited a beat while a guy delivered the coffee. I added

68

milk and waited for mine to cool.

'Bagatelle is a membership-only party site. Potential members must be between eighteen and forty-eight and apply online with a photograph. Only the beautiful are allowed to join.'

I muted my natural response, one of surprise.

'What do you charge?'

'£120 per single, £200 per couple, or there's a gold membership at £1,500 a year.'

Seemed steep to me. 'How many people on your books?

'I have around 20,000 female members.'

'And men?'

She shook her head.

'What? Parties exclusively for women? Isn't that a high-end form of networking? Sounds dull.' And definitely not a label I'd attach to Simone.

She raised an eyebrow. 'You think?'

Somewhere I'd missed the point. Before I could ask another question, she said: 'Would you like to come as my guest this evening?'

I was dubious. I'd wanted Simone to myself. I'd hoped for an evening out followed by an intimate night in. The thought of sharing her with a hundred other females held no appeal. 'The only male?' I didn't know where this was leading. It seemed that with Simone all things were complex.

'No,' she laughed. 'You do not understand. Men cannot be members but that doesn't mean they cannot attend. They may come but only if invited.'

At this I pulled a face. 'Isn't that sexist?'

Simone gave what could best be described as a Gallic shrug. 'Those are the rules.'

'Any others I should know about?'

'You may only watch. You must not touch or join in unless asked.'

I'd like to think I maintained a cool exterior. Secretly, I was fascinated. With Simone, I felt as if I'd met my match. 'Fine,' I said. 'What time do I have to be there?'

CHAPTER FOURTEEN

Simone arranged to pick me up around the corner from Hotel du Vin at 10 p.m. 'Dress code blue, with masks.'

I said, 'Masquerade.' I thought 'steamy'.

Bemused and clean out of suitable face gear, I deposited a chaste kiss goodbye on her cheek and headed into town to a party shop that I thought might be able to assist. The fog had lifted, replaced by dull, featureless light. To me, it looked exotic and beautiful. I wasn't accustomed to feeling this happy, this turned on or open to possibility. Lately, I'd felt nothing much other than boredom coupled more recently with brief snatches of excitement. Was I entranced? You bet.

As I was about to enter the aptly named Party House my phone rang and, believing it might be Simone, I picked up.

'It definitely wasn't Mossad.'

I said nothing.

'Hex, are you there?'

'Yes.'

'And Lars Pallenberg had no significant amounts of adrenalin in his system, I checked.'

'Right.'

'Can you talk?'

'No.'

'Can you meet?'

'No.'

'But we have to talk.'

'We have nothing to discuss.'

'We have plenty to discuss.'

Stalemate. Silence ticked between us like a bomb on count-down.

'Look, I'm sorry. I treated you …' she paused, unable to find the right word to describe how badly she'd used me. I didn't help her out. '… despicably,' she stuttered.

Good, that would do. Even better, she sounded contrite, unusual for McCallen. At the back of my mind it occurred to me that the call, her plea, was a ruse to lure me in so that the argument could recommence. The thought of having another energetic spat with McCallen was as appealing as drinking warm camel's milk.

'So can we meet?'

Too quick with the kiss and make up, I thought. 'I'm busy.'

'I hear what you say about Billy.'

'Good.'

'But someone is out to avenge him.'

'I don't buy it.' I didn't list why I thought she was wrong.

'Are you saying that you don't believe me?'

'No, I believe you.' I only said this because the alternative would lead to more discussion which would lead nowhere.

'I'm telling you,' McCallen said, 'someone is trying to spook us.'

'There is no "us". Don't include me in your mess.'

'Won't you hear me out?'

I stopped to think about it. Someone had definitely tried to kill me. Maybe I could use McCallen to find out who it was. 'Not now,' I said.

'Soon?'

'Maybe.'

'Tonight?'

'Otherwise engaged.'

'Tomorrow.'

Tomorrow I'd be tucked up with Simone. Pessimistic by nature, I suddenly made a happy discovery: I was turning into an optimist. 'Make it noon.'

'Where? You choose.'

And because I was feeling mellow I decided to be nice. 'Queen's Hotel,' I said.

CHAPTER FIFTEEN

Simone showed up in a chauffeur-driven Bentley. Part of me was impressed, the concealed part alarmed. I'd lost count of the times I'd stepped into a car like this so that a paranoid crime lord could conduct a one-to-one conversation. Nevertheless, I beamed and lowered myself inside, the plush leather yielding beneath me.

She smiled and handed me a glass of champagne. 'You scrub up well.'

'That's very colloquial.'

'I had a good teacher. My mother was British.'

'Was?'

'Was,' she said, the tone announcing subject closed.

I knew how she felt, and reached over and squeezed her hand. British mother, French father. I briefly wondered about Monsieur Fabron. Had Simone wished to mention him, no doubt she would have done so. 'You look absolutely gorgeous,' I said.

She wore a dark blue silk and metal dress with a plunging neckline, slashed to her thigh, silk and rhinestone sandals and metal and turquoise crystal earrings.

She threw me another of her trademark smiles. Her whole face lit up.

'Where are you taking me?' I said, sipping my drink. We had

driven some miles out of Cheltenham and into the Cotswolds.

She laughed. 'To church.'

The church was a rectory tucked away in a valley at the end of a long drive. Floodlit grounds revealed every make of luxury car, including a Maybach parked outside the limestone entrance. What really blew me away was a Lamborghini Aventador Roadster in metallic sapphire. Another time I'd have checked out its hexagonal architecture, but I had other visual delights in my sights.

As we ascended the steps a doorman in a beefeater-style coat and wearing a top hat and white gloves stepped out to greet us. 'Good evening, Miss Fabron.'

'Evening, Frederick,' she said, swishing past through double doors and into a hall where bare-chested young men with oiled torsos and silver masks served champagne from silver salvers.

Simone swept up two glasses, handed one to me and walked into a grand hall lit entirely by candles. A blazing log fire took point at each end. Chaise longues and sofas flanked the walls of a room that pulsed with sound and vision. People talking. People admiring. People playing. My spirits rose at the sight of so many beautiful and elegantly dressed men and women.

'Simone, what a fabulous party.'

I turned in the direction of a leggy blonde in a short black leather skirt, her voice shrill above a cacophony of rave music. The guy on her arm was a shade shorter than me, with a mane of dark, glistening hair and very white teeth. I guessed he was of Middle-Eastern extraction.

Simone smiled her gratitude and lightly touched my arm. 'Will you excuse me for a moment? I need to check on a couple of things. 'Zara,' she addressed the blonde, 'will you keep Joe company?'

Zara beamed. 'Be my pleasure'. The Arab also excused himself – to use the bathroom, I presumed.

I shifted the weight of my body from one leg to the other and sipped my drink. Zara pressed herself up against me and idly twisted a lock of blond hair through her manicured fingers.

'Is this your first time?'

'It is.' It wasn't. I'd attended similar gigs in a strictly business capacity, but that was a lifetime ago, or to be more exact, a year. I took a step back. I'd never cared for having my personal space invaded unless I invited it.

'Simone hosts the most divine parties.'

I glanced around me. One black girl in dark blue chiffon was on her knees, tongue darting, going at another semi-naked woman splayed wantonly across a sofa while a man, presumably a husband, boyfriend or lover watched. I turned away, bored. Crime lords have a penchant for gigs like this, the weirder the better. I didn't see anything now that I hadn't seen before. By criminal standards, it was fairly tame. What interested me was Simone. I turned to Zara.

'Known her long?' I said.

'Five years.'

'Know her well?'

'In what sense?' Zara smiled, exposing expensive orthodontics, and tossed her hair back in a clearly provocative gesture. I think she intended me to think that at some time in their history they had got it on.

'In the *nice to see you, how are things going and what are you up to* sense.'

This seemed to amuse the blonde. 'That's not what we are about.'

'Right.' Hitting a brick wall, I glanced around once more, wondering where Simone was and how soon she was coming back. I've never been good at small talk.

'Are you married?' Zara said.

'No. You?'

'Yes.'

'To the guy you were with?'

'Moshe.'

76

I flinched. 'Israeli?'

'Egyptian.'

She inclined towards me, hot breath close to my face. 'You must be special. Simone only has the very best.'

I didn't like comparisons. I was not a vintage wine or prime cut of meat. I wondered what had happened to Simone's last lover. Zara appeared to read my mind.

'Simone gets bored quite quickly.'

'Thanks for the tip. I'll bear it in mind.'

Another slutty smile. 'You're different to the others.'

I arched an eyebrow.

'A man of few words. I like that about you.' She pressed the flat of her hand against my belly. Got up close and very personal. 'Rock hard. I bet you'd be good in a fight.'

'I don't get into scraps. Not my style.' Which was true.

Without warning, Zara's tongue darted into my ear. I guess this was what passed for an invitation. I didn't know what the etiquette was for saying 'no' and wished I'd found out.

'Won't Moshe mind?'

'Not at all. He is probably doing the same.'

I briefly wondered whether his exit with Simone was planned.

'If you're shy we could find a quieter place.' Her hand was now on my crotch.

'Here is fine. Want another drink?' I drained my glass, twisted away and strained to find a passing waiter. A broad-shouldered guy walked past with a gold mask and, instantly, I felt as if I'd swallowed broken glass. I couldn't articulate it, but something in his bearing chimed with me. He had short mid-brown hair, exposing neat ears. His jaw was long, slightly lop-sided. I couldn't place him, but instantly my guard was up. Before I had time to consider, Simone was next to me. She looked smiley and relaxed. Not a hair out of place, her make-up perfect. When she slipped her arm through mine and whispered my name, I felt as if I'd been rescued from a burning car wreck.

'All is well. No cameras, no coke.'

Startlingly different from a crime lord orgy, I thought. Zara, meanwhile, glided off to find another male to molest.

'Let's explore.' Simone slipped her hand through mine and ushered me up a wide staircase and across a landing where a half-naked couple were having sex on an expensive looking Persian rug.

Simone turned to me with a sultry smile. 'Want to watch?'

I shook my head. She smiled some more and led me past a table with a bowl filled to the brim with condoms, and pushed me into a room that was pitch black inside. The door closed behind us. I heard the key turn in the lock. She pressed me up against the wall, much as I'd done to McCallen at the church. Next, I felt something cold and metallic against my throat. My hands flashed up and closed around her neck, prepared to put her in a chokehold, if necessary. Pushing her luck could have far-reaching consequences for the pair of us.

'Scared?' she purred.

I should have been. Fear is a sensible reaction. Fear is also a turn-on. 'Do your worst.' I eased off enough to avoid constricting her breathing, not enough to give her carte blanche.

She laughed, dropped whatever it was she held to my throat and, taking my hand, guided it underneath her dress. 'Do you want to hurt me?' Her voice was drenched in lust.

That kind of thing never appealed to me. Sex, for me, was about fun, not pain. I declined and, releasing my hand, slipped off my mask. My eyes are good at adjusting to night vision, but the room remained stubbornly impenetrable. By touch alone, I could feel pliant strength in her shoulders confirming that she swam a great deal. Now that I was deprived of light, Simone ramped up the action.

'These,' she said, pressing earplugs into my ears. I was now

78

deaf as well as blind, a form of sensory deprivation that left me sensitive to every single move she made. I don't know for how long we stayed in that room. I had never experienced anything like it. I don't take drugs, but I'm certain it was the closest I could get to a trip without dropping acid.

Later, we went downstairs and I found that everyone had dispensed with masks. Zara, her dress around her waist, was having no-holds-barred sex with a guy who wasn't her husband. I paused, pretended that I was enjoying the lurid show and shivered, not because I was turned on but because the man so vigorously fucking her was the man who'd worn the gold mask.

'Are you all right, my love?' Simone said, languidly.

I smiled that I was fine and pulled her away. Inside, I was anything but.

CHAPTER SIXTEEN

I spent the remains of the night prowling and wondering where I'd seen Zara's sex partner before. He had sharp dark eyes above a wide nose and square jaw. He looked moneyed, like the kind of guy who'd be good with figures.

Simone thought me cold and detached.

'You are not happy. Perhaps I made a mistake. This is not what you enjoy.' She let her gaze roam around a room of heaving, panting bodies.

'It's not that,' I insisted. 'I'm sorry. Look, I'll get a cab back.'

'I thought we could spend the night together.' She looked gravely disappointed.

'What's left of it.' I forced an awkward smile.

She let out a slow sigh, placed her delicate hands on her hips and pouted in mock despair. 'I will have no one to breakfast with.'

'Good.' I laughed and crooked a knuckle under her chin, tilting her face up. Caught in the candlelight, she rated as one of the most beautiful women I'd ever been intimate with. She smiled, kissed me long and slow. 'Tell Frederick to order a cab for you,' she whispered.

'I'll call you soon,' I said.

Slightly disorientated, I went outside and, slipping my phone from my jacket, ordered a taxi from a firm I regularly used. I like to be in control of my own destiny and I realised how close I'd come to giving myself over to the Fates. My problem: too many unexplained incidents had taken place in quick succession.

Limbs of moonlight graced the night sky. The Lamborghini had left, as had a number of other vehicles. I hung around, watched people leave – a few of them laughing, some looking as if they couldn't wait to get home and fuck the life out of each other. Two separate couples engaged in full-on rows. The prospect of my meeting with McCallen suddenly seemed like a pure blast of oxygen, certainly a better idea than it had several hours before. It made me feel a little bad for giving her the run-around and such a hard time. I certainly felt more open to the prospect of us helping each other out.

When twenty minutes later a cab arrived and took me away, I was glad.

* * *

Champagne in excess gives me a headache. I had a pain in my brain as if someone was excavating it with a chisel. I swallowed painkillers with orange juice for breakfast, set the alarm for eleven, and went back to bed.

Eventually resurfacing, I took a hot and cold shower, shaved and dressed. Luckily, I looked better than I felt which, in truth, wasn't that bad. Just not fully functioning. Looser in my thinking.

In my less than clear state, I entertained thoughts that in a more sober frame of mind I'd efficiently swept away. The guy in the gold mask spooked me. The fact I'd seen him before meant he was a part of my other life.

I have excellent powers of observation. My previous employment and my survival depended upon it. When researching a target I could follow him for days, work out his habits, routines and who he spent time with. The guy in gold could have been an associate of a victim. More likely, he worked for a former client, or maybe he was part of the crew of another opposing outfit. I had not spotted the light of recognition in his eyes, which suggested to me that, although I'd tagged him, he had not tagged me – advantage plus point. As an isolated occurrence, it signified nothing. Added to the near miss in Berlin, McCallen's predicament, Chester Phipps, it looked like part of a murky picture.

And that brought me back to Simone.

She had picked me up and I, in an unguarded moment, had let her. As classic honey traps went, it ticked all the boxes. My big question was why.

I knew little about her. By her own account, she moved around the world at a moment's notice with only a passport and suitcase in tow. She was singular and fearless. She took control and, had she wanted to take my life, she had created exactly the right opportunity, although I very much doubt that she could have pulled it off. I wasn't complacent. In my experience, women in high positions of power are more ruthless than men. Again, her itinerant lifestyle, her high-tech, mobile, minimalist, unsentimental attitude to life bore certain similarities to the life I had so recently abandoned. Did I think she was a contract killer? Absolutely not, because she'd broken a classic rule: she'd got involved with the victim. Did I think she was on someone else's payroll? Possibly. A quantum leap forward in the suspicion stakes, I knew that however much the woman had crawled underneath my skin and captivated me, I had to take a pace, or even several paces back. If she was the real deal, there was nothing to fear and nothing to be lost. If not, I was going to find out how she fitted and who bankrolled her.

Outside was cold and damp and sunless. Using a popular cut-through, I headed into a leafy road with vast Regency houses and apartment buildings on either side, and crossed into Montpellier, skirting Montpellier Gardens. Only in Cheltenham would you see a man using a croquet mallet to strike a ball for his dog to chase. I paused for a moment and watched as the crossbreed leapt and caught, returning the ball to his master who whacked it once more and sent it flying through the air. Maybe I'd get a dog. The appeal of unconditional love attracted me. It had never been an option before. Now, spending my time in and around one place, I could entertain the possibility.

I arrived at the Queen's a little after noon and was surprised to find that McCallen hadn't beaten me to it. Perhaps she was playing hard to get.

I ordered coffee for two, swiped a newspaper and sat in the lounge. Glancing out of the window, I saw nothing more than the war memorial to those who'd given their lives in the Crimea and people walking down the Promenade, McCallen not among them. Ploughing through the first page, I checked my watch. She was now twelve minutes late. Unusual, but nothing that struck me as strange – she could have been hauled into GCHQ a mile or so down the road for all I knew. The coffee arrived. I poured out a cup with plenty of sugar, read the second page and the third, word for word. Time ticked on. I checked my phone. No word from McCallen. I cut to the sports section, caught up on football, tennis, horseracing and golf, a sport I don't generally follow. My phone remained stubbornly silent. Not so much as a text. She was now running almost an hour late. I poured another coffee and got up, spoke to a receptionist who politely told me that no message had been left for Joe Nathan. Baffled, I sat back down and watched the revolving door like a killer waiting for his victim to show up. At any moment I expected to catch a flash of copper, her pale creamy complexion, the undulating contours of her physique. *Nada*. A blast of police sirens, not an uncommon occurrence, briefly rattled my senses. It felt like an omen. I gave it another ten minutes and then called the last number I had for McCallen. It went straight to voicemail. Rattled, I paid and left.

Standing outside, hands plunged deep into my pockets, face set to an icy cold wind, my phone rang. I snatched at it.

'You're late,' I said.

'For what?'

'Simone, sorry, I was expecting a call.'

'Sounds important.'

'From a potential tenant.'

'You wish me to get off the line?'

'No. I expect they'll catch me later.'

'You left in such a hurry last night, I was worried.'

'No need.'

'Would you like to hook up?'

'For what exactly?' I made sure that the double-entendre sounded clear.

Her voice tinkled with laughter. 'For lunch. I'm hungry.'

'When?'

'Now.'

I wasn't sure about jumping to her invitation, but then if Simone was involved in something that threatened my security, it was high time I found out.

'Where?'

She gave the name of a French fish restaurant five minutes' walk away. I told her I'd be there.

CHAPTER SEVENTEEN

Simone proved a revelation.

She ordered and ate Cornish mussels in a creamy white wine sauce with hunks of bread and devoured both with the same attention to detail and energy she reserved for sex. I settled for steak and triple-cooked chips. Between us, we demolished a bottle of house red.

I played it straight. If Simone was bait, I didn't want her to think I'd tumbled to it. Not yet.

'Are you all right?' She ejected a mussel from its shell and peeped up at me through her long dark lashes.

I frowned. 'Why do you ask?'

'You keep checking your phone.'

'Like I said, potential tenant.'

She wiped her mouth, paddled her fingers in a lemon-scented finger bowl, dried each neatly and gave me a straight look. I sensed that underneath the calm façade she was angry. 'Why did you leave?'

It seemed we both had questions.

I shrugged. She topped up her drink and snatched at her glass. Suspecting that she was the volatile type, it crossed my mind that she might empty the contents over my head. I pushed my chair back casually. Her aim would need to be very good to make contact.

'That is not an answer.'

'It was your gig and you looked busy.'

'Not too busy to fuck you.' Her dark eyes flashed.

I smiled. 'I don't understand why you are so upset.'

She let out an angry little sigh. I don't think she was getting the reaction she expected. 'Did Zara say something to you?'

'Zara?' I made out that I had no idea who she was talking about.

'The blonde I left you with.'

'Oh yes, I remember. Who was the man screwing her?'

'Which man?'

'Wore a gold mask.'

Simone shrugged. 'How should I know? He was a guest. Why do you ask?'

I scratched my chin. 'I thought I recognised him from somewhere.'

She gave another shrug. She looked like she was going to go all silent on me.

'Zara said that she'd known you for five years yet didn't seem to know a thing about you. Odd, I thought.'

'Why? She is not my friend.'

'What is she then?'

'A client.'

'But I take it you have friends. You must make lots in your line of work.'

Simone tossed back her head and laughed. 'Is this what it's all about, this petulance?' She pronounced it with heavy French intonation. 'You are jealous.'

'I'm not the jealous type,' I said, which was true. 'But if I'm sleeping with a woman, I like to know something about her.'

She fixed me with a Medusa-like stare. 'You didn't seem to care when I picked you up two nights ago. I could say the same

86

about the men I screw.'

Touché, I thought, and a fair point. And she'd admitted to picking me up. Perhaps I'd got her all wrong. Perhaps she really was on the level.

'The simple truth – you do not trust me.' Her eyes blazed. She was mad as hell.

'That's not the way I read it.' I'd let her do things to me that no other woman had ever done. I don't play submissive and yet, with Simone, I had allowed her to dominate. I had the bruises to prove it.

Simone wasn't done. 'I think you are not as adventurous as you make out. I think you are a little bit scared.'

'Scared?' This was not something I'd ever been accused of.

'You pretend to be mysterious, but you are not mysterious at all. I have no time for games,' she said, snapping her fingers and gathering up her things. 'Call me when you, how do you say, man up and grow some balls.'

And with that, she flounced out, leaving me to pick up the tab. I stared after her in astonishment and wondered how it was that, in the space of a couple of hours, my life had taken such a nosedive. McCallen had stood me up and now Simone. I guessed this was the type of stuff that happened in the real world.

CHAPTER EIGHTEEN

Two days elapsed. It had been a fortnight since McCallen's path had crossed mine. I called her a dozen times and left five messages. Simone didn't get in touch and I resisted contacting her. Googling Miss Fabron told me little I didn't already know. She'd set up Bagatelle ten years ago, held parties all over the world and was viewed as a successful businesswoman and something of an icon for 'Generation Zero', whatever the hell that meant. Personally, I thought she'd benefit from cooling her pretty little Gallic heels. I was never one for apologies.

The morning of the third day dawned grey and cold. Varying my route, I walked to one of three gyms I used, pumped iron for an hour, showered and returned home and called McCallen again. This time it didn't connect at all. McCallen was a games player through and through, it came with the job description, but she wanted something from me and her silence didn't feel right. A big believer in timing and calculating the odds, what was the chance that someone had knocked off Phipps, threatened McCallen, taken a pot shot at me, and each event was separate and unconnected? Revenge, where I come from, is normally plotted before funerals, but however unlikely, it seemed that Billy Squeeze, dead as he was, held the key.

Billy's monstrous bid for power had kicked up a storm of death and destruction and, in its wake, had threatened the lives of hundreds of innocent people. Not for one second did I regret halting his ambitions and removing him from the planet.

I made a list of everyone I'd talked to in my quest to hunt him down. Three names topped the bill: China Hayes, Daragh Dwyer and Faustino Testa. I hadn't spoken to them since and I was wary of contacting them now. Before I knew it they would be clamouring for my services and all my good intentions would go to rat shit. Based on the strong likelihood that if any had met the same fate as Phipps it would be reported, I quickly trawled the internet. Five minutes later and, as far as I could tell, the trio were in the clear. So far, so nothing, then my eye caught a news item and my blood vaporised.

'Inger McCallen, a senior civil servant based in Cheltenham, has not been seen since leaving her apartment in Montpellier on 28 January. Colleagues first raised the alarm when she failed to report for work three days ago.'

Spies, often referred to as civil servants among other things, only went missing when their luck ran out, when betrayed, or both. The fact that her disappearance had been so swiftly reported indicated that McCallen was in deep shit and that MI5 were desperate. Either she was dead or she'd been abducted.

I remained calm and thought it through. Abduction was a stretch. I'd often been asked to carry them out and I'd always refused. Fraught with risk, kidnapping posed tremendous difficulties. Not only did you have to pull it off, you had to prevent the hostage or target from making an escape. Messy. Unsubtle. Cruel. In my time, I'd known of people abducted for no other reason than to put pressure on others to change witness statements or to cough up obscene amounts of money. In these instances, the victim often escaped mistreatment. Then there were other stories, tales of blowtorches and knives, electric cables and drugs. Sometimes, if information remained the objective, the abductor would play protector, offering kindness with one hand as his torturer in chief dished up unspeakable pain with the other. Most victims did not survive.

An intelligence officer of McCallen's calibre on home ground would be almost impossible to abduct. If, by some slim chance, she were, her training would kick in. She'd play dumb, the innocent, resort to tears, act confused, offer a legend that could be checked and checked again, pull out every toy in the spy's toy box until, lie by lie, her story was broken and her exposure complete. Every professional recognised the inevitability of how these events played out; all break, including the courageous. It was simply a matter of how long they could hold out. Sometimes the cavalry arrived. Most often, not.

The alternative scenario seemed more likely.

And if she were dead …

Breath lurched in my lungs. Sweat exploded across my brow. Sadness swept through me that I believed would never go away. Next up, rage.

Scarily close to dropping off my four-hundred-and-three-day wagon, I knew that if she were dead, I'd kill who was responsible.

The truth was, whatever had befallen McCallen, it wouldn't be long before the security services were chasing down leads, looking at those she'd last hung out with and banging on my door. Without McCallen to offer an explanation, I'd be first in line for the role of prime suspect.

It seemed, to me, that Billy's ghost had unfinished business.

CHAPTER NINETEEN

Hastily packing a bag, I walked swiftly to the train station. Every road was alive with police, cars tearing past, sirens blaring as if a disaster had taken place. Maybe it had.

It took me two and a half hours to reach Paddington, another twenty minutes to traverse slush-coated pavements and reach my lock-up at Kings Cross. It seemed to me that everything had changed and yet nothing had changed. Danger hovered on street corners. Threat in the eyes of every stranger. The last time I'd set foot in the capital was for my final kill – Billy's.

Firing up the generator and looking around the dingy walls at the rack of disguises, the pots of coloured contact lenses and props for the tools of my old trade, I felt like a man whose pockets are filled with dirt and stone. My only saving grace: no weapons. I'd disposed of them the day I jacked in my life of crime.

And that left me vulnerable.

The cash I'd hidden behind loose bricks in a facing wall and was exactly where I'd left it. I counted it out – all ten thousand pounds – and sealed it back up. I also had two false passports linked to a couple of credit cards stashed away. I'd hung on to them as insurance, in case of emergency.

Slipping brown lenses into my blue eyes, exchanging my smart overcoat for a musty leather jacket that smelt of gun oil, and putting on a pair of leather gloves, I headed for the Caledonian Road and a barber's where I knew China Hayes hung out most afternoons.

Fresh snow dusted the pavements. Sleet clung to my hair like a cobweb. The roads were untidy. None of it registered. All I could think of was McCallen.

Sure enough, China Hayes, his face lathered, sat in his favourite seat, two chairs in from the window, bodyguards on point. Before I'd crossed the threshold, three men with *You're dead* expressions reached inside their jackets. To the barber's credit, he didn't flinch, simply carried on scraping with a cutthroat razor, like he'd seen it all before.

China spread the fingers of one hand, signalling to the men to keep their powder dry, their trigger fingers dancing. He gestured to the barber to step aside. I stood dutifully, my hands crossed in front of me, relaxed.

'Search him,' China said without a flicker of emotion.

The biggest of the goons stepped forward, did his thing and, satisfied I was clean, punched me hard on the top of my arm for reasons unknown. I looked into his slab-sided face and read hatred in his expression.

China regarded me with pale blue eyes. 'I thought you were dead, Hex.'

It had certainly felt like it. 'Not me,' I said.

'Is this a business call?'

Seemed a strange question. Surely he didn't think I was going to ask him out for a beer. I nodded, silently maintaining eye contact.

'Give me a few moments,' China said.

I watched and waited while he had his face shaved, steamed with warm towels, his ear and nostril hair taken care of. No amount of cologne could mask the smell of blood that hung around a man who ordered others to wield the sword and fight fire with fire.

Next, he went for a manicure. This gave me ample time to study his poker face and pebbledash complexion, his red lips like raw offal that matched the colour of his hair. It beat me how a man like that could be a narcissist. For years I'd tried to work out why he was called China. Never fathomed it. His goons, meanwhile, stared at me with the detached hostility that comes from years of mindless killing. It didn't bother me. To them, I was the human equivalent of a Swiss Army knife, multifunctional. To me, they were poor rusty blades and about as useful.

The barber whipped away the gown to reveal China's trade-mark tropical shirt, more Hawaii than California, and locked the door and switched the 'open' sign for 'closed'. China stood up and beckoned for me to follow him through to a back room that smelt of liniment and was stacked floor to ceiling with boxes of hair products. At least, that's what the labels said. If the contents were shampoo and hair conditioner, I'd eat my own jacket.

Standing proud, a desk with a telephone and computer and two office chairs – in other words China Central. Hayes sat down in the boss's chair, a beast in padded leather with levers and switches. His back to the wall, he gestured for me to take the only other available seat. I sat. He pulled open a drawer from which he produced a bottle of malt whisky and two glasses and filled both three fingers full.

Pushing a glass in my direction, he took a long swallow and looked at me straight. I thought this my cue to open my mouth. I was wrong.

'Someone tried to kill me three nights ago,' he said.

I did the maths: same night I was at the party with Simone. 'Last time I checked,' I said, 'there are over seven thousand organised crime gangs in the UK. Could have been any one of several.'

China arched a gingery eyebrow. He didn't need to ask the question. I knew what he was driving at. 'Wasn't me,' I said.

'Your style.'

I bit down hard to stop my jaw clenching. Billy back from the dead, someone pretending to be me, McCallen gone – someone had my balls to the wall. 'What happened?'

'The brakes on my car were tampered with. By pure chance one of the boys took it to pick up petrol. Lost control on a nice clean stretch and hit a tree. No other car involved.'

'Your man?'

'Dead, as I would have been.'

'Are you sure about the brakes?'

'I am – proper job.'

He was right. It was my style. I took a drink. 'When did you last use the vehicle?' I wanted to estimate the killer's time frame.

'Early evening, same day. Probably a two-hour gap between me using it and my man taking it.'

Plenty of time. 'Where was it parked?'

'Here.'

Audacious, I thought. 'Any workmen about?' The 'workman' disguise was a popular ploy.

China scratched his chin. 'Maybe. I don't know. I could check. You're asking a lot of fucking questions.'

'You're making a big fucking allegation.'

'Which you haven't yet answered to my satisfaction.' His stare was cold and bloodless.

'Why would I want to kill you?'

'You tell me.'

'I can't because I have no reason to harm you.'

'You're a hired gun. You'll kill anyone for money.'

This had never been strictly true, but I wasn't going to debate it now. 'Not you. You have my word.' I should have told him I was out of the game, but survival instinct made me hold back. I was more useful to China if he believed I was still operational.

China's stare was without expression. To be honest, words didn't count for much in his world. 'You think it was a random snitch trying to muscle in?'

'Could be,' I said. 'The vacuum left after Billy's death has resulted in quite a shakedown.'

China nodded in agreement. 'You heard about Chester?'

'I read about it. Bad business.'

'And Faustino?'

I did my best to stop my eyes from widening. China meant Faustino. 'Faustino Testa?'

'Helicopter dropped out of the sky on a nice, clear winter day.'

'When?'

'Last month.' I blinked, wondering how the hell I'd managed to miss it. Had it been swallowed up by even more grim and recent news? Then it dawned on me. Faustino used a number of aliases and often travelled with a false passport. The police were probably still attempting to unravel his true identity.

'Where?'

'Italy, some place. One of those things, an accident, it was alleged. I heard through my contacts that someone spiked the fuel in the tank. Right up your alley, wouldn't you say?'

I lowered my voice to impress upon China Hayes the importance of what I was telling him. 'Since my last gig I've been out of commission.'

'By last gig, you mean Billy?'

I nodded.

'Then why are you here?'

'Someone tried to kill me on a Berlin street less than a week ago.'

China's top lip curved in imitation of a smile. 'Really?'

'You can check my story. I was in a crowd at Brandenburg Gate. A man standing next to me took a bullet meant for me.'

China leant back in the seat, the leather complaining

beneath him. He looked at me long and hard. I thought I saw something skitter behind his eyes. Doubt, that's what I'd seen, as if he wanted to tell me something but wasn't sure if the timing was right. 'What are you trying to say, Hex?'

'Someone is trying to roll us up.' I didn't need to say why. A cunning man, China could work it out for himself. He gave me another stare that managed to be level and oblique at the same time.

'So what are we going to do about it?'

CHAPTER TWENTY

'First off,' I said, 'take precautions. Double your protection. Skip the barber's, or choose somewhere else. Avoid all the places you normally visit. Vary your routine.'

'Run scared?'

'Lay low.'

'I have my men,' China said. 'They will protect me.'

'Not against a determined killer.'

China flashed a rare smile. 'Could you take me if you wanted to?'

'You know I could.' No point in lying. 'Someone with less experience might not find it so easy, but it's not a risk worth taking.'

China lowered his eyes, took another pull of his drink. 'And while I'm lying low, what are you going to do?'

Search for McCallen. 'Warn Daragh Dwyer and shake some trees.'

'Think someone is out to avenge Billy?'

'Looks that way. I don't know for sure. You knew Billy better than me.' Which wasn't strictly true, but China was more connected to him in a business sense. 'Was there anyone close – an associate, maybe?'

China shook his head.

'A mistress?' I was throwing a line, hoping it would find purchase.

'Billy believed in family, wasn't the kind of man to put it about elsewhere. As for Justine and the kids, they were kept right out of his dirty little deals. Last, I heard, they'd fucked off abroad.'

'Brothers and sisters?'

'None.'

'Back to contacts and colleagues then.'

'You know as well as me, Hex, that at the finish there's wasn't a man left standing who'd defend him.' No surprise. That's what happens when you want to trade in ethnic-specific bioweapons.

'What happened to his assets? I said.

'Billy was one clever bastard. Anybody trying to get their paws on his estate would have better luck breaking into the Kremlin.'

'Somebody must have profited,' I pointed out.

China shrugged. 'Nobody I know got their paws on it. 'Course, plenty have moved into the power vacuum he left behind.'

China included, I thought. 'What about the cops?'

We exchanged glances. It was well known in our circle that the Assets Recovery Agency was slow, unfocused and cumbersome. We both knew of instances where criminals hung onto their ill-gotten gains, mostly because they had the best lawyers money could buy.

'Had a crack at it, no doubt,' China said. 'Mind, you know Billy ...'

'Coppers on his payroll?'

China nodded. 'High up the food chain.'

My mind flashed to Michael Berry, a former police officer, destined for stardom with the Met. Bent as they came, he had murdered my mother and I had murdered him. China was still talking.

'The house was rumoured to have been sold to some charity, although, for all I know, it was another of Billy's clever ploys to keep it in the family. Wouldn't surprise me if Justine and the kids were still living there.'

It was a question I should have put to McCallen. I felt as if I were driving I were driving a fast car down a motorway in fog. China's eyes were like stone. I knew then that I'd failed to convince him that I had his best interests at heart. He knew I could be slippery.

'I'll take your advice,' he said slowly. 'Double up my manpower, lay low, but only for a short time. Man like me can't afford to look soft. Brings more trouble than it's worth. In the meantime, you do your digging – discreetly, mind.'

'Of course.' I made to get up. China's dead eyes told me to stay put. I did.

'Need to sort out another bit of bother.'

'A bit of bother' could only mean one thing. It seemed a poor description for a systematic regime of assassination, but I said nothing and listened.

'I've got a decent bit of business going in the mule industry. You know what I'm talking about, Hex?'

I nodded. A mule meant 'body packer', someone who swallowed and smuggled narcotics. Mules coming into the UK often arrived from countries like Jamaica and St Lucia.

'A human stomach can hold up to half a kilo of cocaine,' China said, uncommonly animated, 'a nice, neat, no-risk method of delivery.'

No risk to the importer, high risk to the mule. I didn't trouble to point this out. Half a kilo could involve around sixty to a hundred pellets in tiny packages; one of those bursts and you're dead. A massive heart attack is not a pretty way to die.

'Except someone is pissing on my patch,' China said.

Realising where this was going, I maintained a neutral expression and wiped my *Fuck, I'm outta here* reaction.

'I've got a proposition for you,' he said, dull-eyed and deadly.

I didn't respond.

'You're the best man to take care of it. I'll pay you the going rate, of course.'

'Wouldn't my time be better spent finding out the identity of the man who tried to kill you, Mr Hayes?' To kill McCallen and possibly me, I thought.

Light flared in his eyes. 'A man of your obvious talents can surely combine a little detective work with a hit. I'd ask one of my own but, like you said, I need to double my protection, so I've no man to spare, unfortunately.'

Wily bastard. China was doing his best to deflect any possible attempt he still thought I might make on his life at the same time as getting me to do his dirty work for him. 'What about Lester?' – a freelancer I knew China used from time to time.

'Lester Marriott?'

'Uh-huh.'

'Inside Belmarsh on a twenty-year stretch. Hadn't you heard? Unlike you to take your eye off the ball.' He frowned big time. The implication was clear. He thought I was deliberately playing dumb. Looking apologetic, I did my best to convey that I was giving his proposal serious and deliberate consideration. Another thought flittered into my mind, and as quickly flittered back out again. 'The target, who is he?'

'She.'

A dark memory rose up and threatened to maul me. A woman's death had been the start of it all with Billy when an unknown client had booked me to kill a female scientist. Someone beat me to it, thank Christ, but little had I known at the time the nightmare that would ensue. It would have turned a lesser man's guts to mush. 'I don't kill women. Sorry.'

'Consider it a test of loyalty.'

I didn't move a muscle and continued to stare him out.

China leant forward. The leather squealed. 'Need I point out that I have three armed men a couple of metres away. One order from me and …' He raised his arm, fashioned his hand into a gun, index finger extended, and silently mouthed 'Bang.'

He had the bite on me, and I had no choice but to accede to his request. 'Tell me who she is and leave the rest to me.'

'Good boy,' China said with an empty smile. 'A French bint. Travels a lot. In and out of airports more times than a priest buggers a choirboy. In her spare time she runs orgies for the idle rich. Her name is Simone Fabron.'

CHAPTER TWENTY-ONE

I walked out onto the street on leaden legs, no oil in the joints. Simone Fabron, sex party girl by night, drug dealer by day, a perfect combination of business and pleasure. I should have worked it out before. Foreign travel, minimal luggage, sex and drugs and rock and roll, what was I thinking? Lust had blinded me and blunted my senses. It was no coincidence at all that she'd picked me up in a cocktail bar in Cheltenham. I wondered if she had any idea that China wanted her out of the way.

To pull a fast one on a man like China Hayes was beyond dumb. Even on a brief acquaintance, Simone struck me as intelligent and streetwise. She did not fit into the usual specification of the people I had removed – nasty, ruthless players with plenty of blood on their hands. This aside, I did not know her, no more than she knew me. I had to smile. As much as I'd been eager to head her off from scrutinising me too closely, she'd been doing exactly the same. Two of a kind, we were equals and certainly more similar than I imagined. It made me wonder whether China Hayes had another more nefarious reason to want her dead.

Maybe she'd double-crossed in love. Involuntarily, I shook my head. Simone having sex with a guy like Hayes curdled my insides. If, however, she was running a drugs outfit all of her own, I needed to know if she was part of a bigger picture involving McCallen.

Overnight Fabron had risen to number one spot in the suspect stakes with regard to the pot shot at me, McCallen's mysterious disappearance and now the attempt on China's life, but how she fitted and why still escaped me. Besides, on the evening the brakes were tampered with and China's car hit a tree, Simone was preparing for the party, or was with me in another part of the country. If involved – and it was a fairly big 'if' – in the vengeance-for-Billy scenario, she had to be an accomplice with someone else jerking her strings. But that didn't make sense either. Fabron did not strike me as the kind of girl who got pushed about by anyone. Moreover, she'd had ample opportunity to entrap me and yet, apart from a few bruises in the throes of passion, I'd escaped unscathed.

Whichever way I viewed my current predicament, it left me with a headache. I had no intention of killing her, or anyone else. That way lay the road to certain destruction.

Unless McCallen was dead and Simone instrumental in her demise.

I headed towards the Tube station, intending to take the circuitous route to Kilburn where Daragh Dwyer hung out. The air smelt of old snow and dampness. Light fast faded in barren-looking streets. People skidded and scurried through the cold, eager to get inside and into the warm. It probably explained why I noticed the two guys walking towards me, heads down, collars up, hands in pockets. They might have been office workers, but the way they walked, beat time together, flagged up that they were not. About to cross quickly to the other side, my boot slipped in the slush. As I stumbled, they came at me as one.

From my crouched position, I punched upwards into the nearest guy's solar plexus, felt the breath surge out of him as he collapsed in agony. The other guy, big and mean, grabbed hold of my jacket. Both his arms encircled me, pinning mine to my sides. I grunted and strained upwards and out, lashing my head back, trying to break his hold. His grip was like iron. I bent my knees, curved my body forward, hoping to throw him off balance. I weighed heavier than I used to, over two hundred pounds, but almost collapsed under his weight. Thinking I might hit the deck and roll him, I heard a man's shout and footsteps. Next, a scuffle, and I was abruptly released and thrown clear. Hands flat to the pavement, face in the dirt, soaked through with wet snow, I lifted my head to thank my rescuer. It gave him enough time to slip a sharp into my neck and empty the contents of a full syringe.

CHAPTER TWENTY-TWO

As I came to, I feared the worst.

I was in a small windowless room, walls the colour of dried putty, strip light running down the centre of the ceiling, table anchored to the middle of the floor. The upright chair on which I sat had wrist restraints and I could not move. Drool slid down from the corner of my mouth and into the collar of my shirt. My head felt like it was full of foam rubber and my eyes had difficulty focussing. I had a thirst like a guy who has popped too many E's at a rave.

Someone pushed a plastic beaker to my lips and told me to drink. Water, pure and clear, trickled down my throat and I was grateful. I was also glad not to be suspended from a hook in the ceiling. Things could be worse.

I shook my head to clear my brain, rolled my eyes, and narrowed them against the yellow artificial glow. One man perched on the table in front of me, close enough to intimidate, not near enough for me to raise my legs and kick him hard in the groin. As my brain processed his face, recognition dawned. He had piloted McCallen that last time I'd seen her in London. The memory of our conversation flooded back as if it were yesterday.

'*Not sure how I'm going to explain you away.*' She gave an awkward glance back towards the pilot.

I turned to go. '*You'll think of something.*'

But she hadn't. She'd told him, and now I was here. This was not my only problem.

'My name is Titus,' he said. 'I'm an intelligence officer for MI5.'

'I know. I remember.'

Pleasantries over, he said, 'Where's McCallen?'

'Who?'

'Don't piss me about. Where is she?'

'I could ask you the same question.'

'You deny having any connection to her disappearance?'

'I do.'

'But you were the last to see her alive.'

'Who said she was dead?'

Titus cleared his throat. 'All right, if you must split hairs –'

'It's a pretty big hair to split.' If they wrote her off that easily she stood no chance.

'You were seen at a party several nights ago.'

'So were you,' I said.

He mostly looked unfazed. It's difficult to mask natural physical responses. Titus was good, I'd give him that, but not that good. I pressed home my advantage. 'Why would an intelligence officer go to a sex party?'

'To keep my eye on scum like you.'

Inside I sneered. Outside, I remained impassive. 'Screwing a stranger in the line of duty? What an interesting and varied job you have.' Busy considering whether McCallen also involved herself in sex parties, I nearly missed the next question.

'Where did you go after you left?'

'You're the spook. You tell me.'

The blow powered through my jaw and loosened a tooth. I spat blood onto his shoes and felt better for it. He didn't even glance down, his piercing eyes suggesting that it was all in a day's work. 'Let's try again, shall we?'

I gave him a *suits me* look. 'I took a cab home.'

'Where's home?'

'Cheltenham.'

'Be more precise.'

'St Paul's,' I lied.

'Not Montpellier?'

'No.'

'Are you sure?' His eyes narrowed.

'Positive.'

'Funny, because McCallen was last seen going into an apartment there.' He reeled off the address of the rental. Something crawled across my skin. Must have showed in my expression. 'Your property, I think.'

'And you're bluffing.'

'You deny she was there?'

'I know nothing about it.' Which was true.

'When was the last time you saw McCallen?'

'A year or more ago.'

This time the blow came with a double slap. 'If you know the answer, why ask the question?' I complained.

'Checking to see where we are on the page.'

I could have come back with a smart remark about chapters apart, but couldn't be bothered. 'For what it's worth, I admit I saw McCallen a couple of weeks ago.'

'Why?'

'She likes me.' I braced myself for another blow but it didn't happen.

'She came to you?'

'She did.'

'She disclosed classified information?'

'She did not.'

Titus leant his rear against the table, arms crossed. 'So she looked you up for old time's sake, is that it?'

'Pretty much.'

'I don't believe you.'

'Your call.'

He waved a finger in my face. 'You don't seem to understand the seriousness of your situation.'

'Neither do you. Do your superiors know you've got me locked down here?'

Titus tipped his head back and laughed. I thought the gesture staged. I couldn't be at all certain that he wasn't working a number of his own, perhaps to cover his seedy private life. If MI5 had a line on me, there would be another more senior player in the room, maybe two of them. 'It's all recorded and on camera,' Titus assured me.

I glanced up, spotted the screens at each corner, all switched off. I turned my attention to the light. Was that how they did things now? He was bluffing. 'The time spent pumping me could be more usefully employed looking for McCallen,' I snarled. 'Why not start with Simone Fabron.'

'Simone Fabron is not important. The men who occasionally grace her parties, now that's a different matter.' My mind flicked back to Zara's husband, the Middle Eastern guy. Okay, maybe Titus had a point. The fact he hadn't named Fabron as a drug smuggler made me reconsider Fabron's position and China Hayes's order to kill her. Had China been spinning me a line?

'What were you doing in Berlin?' Titus said.

Either he'd been a busy boy or McCallen had confided in him. I was disappointed; I'd believed, foolishly perhaps, that I was the only one in her personal loop. Vanity, I was once told by the mentor who'd finally betrayed me, was man's greatest enemy. 'Visiting an old friend,' I said.

'Scoping your next target?' Titus's accompanying smile was nasty.

'I've packed it in.'

Titus leant forward, his breath sour. 'A leopard never changes its spots.'

'While you're dishing out clichés, McCallen could be breathing her last.'

'You really believe she's alive?'

'Have you found a body?'

'We often don't in our line of work. Similarities abound,' he added smartly.

'She's not dead until you can prove it,' I said, stubbornly. 'She went missing in Cheltenham, not a black hole in the Middle East. She has to be somewhere.'

He looked at me in a way I found difficult to fathom. I'm usually good at reading people, but, having been out of the game, I was out of practice.

'She'd received threats,' I said.

'Who from?'

'A dead man.'

Again, the unfathomable look. Titus had a soundtrack running through his brain quite separate to the movie action in my own. That's spooks for you.

'Would you like to expand?'

I shrugged. 'That's all she said.'

He knew that I was lying. To my surprise, he didn't push it. 'Think you can find her?'

I glanced down at the restraints, issued Titus a square look. 'You want my help?'

'From where I'm standing, you have no choice.'

'There are always choices.'

The muscles in his face flexed and he released a catch half submerged in the wall. The restraints snapped apart. I lifted my arms clear, rubbed my wrists, ran a tentative hand over my jaw and stayed seated.

'Does this mean you believe me?'

His lopsided face contorted into an approximation of a smile. 'Jury's out. I'll be keeping an eye on you.'

'What a chronic waste of resources. Am I free to go?'

'You are.'

I stood up. 'Is that it?'

'You've got forty-eight hours.'

'Until what?'

'Until you unearth a lead, or tell us where the body is.'

My head spun. I had to warn Dwyer, interrogate Fabron and find McCallen. Titus pitched into my thoughts. 'To make things easy, I'll meet you on home turf.'

'That's very good of you.'

His insect eyes locked onto mine, 'Two days, Hex. 10.00 hours. St Mary's and Matthew's – I believe you're familiar with the place.'

Either McCallen had told him or he'd been tracking her movements, neither good from my perspective. 'And if I don't show?'

He looked like a gunman with the trigger cocked. 'I have friends in Mossad who'd be most happy to make your acquaintance.'

CHAPTER TWENTY-THREE

Without another word passing between us, Titus led me through a warren of empty corridors with digital locks and pin codes and finally ejected me out onto a back alley that discharged me into Pimlico. The night air felt good on my skin. Too late to get a Tube, I flagged down a cab and asked to be taken to Kings Cross. Back at the lock-up, I had an old campaign bed I'd once used for emergencies. Once I got the gas heater up and running, it wasn't too bad, although I had to admit that I'd grown soft in the intervening months.

At first light, around seven, I shook myself awake and headed off to Kings Cross station to take a shower in the public conveniences. Next, I bought a pay-as-you-go phone and contacted Daragh Dwyer.

'Daragh, it's Hex.'

'Fuck me, thought you were dead. Nobody's heard a squeak out of you for months. How have you been keeping?'

With no time to explain, I said, 'Can you talk?'

He let out a rich fruity laugh, his voice smoked and cured from endless cigarettes. 'Now what sort of a daft question is that? I can talk for Ireland, so I can.'

'I meant, are you alone?'

'Just the missus and me. What the problem? You sound tense.'

'Your life is in danger.'

'Jesus, Hex, my life's been in danger since the day I was born.'

'It's a heads-up, Daragh, a credible threat.'

I heard the sound of a match being struck, a set of lungs drawing on a cigarette. 'Want to tell me what this is all about?'

'Billy Squeeze.'

Daragh, so garrulous, fell silent. I didn't know whether Billy still commanded that level of respect from beyond the grave, or whether Daragh was privy to information that I didn't have.

'Are you still there?'

'I am that,' he said.

'You know about Chester and Faustino?'

'To be sure. Bad business. You think I'm next, is that what you're saying?'

'You need to watch your back.'

'Are you up for a meet?'

I hesitated. There was so much I needed to do, but Daragh Dwyer could yet shine a light on a dirty corner. 'Stay where you are. It's safer that way. I'll come to you.'

* * *

Having moved to London as a young man, Daragh had never left his Kilburn roots. In common with other crime lords, his business was drugs and arms and associated mayhem, his fatal weakness cars, the more expensive the better. In his time he'd owned Astons and Ferraris, Bugattis and Bentleys. If you met him in a pub, you'd never suspect that the warm and generous Irishman buying a round of drinks was, in reality, a rattlesnake that protected his corner with a viciousness that battered the senses, and that he routinely had people flushed away.

I walked the short distance from the Underground station to his home. Set back from the road, behind electronic gates and a security system that could rival that of GCHQ, was a large Gothic-looking pile – three floors and six bedrooms, over three and a half thousand square feet of real estate in all.

I pressed the keypad and spoke into the entry phone. Daragh emerged from the house, stocky frame caught in a shaft of raw morning sun. Dough-faced with a big moustache, he grinned and winked at me, rattling a set of keys in his hand and pointing to his latest toy.

'Open the gates, Daragh,' I shouted. But Daragh was gone, full craic, 'A masterpiece of engineering and as solid on the road as …

My eyes swivelled to the low-slung Pagani – silver, muscular and menacing. 'Daragh, stop,' I yelled as he bounded down the flight of wide stone steps from the front door to the driveway.

'Hex, you're a funny man, so you are.'

All at once the air around me shrank and the light darkened, like seawater receding over sand and beach, sucked dry before the onslaught of a tsunami. A white flash and then noise so loud it eclipsed a one hundred gun salute, I was lifted bodily off my feet and thrown back against a car parked a metre away. My jacket torn, warm liquid trickled down my left arm, bicep burning. The smell of cooked and charred flesh invaded my nostrils. Deafened, my ears buzzed, then a high-pitched whine pierced my hearing followed by an inner noise like a weir in full roar. Half-blinded, I looked up through gritty eyes and saw the mangled gates, the silver car reduced to a blackened, crumpled, unidentifiable wreck. Grisly body parts lay scattered across the drive. A severed arm, wristwatch still attached, and a leg caught in the branches of a tree, the only identifiable remains of Daragh Dwyer. A stout, middle-aged woman with dyed blond hair stood outside the front door, both hands over her ears, her mouth wide open, her scream inaudible.

I looked around. People with frightened faces ran towards me in slow motion. Some ran away. I couldn't hear a thing, but I can lip-read, and a young guy crouched down and asked if I was all right, if I was hurt. I shook my head, made to get up. Pain screeched through my arm. He pushed me back down, told me to take it easy and stay where I was. Someone else mouthed, 'Call the police. Get an ambulance.' Another guy, wearing a bobble hat, stood as close as he could to the carnage. He held a mobile phone high in his hand and took pictures. I imagined Daragh's mortal remains uploaded and posted on YouTube.

I shook off my young Samaritan, staggered to my feet, pushed my way through a gathering crowd, knocked the phone out of bobble-hat man's hand and stamped on it once. Before he could react, I stumbled away and broke into a run before the cops turned up.

CHAPTER TWENTY-FOUR

'How did it happen?'

I lay on a couch in a cramped room off a poky street off the Grays Inn Road. The instruments and operating facilities inside could be found in any doctor's surgery, but with a little added extra. For the right price, bullets could be extracted, stitches inserted, knife wounds cleaned, no questions asked.

Dr Jeremy Mason, or plain old Mr Mason to the outside world, was a real gentleman of the old school with a calm and kind bedside manner. He had the expertise of a brain surgeon, the temperament of a hostage negotiator and the disposition of a habitual drug user. Struck off many years before, he was the gangster's friend. Not only could he stick men back together again, Humpty Dumpty style, he was a sound source of information. None of it came cheap, but he'd once saved my life and any investment in 'Mace', as he was known, was worth it.

I flinched. My pain threshold is high, but my leather jacket, which I'd had for years, lay in tatters like a dead animal on the floor. When Mace had peeled it off I thought he was flaying me alive.

'A bomb,' I said, and before Mace could respond, I added: 'Not mine.' My voice sounded strange. I still had trouble hearing.

'Meant for you?'

'For Daragh Dwyer.'

Mace peered at me once through hairy eyebrows and said nothing more. He was used to such events, I guess. He expertly cleaned up the wound, which now hurt like fuck.

'Someone had it in for China a few days ago,' I said speculatively. 'Heard anything about it on the grapevine?'

'Not a word.' Mace sprayed the raw wound with God knew what. My eyes watered.

I tried to come at things from a different angle. I'd often thought that visiting Mace was a bit like a trip to the barber's. Pitch the conversation right, along the lines of 'What did you think of the match last night?' and all kinds of stuff got disclosed. 'Remember Lester Marriott?' I asked.

Mace's patrician features cracked into a smile. 'I've stuck so many bits of him together he should be called the bionic man. Isn't he down for a stretch?'

I repeated China Hayes's statement, parrot-fashion. 'Belmarsh – twenty years,'

'Main or HSU?'

'HSU, I reckon. He's got to be a Category A.' I pictured the grim, windowless building. Steel doors. Fingerprint recognition. CCTV. Body scans. Four officers to every prisoner. Marriot and me had been cast from the same furnace, smelted in the same fire. Shit, it could be me banged up in there.

'Poor bastard,' Mace said. 'Didn't he have a brother in the game?'

'Yeah,' I said. 'Darren Marriott. Petty crook and foot soldier.' And once upon a time, he'd worked for Billy Squeeze. Now I came to think of it, it surprised me that China had made no reference to him. Perhaps he was too distracted by the thought of imminent death.

'You're absolutely right,' Mace said in his fruity accent. 'Also suspected of being a nark. Off the record, you understand, old

116

boy?' he said, bandaging my arm.

I tapped the side of my nose with the index finger on my good hand. 'Of course. Any idea where I can find him, doc?'

'Pentonville.'

I suppressed a smile. The best place for finding out the word on the street was inside a prison.

* * *

There were all sorts of rules governing prison visits. You couldn't simply pitch up and ask to see an inmate. Most prisoners were allowed two visits a week as long as they behaved themselves, two a month for serious offenders, but they had to book the visit from the inside twenty-four hours in advance, and the designated visitor had to jump through all kinds of security hoops to prove identity, relationship to the inmate and confirm the date and time of the visit. With Titus's deadline looming, I didn't have enough man hours left for bureaucracy.

Back on my feet by noon, I took my walking-wounded self to a burger bar where I demolished a cheeseburger with fries and coffee that tasted sour. Next, I collected another jacket and a roll of notes, and headed out to Tufnell Park. It was a gamble. Having had my head almost blown off that morning, I wasn't due for another slice of luck that year, never mind that day.

My destination was a three-storey house between a butcher's and a newsagent's. There was a strong possibility that the occupant would be at work, out sunning himself in foreign climes or cutting slimy deals with a crook that wanted favours. He could also simply be at home and would answer the door, take one look and slam it in my face. In the old days I'd turned up armed, and this usually gained me entry to most places. This time, persuasive words and hard cash were the only weapons in my armoury.

The property had received a fresh coat of paint in my absence, the front door a fashionable light aquamarine to match the French

Riviera shutters. Very Farrow and Ball. I reckoned the whole lot was worth at least £500k, not bad for a screw. A security camera, positioned high and sensitive to movement, swivelled in my direction. I looked up and grinned, then, using the chrome knocker, battered on the door as though I was a member of a firearms team. A dog barked. Sounded big. I listened to the heavy lumber of footsteps and imagined the occupant staring through the fish-eye lens. More heavy tread, followed by a minor scuffle and the noise of a reluctant dog manhandled into a room.

The front door swung open. Barry Wall, six feet six, loomed over me. Even in his prison officer's uniform, his physique looked like a geometric diagram, a series of large concentric circles with an isosceles triangle for a head. Tiny dark eyes squinted out from behind a mound of flesh and above a Cupid mouth. His dark, receding hair looked as though it had been drawn on in black biro. He wheezed hello and let me in.

Usually people freeze when they recognise my face. Perhaps elective retirement had softened my hard edges, maybe word had got round that I was out of the game, or possibly Wall's newfound wealth had given him false confidence. As I followed him down the hall, throaty snarls vibrated from the other side of a door combined with the noise of paws wood. I don't know why Wall kept a dog. He only had to fall on a man to kill him.

'What you got in there?' I said.

'A Ridgeback. Her name's Helga. She doesn't like men.'

Predictably, we finished up in the kitchen.

'Just eating,' he said, indicating a half-eaten mound of fried food.

No shit, I thought. 'You carry on.' I drew up a chair.

'Tea in the pot, if you want it,' he muttered in between chews.

'I'm good, thanks.'

He looked at me with his piggy, watery eyes. I came straight to the point and counted out two thousand pounds. Wall popped a piece of sausage into his mouth, imperturbable.

'I need a visit.'

'Who?'

'Darren Marriott.'

He didn't say no and he didn't ask why. 'When?'

'This afternoon.' I wanted to be on a train back to Cheltenham that evening.

Wall shook his head. A trickle of grease slid down his chin. He started to count off on his dainty little fingers all the reasons it would not be possible at such short notice. I waited for him to finish his wheezy monologue.

'That's why I'm paying you – to make sure it *is* possible.'

He rolled a fold of skin in his forehead. I imagine this was his way of raising his eyebrows. Trouble was, they were obscured by flesh.

'Would more cash work for you?' I said.

Wall chewed some more, took a swig of tea from a mug that said 'Every Dog Has Its Day' and said, 'Five.'

I snorted. 'Five thousand?'

'That's my price.' He shoved a piece of bread between his porcine lips as though it was the end of the subject.

'Four.' I counted it out, thinking that it would buy him a heck of a lot of paint. At this rate he could erect an extension.

He eyed the loot in the same way he viewed his lunch. I clocked the greedy gleam in his eye. Money in that quantity looks nice and tempting when it's laid out.

'And I'll need you to fix it for Darren to contact me direct by phone,' I added. It was absolutely forbidden for an offender to receive calls.

'Four and a half,' Wall said.

I don't like people pushing their luck, and scraped back the chair and stood up. 'Forget it.' As I went to sweep the cash back into my jacket, Wall's clammy hand came down on mine. It was not a nice feeling.

He looked up at me with his small wet eyes. 'I am not an

unreasonable man. Make it three o'clock, 'F' wing.'

The detox unit, I registered. How Wall would manage to pull it off was of no concern of mine. Did I trust him? Yes, I did. He knew the consequences should he fail to deliver.

CHAPTER TWENTY-FIVE

Darren Marriott looked petrified. I don't know whether he was expecting to see his brief, but he most definitely was not expecting to see me. Somehow, Wall had managed to get us into an interview room alone with no glass between us, simply a low table, two chairs. No rubdown, no metal detectors, no sniffer dog. The lens on the camera in the corner was blank, unseeing.

'Hello Mr Hex,' Marriott said, eyes darting, left leg twitching, fingers tattooing a drum roll on the formica.

I overcame my natural aversion to sitting in a place that I'd spent my adult life avoiding, and leant back, hands in my pockets, and smiled. Marriott junior was a good-looking guy. Dark, with even features, he had a strong jaw line, liquid brown eyes with unusually long lashes for a man. In another life, he could have been a model. I wondered if he was having a bad time inside. Lester, his nondescript brother, was nothing like him. It doesn't pay to stand out too much if you're a button man.

'Darren, I want to talk to you about Billy.'

Darren's face clouded. His neat nose twitched and his eyes watered. For a moment I thought he was going to burst into tears. I can be frightening but I couldn't understand why Darren should fear me in here. He couldn't know that I had pushed Billy under a train. Even if he did, I was there illicitly, the equivalent of Daniel in the lions' den. Wall could get rumbled. I could get rumbled. If anyone was in danger, it was me. Then it dawned on me. Darren was genuinely upset that Billy was no longer with us. I waited for him to compose himself.

'Billy was like a dad to me,' he snivelled.

Yeah, he did that caring, sharing thing so well, I thought.

'Treated me like one of the family. And his poor girls,' he gulped.

I arranged my face into one of open compassion.

'You know,' Darren said, big-eyed, 'We was really getting some-where in the film industry. You know Billy helped me, Mr Hex?'

'I'd heard.' Rumour had it that Billy had once tried to get Marriott Junior into films in the US. I think the pinnacle of Darren's career was a minor role in a porno version of *Snakes on a Plane*.

'Got me an audition for a film, a proper one,' he said, flashing me an honest look, 'a gangster movie, low budget, British, know what I mean?'

I nodded. I didn't need to go to the movies to see stuff like that. I had enough pictures to last me a lifetime.

Darren reeled off a list of names of actors, a director and a couple of producers; people I'd never heard of and was never likely to. I did my best to look in the know and impressed.

'When he died everything went tits up. Got myself into a bad place, booze and drugs and that. Couldn't pay my way. Couldn't see a way out.' Darren pushed the heel of his hand into his eyes. He was actually crying. He looked at me with his big, pleading spaniel eyes. 'Got any blow on you, Hex?'

I shook my head. 'I'm sure Barry will see you right, if you ask him nicely.' Barry was not averse to smuggling in the odd bottle of vodka, cigarettes or drugs to the right people as long as there was something in it for him.

Now we'd got the small talk out of the way, I got straight to the point. 'Darren, you're obviously upset about Billy, I appreciate that, but do you know anyone on his team, someone who stood to lose, maybe a supplier, who'd want to exact vengeance?'

'Vengeance?'

I blinked. He had to rate as the only guy in town who didn't know that men like Billy don't die through natural causes, or by 'accident'. Darren might rate highly in the looks department, but his intelligence was severely impaired. Maybe drugs had stunted his brain. I leant forward conspiratorially. 'Rumour has it he was pushed.' I should know, as I did the pushing.

Darren's eyes widened. He opened his mouth to speak and closed it again. I could almost hear the cogs slowly turning and misfiring. 'Shit,' he whispered finally, 'wasn't my no-good brother who did Billy, was it?'

I shrugged, wide-eyed, spread my hands. Darren, in his addled way, thought that Billy's killer was the same guy wreaking havoc now. It suited me not to put him straight. 'Thing is, Darren, someone is out to make trouble, someone professional. All kinds of people are getting whacked.' I reeled off the names of the most recent players, counting them out on my fingers.

'Can't be Lester,' he said. 'He's inside.'

But there could be any number of others. It wasn't one of the new guys who'd knock anyone off for a few grand – this was an expert, someone who'd studied my methods, and someone trained to fill the void I'd left behind.

'You've not heard anything on the wire?'

He shook his head.

'Of course, there could be another explanation for the current spate of killings.'

'Yeah?' he said, hopeful.

'Could be Billy's wife, one of his kids seeking revenge.' China Hayes thought otherwise but it always paid to corroborate facts.

'Nah,' he said without hesitation. 'They haven't got it in them. His girls are barely into their teens.'

'Did you ever discuss business interests in front of the family?'

'Billy was always careful about that. He'd have killed me if I'd let on about work. We only ever talked about me breaking into films.'

'Did he have any other women in his life?'

'No way.'

'Rent boys, prostitutes, anyone at all?'

Darren's eyes blazed with indignation. I was obviously trampling on precious memories. 'That's a filthy suggestion.'

'Business associates who'd go down the pan without him?'

'I wasn't close enough to know.'

'Right,' I said, disappointed.

Darren thought for a moment. He'd stopped drumming the table and his left leg was still. Suddenly, his face darkened. 'But if someone is out for revenge, that's good, isn't it? Man should get a medal. Billy never deserved to die like that.' He gave an involuntary shudder.

Perhaps I needed to modify my opinion. Darren wasn't as empty-headed as he seemed and not quite so easy to manipulate as I'd imagined. 'I agree, but it's getting out of hand. You know what it's like. A guy gets killed. Another guy takes revenge. Fair enough, but when it turns into a cycle of violence, it's not good for anyone. How long are you inside for?'

'Got another thirteen months.'

'You'll need somewhere to work once you're out of here and if all the main players are pushing up daisies, where does that leave you?'

Darren frowned. His tongue peeked out of the corner of his mouth as he was thinking his position through. It always paid to push the *numero uno* argument. Won every time.

'I'll make it worth your while,' I said, appealing to the

acquisitive side of his nature. He glanced at the door and lowered his voice even though it was just him and me in the room.

'Want me to ask around?'

'If you could, but take it easy. Be cool. Don't push too hard. I need to know who is giving the orders and who is carrying them out.' I pushed two twenties and a ten across the table. It wasn't enough for what I wanted him to do, but any more could look suspicious and draw attention. People might start asking questions. Besides, fifty quid in jail is worth a lot more than on the outside. 'Barry is going to fix it for you to contact me,' I added.

Darren scooped up the cash. 'You can count on me, Mr Hex.'

'Any whisper in the wind, I'd be grateful if you could keep me informed.'

CHAPTER TWENTY-SIX

I picked up a coffee and caught the 17.40 from Paddington via Stroud and arrived back in Cheltenham nearly three hours later due to problems on the line at Reading. Four days had passed since McCallen had disappeared. The longer it dragged on without negotiation or, more commonly in terrorist circles, a threat, the greater the likelihood that she would be killed. I hoped, for her sake, that she was drugged. Spirited by nature, she'd be less inclined to give her captor or captors' grief.

Titus rattled me. He knew things about McCallen and me and yet he seemed to be boxing in the dark. I didn't know whether or not he was bluffing. I didn't know whether he was on official business or simply watching her back. I couldn't work out why he'd left me to run when he appeared to tie me to McCallen through the Montpellier rental. What was his game?

As for the hits, there was no secret club where button men hung out and compared notes. Its shadowy world relied on secrecy. It also relied on a code of honour, along the Mafia lines of *omertà*, or keeping your mouth shut about criminal activities as well as targets. It was just possible somebody knew something that somebody else had heard about, which was what I hoped Darren Marriott would be able to unearth. Find the shooter, the bomber and murderer and then follow the lead to the guy issuing orders. I let out a weary sigh. Having been here several times before, I'd sniffed out every lead to Billy Squeeze – bending ears, greasing palms, threatening reprisals – and look where it had got me.

And now others were paying the price.

I walked back home from the train station, dumped my gear, washed and changed into a suit and tie, put on an overcoat and leather gloves, and was back out around ten, the night still young. I went straight to the rental. I expected signs of forced entry, blood on the carpet, proof of a scuffle, overturned chairs and smashed ornaments. The place was as silent as a monastery at prayer. Everything was as I'd last left it. McCallen had not been abducted from my property. On this, Titus was wrong.

Working a hunch, I cut into town and back to Cambray Place and Coco's. A group of eight guys built like rugby prop forwards piled out of the basement restaurant and, planning to make a night of it, headed upstairs to the cocktail lounge. I joined their party, inserting myself at the back for long enough to get a good eyeful. Sure enough, Simone was sitting, her back to me, wearing a crepe dress of dusky pink, long legs crossed and to the side, pink heels to match. Was she waiting to pick up some other unsuspecting male, or was she hoping to corner me?

Slipping away, I crossed to the opposite side of the square and took up residence in a pub, the bar seven deep with drinkers, my face glued to the window, watching. It took Simone Fabron a little over an hour to emerge. I watched as she paused on the highest step, fastening the top button of her coat, looking right and then left, before setting off for the main drag. I gave her ten seconds and went after her.

She walked with an easy gait down the High Street, turning left and finally veering into Montpellier Street. No nightclubs, no late-night bars or stop-offs tonight. She didn't so much as exchange words with a passing stranger, speak on a mobile phone, collect or exchange a thing.

Taking a detour, she headed into another main road and up the incline towards the Montpellier Chapter, a restored and extended villa, its large glass-fronted conservatory the most visible feature. To me, a chapter is either a division in a book or a division in Hell's Angels. In Cheltenham, it's a posh hotel. Fabron was either staying there or visiting. If the former, I had her down for a penthouse kind of girl. She might be a minimalist but she appreciated glamour. The other thing about the Chapter was that the second-floor penthouse suite has its own private staircase and entrance, perfect for those engaged in things they shouldn't be.

I watched as Simone crossed the car park and approached a vehicle. I hung back in the shadows and clocked exactly where it was. She bleeped open the passenger door, reached inside the glove compartment, took something out and, locking the vehicle, walked away. As soon as she was out of sight, I checked out the Alfa-Romeo 4C, a fast car that rivalled the Porsche, and made a mental note of the registration.

I crept up a set of stone steps, passed through a double set of softly-sprung doors and hung back in the lobby. Ahead, an open-plan reception area, minimalist, with a single laptop balanced on what looked like a piece of contemporary sculpture instead of a desk. Within earshot, I overheard a brief exchange between Simone and a male receptionist, after which Simone walked down a corridor and stepped straight into a lift. I waited until the doors closed then breezed through the reception area as though I was a paying guest and took the next lift to the second floor.

The entrance to the suite offered totally privacy. I listened hard and hesitated. There was no way of knowing whether or not she'd simply walked inside without a knock or greeting, or whether she'd called out 'Honey, I'm home.' Estimating it might take her ten or so minutes to take off her coat, kick off her shoes and slide into something more comfortable, I counted down and tapped on the door.

'Hello, who is it?' She called out.

'It's me, Joe.'

'Wait one second.' Hundreds of seconds later, she'd still not emerged. As I was about to tap again, the door flew open. Simone was standing there, fully clothed in her pink dress, high collared and prim. Her hands rested on her hips and although she did her best to scowl, her eyes told me that she was pleased to see me.

I smiled. 'Am I forgiven?' My only intention was to get inside the room. After that I expected straight answers to straight questions.

Her hands dropped. She broke into a magnificent smile and reaching out, grabbed my tie and yanked me into the room, caveman style. I kicked the door closed behind me and before she could get down to business, I grabbed hold of her and pinned her to the wall. Her breasts heaved beneath me and, misreading my motive, the tip of her tongue darted out, touching her top lip. She gave me a slow, wanton smile. It took half a second for her to register that urgent sex was not what I had in mind.

'We need to talk,' I said.

'You bastard,' she snarled. 'Let go of me.'

'Not until you tell me about your drugs operation.'

Her eyes shot wide. 'What?'

'You heard.'

She wriggled in my grip. 'Are you crazy? I don't know what you're talking about.'

'Yes you do.'

'I will scream the hotel down if you don't take your hands off me.'

'Scream away. I'm sure the management would love to know

that they have a drugs smuggler for a guest.'

'I am not a drugs smuggler.'

'I'm only surprised there were no bowls of cocaine alongside the condoms at your party.'

She flashed with temper. 'Are you deaf and blind as well as stupid? I don't allow drugs at my parties. It is the most important rule. It's why I make a point of checking.'

All is well. No cameras, no coke.

I eased my grip slightly. She panted with fury. Her eyes like polished black seed pearls narrowed with suspicion. 'For a property developer, you ask very strange questions.'

True, and I was about to fire another. 'Know a man called China Hayes?'

'*Chinois*, what sort of a name is that?'

'The sort you swindle.'

'You are talking nonsense.'

'Or maybe you work for someone else.'

Enraged, she unleashed a volley of French. Had I paid attention at school, I still doubted I could translate.

'Who is it, Simone?'

'When you are done,' she said coldly, 'I am going to pick up the phone, call reception and ask them to alert the police.'

I searched her face for deception. Couldn't see it. She jutted out her chin, drew a deep breath in through her pretty nose. 'Just who the hell do you think you are to question me?'

In an instant I understood why it had always been better to blindly follow orders with no deviation. There were some who became involved with their victims, either sexually or as a fake work contact, simply in order to kill them. I'd never favoured that approach. Aside from being underhand, it led to too many questions. If you were any good at the job, and I was the best, you got in, did it and got out. Truth was, I never intended to kill Simone, irrespective of what Hayes wanted. By trying to nail her, however, I'd wildly opened myself up to exposure.

I let her go. 'There's no need to call the police.'

She rubbed her wrists, eyeing me as if she no longer recognised the man she slept with. I felt like a guy who has just hit his girl. It wasn't a good feeling. I wasn't sure how were going to make it back through the debris to more solid ground. Luckily, Simone was forgiving. Her face suddenly softened. 'Joe, what is this all about?'

How I wished I could tell her.

CHAPTER TWENTY-SEVEN

She poured out brandy from the minibar.

'Do you swear there's no truth in it?' I loosened my tie and collar.

She handed me a glass, chinked hers with mine and gave me a level look with the smallest hint of a smile. 'I do not swear, no.'

I thought I'd misheard, something lost in translation. 'But you said –'

'That I am no drug smuggler.' Simone's smile widened. Enjoying the moment, she appeared to be revelling in my confusion. She parked herself on a low sofa, flicked back a lock of hair and patted the place next to her. I sat down, snookered.

'I travel a great deal,' she began. 'I often fly into Heathrow. Five years ago, I sat next to a girl on a flight from Jamaica. She was a mule.'

I frowned as though I had no idea what she was talking about.

'A mule carries drugs within her body. She swallows it, usually cocaine, in pellets contained in supposedly leak-proof latex.'

I nodded for her to continue.

'While on the flight I thought she seemed nervous, frightened really. She was perspiring a great deal and kept asking for water. Mid-flight, she became ill and told me that she was carrying eight packets of cocaine inside her.' Simone took a deep swallow of brandy. I could see that it was not an easy tale to tell.

'I told the cabin crew and, as she collapsed, they did all they could to save her, but she died,' Simone continued, her voice suddenly small and grave. 'She was nineteen years old and the best job she could get back home was the one that killed her.'

Simone took another drink. 'Since then, I've been on the lookout. I see it as my, how do you say,' she frowned, 'my personal duty, my crusade to seek out these women and persuade them to turn themselves in. These are women who have no other choices,' she said, impassioned. 'They are poor and desperate. Have you any idea how many women fly into London like this?' She said it as a challenge – as though I, a mere man, had no idea of the suffering of women.

I shook my head, sorry I'd asked. Someone like China Hayes would simply view this woman's death as theft of merchandise, to hell with where the drugs finally fetched up, even if it was down a municipal toilet (because that's how Customs 'extract' the drugs from mules) only to be then impounded by the police.

'Does this answer your question?'

Simone the Good Samaritan? I wasn't so sure, but nodded with conviction.

'So, Joe Nathan, my turn to ask. Who is China Hayes and what is your involvement?'

As a man with plenty to hide, I could hardly tell her that I had 'assassin' on my CV, that I'd been asked to kill her, that I'd committed myself to a life of violence and had decided to go straight, only my past was dragging me back. Neither did I want her running away with the idea that I was an associate of a guy like China Hayes.

'I can't tell you,' I said.

'What? You force your way into my room –'

'You let me in,' I protested with a cool smile.

'… make these ridiculous allegations based on lies –'

'Based on truth.'

'And you don't owe me an explanation?' She drained her glass, got up and did that thing that women often do when they are mad. She put as much distance between us as humanly possible without venturing out onto the terrace, rested her back against the furthest wall, crossed her arms across her chest and glowered. Indignation personified.

I got up and followed her. 'Simone, darling.'

'I am not your *cherie*.'

I glanced away as if weighing up how much to disclose.

Her foot gave an angry little stamp on the carpet. 'You do not trust me.'

No, I didn't. I didn't trust anyone.

'I work in intelligence.' Impossible for her to check, I thought it my best snap cover.

Her mouth dropped open a little. Her shoulders relaxed. 'You are not a dealer, a bad man?'

'Certainly not.' I took off my coat and jacket, pulled out my shirt and, undoing the buttons, slipped it off. She took a step forward and examined my freshly bandaged arm, my wounded status lending credence to the lie.

'You are a spy?' She broke into the broadest smile imaginable. 'Like James Bond?'

'Like James Bond,' I grinned back.

'In that case,' she said, her fingers slowly tip-toeing across my chest. 'You can take me to bed.'

CHAPTER TWENTY-EIGHT

I left before she woke up. I felt both used and abuser. Having sex with Simone felt plain wrong when I knew that McCallen was out there alone somewhere. As long as I stayed alive, dodged the bullet with my name on it, I stood a chance of finding her. I had less than twenty-four hours before I hooked up with Titus. I needed to give him something if I was to keep him off my back and I needed him off my case if I were to find McCallen.

I crossed town in the pouring rain, wondering if she was wet and cold, if she was hungry and beaten, and how Lars Pallenberg fitted into the picture, if he'd been used as bait. I was looking at one story when there was another rotting narrative beneath. I had strands and events. It was clear to me now that China Hayes was working his own agenda while trying to stay alive, but nothing quite gelled in my mind. I needed McCallen. Our shared history with Billy Squeeze meant we were inextricably linked. We bled the same. She was the key and today I had to find her.

I passed the watchmaker's and turned as usual to greet him. He looked up, laid aside the timepiece he was working on, took the magnifier from his eye, climbed to his feet and tapped once on the window. I met his eye, nodded thanks, didn't break stride.

Cutting down a side street, I entered the back alley, walking on the balls of my feet past rear entrances and garages until I reached the back of my own house. The only way to get inside without a key was to vault the gate. Easy for a ten-stone burglar, not so easy for a fifteen-stone assassin. A scrap of cloth attached to the top spike told me that my intruder was heavy, athletic and determined.

I unlocked the gate and slipped inside. The Z4 was parked in the carport where I'd last left it. It was pretty filthy, and any handprints would be easy to distinguish. There were none. Taking no chances, I stayed back, looked for tripwires, booby-traps, cables protruding from somewhere that couldn't be explained. I moved in closer, dropped down on my haunches and checked each wheel for pressure switches – all clean. Next, I examined the underside. It was still possible that unlocking the car would trigger an explosion, that hidden trigger wires were secreted inside the doorframes or an electrical circuit trigger had been inserted into the steering column. I wasn't going to open the car. Not yet. What had happened to Daragh Dwyer was not going to happen to me.

Odds-on, my intruder banked on me coming home in the usual fashion, through the front entrance. If I were he, I'd be sitting at the rear, away from the window, in the living room, gun cocked, eye on the door. I had no idea how long he'd been there. He could have been waiting a couple of hours, all night, or a couple of days. I hoped he'd been there a long time. Boredom makes people restless, then lazy.

Staying down low, I moved like a crab across the patch of grass that passed for a lawn. Rain had softened the edges, muffling my tread. The back door was double-locked, but as I'd anticipated, he'd shot through the bolts and shattered the wood and stupidly left spent cartridges as evidence of his crime. Not a pro then. I picked one up, sniffed it. Large calibre, recently ejected, it had travelled from something heavy, like a Smith and Wesson Magnum, and as Dirty Harry said *probably the most powerful handgun in the world*. Gunfire in Cheltenham is as rare as witches' brew, the blare of sirens commonplace. A smart man would have timed his entry. I didn't think he was that clever. This was no heavy-duty visit from the security services. More likely, a call from organised crime.

I had two weapons at my disposal: surprise and knowledge, not much of a defence against a man armed with one of the most formidable revolvers there is.

Undeterred, I sneaked in through the broken door, took a saucepan from the drainer, crossed the floor and moved up the two steps to the hall corridor and waited. It could have been my imagination, yet I was as sure as I could be that my contract killer was sitting on the other side of the wall in my best easy chair, feet apart, locked and loaded.

I threw the pan high and hard. It soared through the air, smashing against the front door and dropped with a tremendous clatter. A figure shot out in front of me, his entire being focused on the entrance, his back to me. I launched myself at him, my right arm around and across his throat, my left hand clasping my right to apply maximum pressure. Thin, penetrating pain in my left arm seared through my body, yet I hung on. I needed him alive and co-operative to find out who his paymaster was.

'Who sent you?' I shouted in his ear.

His answer was to shift his weight and attempt to curve his body forward. I tightened my grip, repeated the question. Still he bucked and writhed, his strength convincing me that, at any moment, he would break my hold and I'd be finished.

'Tell me!' I yelled. A shot exploded from the gun and into the wall. The recoil was so strong it powered through his hand and up my left arm, the pain excruciating. 'Was it one of Billy's mates?' I gasped.

He smashed the barrel of the gun against my right arm to weaken my grasp. Still I clung on. My desire to talk did me no favours. His reluctance to oblige made me weak. Ironic that by trying to be good I made myself more vulnerable.

Pumped up, he went for my left and wounded arm just as my survival instinct kicked in. No way was he going to utter a single word. Desolation swept over me as I realised that I had no choice.

With one chance left, I had to be as accurate as powerful. Clamping my gloved hands both side of his neck, I exerted maximum force and twisted hard, heard the crack and thunder. As I let go, doubled over and retching, he tumbled to the floor.

Adrenalin spiked my system. Nausea, in sickening waves, forced burning bile up and into the back of my throat. I hadn't wanted to kill, but there'd been no alternative.

Toeing the dead man over with my shoe revealed China Hayes's attack dog, the goon who'd frisked me and punched me hard.

It made no sense to me.

CHAPTER TWENTY-NINE

I didn't get it. Why send a man to do a job and, before he's carried it out, send another to kill him?

Unless China Hayes had lied about the threat to his life. I scratched my ear. Why would he do that? Then, like a clear view on a sunny day, it hit me between the eyes. China was coldly and cynically wiping out his competitors. Maybe he was also fabricating a Billy revenge story. No sooner than I thought it, my sunny view abruptly vanished. China knew nothing of McCallen's existence, let alone her involvement in Billy's death and, if he'd wanted to kill me, why didn't he do it when he had the chance?

Parking the *why* of it for now, I studied the goon lying dead on my relatively new hall carpet. Whatever his motivation, he lacked subtlety. This was no sophisticated contract killer. As hitmen went, he ranked in the Z list. Not that this made any difference to my situation. He'd left me with a monumental problem. How was I going to dispose of him?

On top of that I was running out of time.

When I bought the Z4 I had not factored in that I'd be transporting dead men in the boot. With a 180-litre luggage capacity, the car was effectively useless for this purpose. Renting a van would not work. Paperwork left a trail. I didn't have time to steal one. Body disposal was not part of my local friendly builder's repertoire but, I realised as inspiration struck, he had the right kind of vehicle.

Crossing into the living room, I glanced out of the window. It was still sheeting with rain, which was good. It meant that Greg might have a van to spare. I slid out my phone and called him.

'Yep?' he said after ten rings.

Against competing noise from a television or radio, I explained that I needed to borrow a van.

'What for?' he said.

'Got to move a bed and other bits of furniture for a mate.'

Greg sucked in air through his teeth, already framing a 'no' answer.

'While you're on,' I said. 'I've got a cracking little job for you and it's inside work. Remember the student house in St Pauls? I want to put in a new bathroom and turn the cupboard downstairs into a cloakroom. Can you give me your best price?'

'Erm … yeah, right you are. Do you want me to pop round?'

'No rush. I'll have to let the lads know first. Now, about the van?'

'Oh, yeah, right. Today you said?'

'I've got a bit of business to attend to, but I can collect from yours in about an hour.'

* * *

The 'bit of business' took longer than intended. I arrived at Greg's on foot, soaked through, and sweaty. Dead men weigh heavy. Heavy dead men are back breaking. It took me over half an hour to find enough thick polythene from a stash in the garden shed and wrap and roll him in it. I was right about the gun and, though it felt tempting to keep it, I decided to break it up and dispose of the pieces separately. Most likely it had a dirty history attached and I didn't want to face the prospect of going down for a crime I hadn't committed. For a moment I closed my eyes. Echoes from the past reverberated through the present.

I collected the van, drove it around the back, opened both rear doors and manhandled my human cargo inside, sending up a cloud of cement dust. Looking around and checking I was alone, I closed the doors, jumped into the van and set off for Leckhampton Hill and the aptly named Deadman's Quarry. I had never deliberately left a body out in the open before unless instructed to do so. (Some clients like to leave their calling cards as a warning.) I wasn't delusional or seeking self-justification; taking a life was never a good idea. But now, it made me irritable and angry with myself. I wished I'd persuaded China's man to talk. I regretted that I'd failed to do so.

Around three in the afternoon, I got caught up in the school run and high-maintenance mothers in 4 x 4s taking over the roads like tank commanders. As I sat in a queue, fingers drumming on the steering wheel, my phone rang. I glanced at it. Simone. Not keen on getting picked up for a minor offence, I let it go to voicemail.

Thirty minutes later I passed a distinctive architect-designed house and arrived at Salterley car park. Beyond this lay a farm. Other than these two buildings, it was remote, muddy and deserted. Rain continued to fall in large heavy drops from a sky fast turned to indigo. Only a fool would be out in weather like this. Or a killer.

I waited another half an hour until it was fully dark before setting out on my grisly mission, the body hoisted fireman-style over my shoulder.

Crouching on the left of the entrance to the car park there was a public footpath, more quagmire than path, which I followed. A walk, that in normal conditions would take fifteen minutes, was a test of endurance tonight.

Wind whipped up from the north. My trousers flapped and

my boots slipped and squelched in the sucking mud. Rain slammed into me, stinging my eyes and drenching my hair. My bad arm was on fire with pain. Trudging uphill along the Cotswold Way, my breath came in short, hard bursts. No moon, no stars, only dense, crushing cloud.

A signpost marked 'The Devil's Chimney' loomed out of the night. I took this path and turned right to the quarry, felt the earth beneath my boots turn to scree. Wind battered the land and at any and at any second I expected to be lifted off my feet and the two of us to be plunged down the one hundred and twenty foot cliff face.

Eventually at a place I deemed suitable, I squatted down, dumped my load, and separated it from the plastic. Dragging the body as near as I dared to the vertiginously high ridge, I kicked the fully clothed corpse over the edge. A brief rush of air was followed by the dull thunk of flesh and bone meeting limestone. Perhaps a keen geologist examining the Jurassic formation of rock would find the man who slipped or, possibly, committed suicide. By the time an eagle-eyed pathologist established a murder had taken place, I'd have covered my tracks. By then I hoped to have solved the mystery of McCallen's disappearance. I hoped to have found her.

Dead or alive.

CHAPTER THIRTY

'I've missed you,' Simone said simply.

'Hey,' I said.

'Are you all right?'

'I'm good. It's been a busy day.' An understatement. I'd returned the van and slipped the gun parts into the lake at Pittville Park, disturbing a family of water rats.

'Want to hook up?'

'Not tonight.'

She dropped her voice to a sexy growl. 'You don't want to chill?'

Sex with Simone was never a matter of relaxation, more like armed conflict. Was I tempted? Yes. Did I give in? No.

I muttered an apology, regret in my voice.

'Work?'

'Afraid so.'

'A pity.' She paused. I could almost hear her thinking out her next move. 'There's another party.'

'Here?'

'London.'

'When?'

'Two days' time.'

'Am I invited?'

'That depends.'

'Simone, I'm sorry. I really can't make it tonight.

'I know,' she said simply. 'It's okay. I will call you. Promise.'

And that was that. Ten seconds later, my phone rang. An unknown number. I picked up. 'Yeah?'

'It's …'

'Who?' His voice was so low I had to strain to hear.

'Darren.'

'You've got information?'

'There's a guy who has a real hard-on for you.'

'Go on.'

'A Russian.'

I choked off a curse. Russians, by and large, had been the bane of my life. Fantastic drinking partners, funny and entertaining, the particular breed with which I'd had dealings made Mafiosi look like pussies. 'Be more specific?'

'His name is Konstantin. Used to work with a guy called Yuri, his cousin or something, for another big Russian.'

They were all called Yuri, but I didn't trouble to say this. Events of twelve months previously flashed through my brain in Blu-ray. One such Yuri had worked for a Russian who occasionally engaged my services.

I had a bad feeling that I knew exactly where this was going and I didn't like the destination.

'His boss disappeared,' Darren said.

I remembered and it wasn't me playing magicians. Yuri had wiped out his own Russian paymaster to get into bed with an American who'd been in partnership with Billy Squeeze.

'Then Yuri was murdered,' Darren continued.

This I knew. Having done the dirty on his boss, Yuri decided to attempt to pull the same stunt on me. Inevitably, Yuri lost. If a man tries to kill me they don't get a second crack at it.

'So Konstantin joined China Hayes's outfit,' Darren said.

The guy lying at the bottom of the quarry, I realised, which was good in one way and not so great in another. I didn't doubt that the Russian hood was in the UK illegally, probably had false papers and, consequently, would be difficult to identify. It would possibly get me off the hook. However the connection to current events was tenuous to the point of insignificance. It was not going to lead me to whoever had set a programme of revenge in play. Essentially, I'd travelled down a one-way street.

'You need to watch your back,' Darren said.

I told him that he'd done well. 'Anything else?'

'You'll see me all right?'

It wasn't quite the answer I was expecting, but I assured him that I'd keep my side of the bargain, pay Barry a visit and see he was suitably rewarded, and Darren hung up.

I pulled out my laptop and fired it up. After a rapid sequence of data processing I checked a bank account I hadn't used in over a year. Sure enough, China Hayes had deposited the correct initial payment for the 'Simone' job not long after I'd been coerced into taking it on. Perhaps this was designed to lull me into a false sense of security. I logged out, closed my eyes, rubbing the lids with the tips of my index fingers, my entire focus on McCallen and the absence of a body or a ransom demand. I ran through our most recent conversations, hoping something would emerge, strike a note, or break. Zero. I had nothing to give Titus the following morning – not a lead, not a whisper, not even a rumour. I wasn't sure how he'd react. What worried me more was McCallen's continued silence. In blind desperation, I punched in her number again, knowing that her phone was dead, switched off, and that my call wouldn't even connect.

But it did.

It rang several times and then went to voicemail. In a low and mellow tone, she asked the caller to leave a message. I blinked, killed the call. McCallen was perfectly capable of winding people up and letting them loose to see where they led. Manipulation was in her DNA. So while I was running around trying to find her, was she alive, in rude health, and playing her damn silly games? I sat back and thought about it and realised that it didn't tally. McCallen would never fake her own disappearance and set her colleagues on a fruitless mission to find her. There would be too much explaining to do and it would screw her career. Only one possibility sprang to mind.

Someone had the phone she used for me. Someone had switched it off and switched it back on. I refused to think about McCallen as anything other than alive. If she was still being held, it was only a matter of time before negotiations for her release began. Hope, a bright burning light, flared briefly inside me. This was progress at last and it provided me with something to hand to Titus the next day.

CHAPTER THIRTY-ONE

The rain had taken a break and was replaced by cold, wintry weather. Sky the colour of wood ash suggested that it might snow. Wrapped up in a heavy overcoat and wearing a beanie, I headed into town and called Simone en route. She answered sleepily after several rings.

'What time is it?'

'9.45 a.m. – time you were up.'

She let out a groan. 'I didn't get to bed until four.'

'What the hell were you doing until that time?'

'I worked on a guest list until late and then had drinks with friends. You could have joined us,' she added, clearly awake enough to throw in a barb. 'Did you get your work sorted?'

'Still on it.'

'Oh,' she said, disappointed. 'Are you still free tomorrow night?'

'Is this a formal invite?'

'*Mais oui*, it is.'

'Do I get you on my own or do I have to share you with dozens of others?'

She let out a wonderfully raucous laugh. 'I'm sure I could spare you half an hour or so.'

'Good. Where do we meet?'

She gave me an address in Belgravia. I knew the street. Once again, memories rose up from out of the deep like the ghosts of the shipwrecked on phantom vessels. One of my former Russian paymasters, now deceased, as Darren had reminded me, once lived in the same area. I told her I'd be there. 'Should I book a hotel for afterwards?'

'Leave it to me,' she said.

'What's the dress code?'

'No masks this time, but the theme colour is purple.'

Purple – the colour for mourning, I thought – dismissing the connection as too maudlin and weird. 'What time is kick-off?'

'9.45 p.m. I'll meet you there.'

By the time I reached the church, I was running late, but it was quiet. The office workers would be at their desks with their first coffee of the day, the shoppers already in the warmer environment of the Beechwood or Regency arcades. The porch was empty and I stepped inside out of the cold. Under the cover of studying the parish notices, I kept lookout for Titus or anyone else. After a few more minutes admiring the fine Victorian woodwork, I tried the heavy door and pushed it open, the noise of the ancient hinges enough to announce my presence. Craning for signs of Titus, I closed the door after me and walked into the main body of the church, my footsteps ticking loud in the dusty silence. Uncomfortable in such a holy place, I soon concluded that Titus was not sitting spy-like in a pew, gaze fixed ahead and towards the altar, waiting to interrogate me.

While I was wondering what to do next, a loud creaking sound shattered the tranquillity and a middle-aged woman stepped inside with a bunch of flowers in her hand. Making eye contact, she smiled. I smiled back, every inch of me on alert, working out what might lurk beneath the flowers and, more importantly, what I was going to do about it, but she soon passed by and the sudden spark of adrenalin inside me

148

died.

Back outside, clapping my gloved hands together to force warmth back into my fingers, I turned left out of the porch, past the magnificent rose window, and walked a circuit of the graveyard. On the second round and thinking I'd return home, I noticed something in the frosted grass. Crouching down, I picked up a discarded pack of opened cigarettes, noted the brand and pushed them into my pocket. Still on my haunches, I took a long look over my shoulder. The sight of iron railings and stone steps reminded me of my last foray with McCallen. Chill crept over my bones.

I stood up, took a lungful of cold air, and crossed the grass. At a glance I saw that the padlocked door to the crypt was broken.

Descending the stone steps on the balls of my feet, I took out my smartphone, switched on the torch facility and entered the void.

I was standing in a stone chamber. Directly ahead were two pillars and an archway of bricks that housed a sarcophagus. Upon the tomb lay two skulls with two sets of sightless eyes that seemed fixed on me. I didn't approach to find out whether the bones were recent additions, or part of the deathly furniture. I wanted to get the hell out.

To my left, the vault opened up in a dogleg. Shining the torch directly onto the floor revealed that it had been badly scuffed; deep marks were gouged into the stone like lashes across naked skin, a clear sign of human activity. Puzzled, I walked deeper inside the tomb and followed the trail for around another three metres then stopped.

The smell of shit after a hanging is like no other, but this was different. Pain, brutality and fear combined with the primary odour.

Up ahead was a naked body, face down, rope around the neck and pinioning the elbows and around the ankles so that the feet were crossed. Another rope ran from the victim's neck to the feet. This had Billy Squeeze's signature written all over it. A buried memory from my previous life when I'd been hogtied, incapacitated, with any sudden movement risking my own slow and painful demise, threatened to knock me off my feet. Another memory surfaced of the woman who'd saved me. McCallen. And here she was, her mid-length red hair revealing that she was another victim of revenge.

CHAPTER THIRTY-TWO

I could not move. I had a vile, acrid taste of something rotten in my mouth and I found it difficult to breathe. Not often stuck for ideas or thoughts, this time I was clean out. I don't know for how long I stayed, my feet planted to the spot, my torch flashing aimlessly around the sides of the vault. Along with the grief and rage, the burning sense of abandonment and loss, I had one desire and that was to cover her up. I couldn't let her be found like that, without dignity.

I reached out towards her. Stupid, of course – it would make no difference to McCallen now that she was dead, and the professional in me said that there was no way could I risk so obvious a connection to her. I had to leave. I had to go and never come back. Despite this, I took one step then another, forcing myself forward. Within a metre or so, I halted for a second time and registered that something else was very wrong.

Chill freezing my spinal fluid, I glanced back, awkwardly, over my shoulder. I don't scare easily. I don't believe in the concept of evil, no more than I believe in coincidence and superstition and men in colourful robes swinging incense, yet the way in which McCallen had been dispatched, the symbolism behind the death tableau did not escape me. Darkly, I wondered if Titus had played a hand in it. Was he still here?

A final couple of strides and I was close enough to stretch out and rest my hand on her hair, feel the softness between my fingers, entwine a lock and feel it shift within my grasp. Alarmed, I gave a tug and the entire head of hair came clean off. Dropping the wig on the ground, I stared more closely at what lay beneath. Short hair, muscular shoulders and narrow hips. Lifting up the dead man's head told me all I needed to know.

I backed away and headed for daylight. At any moment the padlock would be reinstated and I'd be left here entombed. To my surprise, the door yielded easily and I sped outside, up the steps, and glancing left and right saw that by some miracle I was alone.

I remembered nothing of my journey home. One moment I was fleeing, head down, hands in pockets, the next I was packing a holdall. As a last-minute precaution, I picked out a skinny vintage tie made of leather, very Sixties, and popped it into my jacket pocket.

I now knew that, with Titus's death and another intelligence officer missing, my home would be swarming with police and MI5 and God only knew who else. If Titus had acted with the full knowledge of his superiors, I was a dead man.

I piled out of the house, mind screaming. The wig was a nasty touch and undoubtedly contained a message. Something I'd paid so little attention to at the time darted into my brain: '*What if he was killed to get to me?*' McCallen had meant Lars Pallenberg. Was Titus killed to get to me? If the wig trick, a blatant and sick joke, was also designed to stir my blood, it had worked. God help whoever was responsible.

Whatever theory or scenario crowded my brain, every one of them was coloured by China Hayes. It was Hayes's man who had come for me, Hayes who had the motive to wipe out his competitors, Hayes who'd sent me to kill Simone. Yet the connection to Simone, the coincidence of her association with

Titus, the fact that she'd picked me up, continued to bug me. When questioned she'd had an answer for her activities and denied having a close relationship with Titus or knowing Hayes, yet the grim thought that there was something Simone wasn't telling me poked me hard in the gut. Again, it came back to motive. The thought of her running around town bumping off experienced intelligence officers was mad to the point of absurd. No, Simone would keep until the following evening. It was time I paid China Hayes a more personal visit.

CHAPTER THIRTY-THREE

I knew where Hayes would be holed up. Avoiding his main residence in the capital, he'd be lying low at his penthouse apartment in Kingston upon Thames. With its glass balconies and river views, it was a grand place to lose yourself and still be connected to the action thirty minutes away.

Security was tight, and a couple of his men did a thorough search before allowing me in to see the main man. When China prised himself away from his laptop, he did not look surprised to see me – anxious, perhaps, but there was no 'tell' in his expression that suggested he'd believed me dead.

He told me to take a seat. I did. The room resembled a goldfish bowl. Floor to ceiling bulletproof glass, smoked-glass coffee table, glass dining table, glass doors, all soundproof. Thanks to my lip-reading skills, I knew that the goons on the other side were chatting about football.

While China clicked out of whatever window he was looking at, I stared idly ahead at a couple of modern arts prints, the patterning resembling China's shirt. Having had more than a couple of hours to work out what needed to be said, I felt confident. Screw the goons with their guns.

China turned his slow gaze upon me. I didn't wait for him to speak. I got in first.

'Job's done.'

China is not a man to show emotion. Smiling is not part of his repertoire. He smiled. His face looked like a piece of pottery with a crack in it. He also let out a deep sigh, one of unusual relief.

'What I don't understand,' I said, 'is why you sent one of your men to kill me.'

The smile vanished. 'I didn't.'

'Are you sure about that?'

'Which man?'

'The Russian.'

'Konstantin?'

'I have no idea how many Russians you have on your payroll. You tell me.'

China's eyes thinned. 'I don't like your tone.'

'I don't like being shot at in my own home.' I slid my hand inside my jacket and let him think for a second that I had a weapon tucked away. China knew he stood no chance if I was armed. He might manage a shout before I shot him but that would be all.

He put up both palms, defensive. 'Konstantin disappeared.'

'When?'

'After your visit.'

'And you didn't think to question it?'

'I might have done, but I saw no connection to you.'

I threw him a spectacularly cold look.

'A man like you can more than take care of yourself,' China shrugged. I remembered that McCallen had said the same thing. 'I have no reason to kill you, Hex. We are in this together, remember?'

I stifled a snort. In common with all the other bosses I'd ever worked for, China was never 'in' anything with anyone.

'What happened?' he said.

I gave him the headlines.

'And you've taken care of it?'

'Yes.'

'I can only apologise. I'll see you're reimbursed for your trouble.'

Did I believe him? Yes. I made to get up to go. China returned to his laptop. 'One other thing,' I said, 'Simone Fabron.'

'What of her?' Almost imperceptibly, his right eyelid flickered, and I didn't think it was due to eyestrain.

'A drug dealer, right?'

'Yes.'

'You're sure.' I wasn't treading on thin ice. I was about to plunge through an ever-widening crack.

'What's your point?'

'My information doesn't tally.'

'Your information?' he snorted. 'Since when have you researched your targets?' All the time, as it happened, but China didn't need to know this. Fact was, he had me. I was showing too much interest and it was bound to raise suspicion. 'Word on the wire.'

China broke into another big smile. 'Are you going soft? And in any case, what do you care? She's dead, isn't she?'

'And buried.'

'That's my man. You know, I could always do with someone like you permanently on the team. What do you say?'

'I'm flattered.'

Just then, his phone gave a bleep and he glanced once more at his laptop. It took him five seconds to change from Mr Congeniality to Mr I'm Coming to Get You – not that it was obvious.

He beamed, stood up, stuck out his hand, clasping mine in his.

'You'll give it serious thought, Hex? I could make it an attractive package.'

'I will.'

'We'll talk in a few days, yes?'

'Fine.'

'You're going to be in the city for a while?'

'I am.'

As I left, China called to one of the guys on guard duty, a nondescript, bland-featured man who I took to be another Russian, his name Leonid. The door closed, effectively soundproofing the living room and sealing off all conversation. Picking up my coat, I looked through the glass, caught sight of China deep in conversation and lip-read his instructions. Four words glanced across his lips: 'Follow and kill him.'

CHAPTER THIRTY-FOUR

When you catch a man in one lie it's a given that there are others. China had lied to me about the absence of killers on his payroll. He had also lied to me about Simone. My first priority was to trap Leonid and discover what China was up to, my second, to find out what was on China's laptop. Something had spooked him but I didn't know what.

I made my way out of the building and headed for the train station at a leisurely pace. I couldn't fault China's choice of assassin. Of average height, average weight, hair neither too short nor too long, and with colourless, nondescript features, he was Mr Forgettable. In his jeans, sneakers, T-shirt and leather jacket, he could be mistaken for any number of individuals. I wondered what he packed. Taking a punt, I guessed a Makarov with silencer, the perfect toy for the type of work he had in mind.

Reaching the station, I caught the next train to Waterloo. Leonid boarded at the same time but sat in a different carriage – his strategy, no doubt, to kill me in a quiet street without an audience. I sat back and decided to play to the man's tune, but with me writing the finale.

I stepped out at Waterloo and took the Jubilee line to Green Park and from there, the Victoria to Kings Cross. In the old days, he'd have tried to pop me on the Underground, but with all the extra security it was unlikely he'd be that audacious. To be certain, I speeded up and fell into the unrelenting flow of workers, tourists and students, keeping my head down. A memory of another time, when I'd been the hunter, flashed through my mind. In the minutes before Billy's death, I'd joined a similar flow of folk and tracked my prey, Billy unaware of me until the final moment. It was karma, perhaps, that I was now the hunted.

Out in the open I rolled up the collar of my jacket, slipped a hand in my pocket, felt the warm length of leather, entwined it around my fingers and, certain my would-be killer had caught up, set off.

The lock-up was a no-go so I tracked in the other direction towards Regent's Canal. Once a slum area, much of the basin had been cleared for apartments and leisure boats, another case of regeneration changing the urban landscape for the better. If my Russian thought he could knock me off and dispose of my body in the drink, he was mistaken.

Up ahead was a narrow walkway in between two towering office blocks with windows facing the Battlebridge Basin. Not too many cyclists and joggers out today. Quiet and soulless, it would be the perfect place for my man to strike. I had other ideas.

The temperature had dropped several degrees to a malicious minus. Damp intensified the bitter cold. The light was poor. My footsteps marked time in a strange syncopated rhythm with my prospective assassin. If I got this wrong, if I had not read him right, I was a minute away, maybe even seconds, from certain death.

Out on an open stretch of moorings, it would be hard for my killer to take a shot unseen. Perhaps he was a gambling man. Maybe he was reckless. I didn't think so. He'd hung back at the requisite distance. He hadn't forced the pace. He hadn't lost me. I respected him for that. An early lesson in my killing career was never to underestimate the enemy.

My destination was a brick-built arch, dark and low lying with black, icy water beneath, the ultimate place for a kill. I increased my stride, eyes straight ahead, determined not to show out even though the guy probably had his hand on the pistol, safety off on the left of the slide, finger twitching on the trigger. It gave me enough time to get ahead and tuck myself into a narrow hollow where the bricks had crumbled. My eyes are quick at adjusting to poor light and I wondered how well my Russian would fare.

Pretty well, as it happened.

He burst through the tunnel and let off two shots, the put-put sound confirming the use of a silencer and that he meant to carry out his orders with a certain amount of finesse. Luckily for me, as he fired, he continued to move forward.

I darted out and wrapped the leather tie around his neck with all the agility and speed of a black mamba. Leonid gasped, dropped the pistol, hands flying to his throat. He obviously hadn't been instructed in the 'never underestimate the enemy' school of contract killing. One kick from me and the pistol hit the water. Put the odds back in my favour.

I shouted above the clatter of boots scraping, limbs flying, the noise of a man caught in the grind. 'Stop struggling. I'm not going to kill you.'

He relaxed and I eased off the pressure. Next, he lowered his head, and as I cut him some slack, he lashed his head back, the strongest part of his skull butting me smartly on the nose. It caught me exactly on an old break, a souvenir of a game of rugby. Pain almost blinded me. A rush of warm blood cascaded over my chin and down the front of my jacket. I hauled hard to temporarily cut off the oxygen to his brain – enough to keep him quiet, not enough to kill him. But the wiry Russian wasn't ready to give in yet. With a tremendous display of power that reverberated through my body, he bucked and twisted his muscular shoulders. I hung on with a terrible sense of déjà vu. What was it with these guys?

'I need answers to questions.'

'*Nyet.*' His breath, sour and tainted with garlic, was too close for comfort.

'Don't give me that crap,' I snarled. 'Speak English. You understand what I'm saying.'

Clearly he didn't because he lifted his right foot and ran the heel of his boot painfully down my shin. It hurt. Properly cross, I twisted the leather in both hands, turned up the pressure, felt the guy gurgle. He tried to dig his fingers underneath my makeshift garrotte in a doomed attempt to release the pressure, but I wasn't budging. Any moment his hyoid bone would fracture. I felt like a guy on a high wire, desperate to keep my balance. I wanted answers. I wanted to send a strong message back to China Hayes. I genuinely did not want to kill Leonid. He wasn't like Konstantin. He was unarmed.

'Screw this, talk to me.'

'Okay, okay,' he gasped. 'I'm fucked anyway.'

This was the equivalent of a symphony orchestra to my ears. I loosened my grasp enough to let him speak, not enough for him to try anything clever. Had anyone seen us together, we would have cut an odd picture. They'd possibly think I was getting up close and personal in an entirely different way to the one intended. 'Did China send Konstantin?'

'*Nyet.* Konstantin had his own score to settle.'

So Darren's information checked out, which was good. I intended to pay Barry Walls another visit in the hope that Darren would have more high-grade information for me. 'Did China kill Daragh Dwyer?'

He delayed for no more than a fraction of time. 'No.' I didn't believe his hesitation was due to Leonid translating a Russian negative into an English negative.

'But he knew it was going to happen?'

'*Da*, yes.'

'Faustino Testa?'

161

'The same.'

'China was party to it?'

'Party? I do not understand.'

'He helped someone else do it.'

'I do not know. Maybe he give out information.'

Yes, that worked, I thought. China, the scheming bastard.

'Chester Phipps, did China help with that too?'

'I do not know for sure.'

I tightened my grip infinitesimally.

'Maybe,' the Russian growled back.

'Someone tampered with the brakes on China's car and tried to kill him.'

'I know nothing of this.'

'One of his men was killed.'

'You are one crazy man.'

'Who is China working for?'

'This I do not know.'

Again, a tweak.

'You cannot squeeze information out of a man who knows nothing,' he rasped.

Leonid was correct, probably because I wasn't asking the right questions. 'Why did he tell you to kill me?'

'It is not my place to ask. I do as I am told.'

That figured. 'Have you heard the name McCallen?'

'Never.'

'Titus.'

'No.'

'Simone.'

'*Da*, China wants her dead.'

'Why?'

'Because she is in his business, in his face, taking money, cutting deals.'

'You know this for a fact?' I eased off a little.

'I know this is what China tells me,' Leonid said, exasperated.

'I am from St Petersburg. Asking questions gets you killed.'

With this I could identify. 'Tell me about China.'

'He is good man to work for. He pays good money. He –'

'Is he under pressure?' I didn't want a CV or to know whether China paid into a pension plan for his employees. I wanted to find out who was pulling China's strings. 'Is he nervous, irritable, unpredictable?'

Leonid let out a rough laugh. 'All bosses are like this. Never happy. Believing someone is out to rip them off and take their business. They are all paranoid. It is what they are.' I had to hand it to Leonid; he understood the idiosyncrasies of crime lords well. I was beginning to think I was running into a dead end. Maybe Leonid was getting as cold and miserable as me, maybe he wanted to go home to St Petersburg. A smart guy, he understood that if I were to release him, he had to trade. He fell silent for a moment. I gave him time to think out his position. It took all of ten seconds. Like I said, he was on it.

'China mentioned someone.'

'Who?'

'A man, a German.'

The light of recognition flared briefly inside my mind. 'His name?'

'I do now know. China only referred to him as the German.'

'When was this?'

Leonid gave a big shrug of his shoulders. 'Many months ago.'

Pallenberg, I thought.

'Tell me more.'

'Nothing more to tell.'

'In what context did he mention the German?'

'Same time he was bitching about Simone.'

A connection between Simone and Pallenberg? I sifted through my conversation with Mathilde in Berlin. Then it hit me. *I put it down to his increasing success and new circle of friends.* Had Pallenberg fallen in with the smart set and frequented one

163

of Simone's sex parties? How likely was it, and how much of a coincidence was that?

'One other thing,' I said, 'where will China hole up when he flees his riverside view in Kingston?' If I were Leonid, I'd stay far away from Hayes and get the next flight back to the motherland. Leonid's failure to report back to base with the equivalent of my head on a plate would be enough for China to realise that Leonid, like Konstantin, had failed in his task. He would be punished severely.

'I do not know. Maybe the warehouse.'

'Where?'

He told me the name of a trading estate in Deptford. If China was this stupid he deserved everything that was coming to him. I released my grasp, pulled out a handkerchief and did my best to mop up the blood. Leonid took a step to the side, put a hand to the raw weal on his neck and looked at me with curious eyes. 'You are letting me go.'

'I am. If you see China, warn him that the next time our paths cross, I'll kill him.'

'But not me?'

'Not you. You are free to go.'

He gave me another quizzical look. If I were Leonid I'd have said 'thanks very much' and fled. The Russian was made of stronger, more resilient material. 'People call you Hex, the magician.'

They did once, not now. I nodded assent.

'You are not what people say you are.'

I smiled and walked away.

CHAPTER THIRTY-FIVE

I returned to the lock-up, changed my shirt, put money in my wallet and called Mathilde Brommer, Lars's ex-girlfriend and the lady who'd collared me outside the Pallenbergs' apartment in Berlin. She sounded tired or as if she were in the middle of something and I'd interrupted. I couldn't claim that she was pleased to hear from me. Once we'd got basic civilities out of the way, never my strong suit, I launched in.

'Mathilde, you mentioned Lars had got in with a new crowd of people in London.'

'Yes.'

'Who were they?'

'People in the art establishment.'

'Any particular names?'

She rattled off a list of people I'd never heard of bar one: a BBC journalist specialising in the arts.

'Did Lars ever talk to you about a man called China Hayes?'

She waited a beat. I could almost hear her trawling through her memory bank for an elusive connection. 'No,' she said. 'Who is he?'

'A bad guy.' I wondered fleetingly if Hayes was responsible for Lars's death. How the hell did that fit together? Mathilde followed my line of thinking and asked the same question.

'I don't know,' I said, 'but I'm going to find out.'

'Really? I thought you were an art dealer. Does this man, China Hayes, paint?' Mathilde's tone was caustic.

There followed an awkward silence in which I thought she'd hung up. Eventually, she spoke. 'You are most persistent.'

She had no idea. 'Mathilde, what did Lars do for fun?'

'Lorna Spencer,' she said, no trace of humour.

A name assumed by McCallen. I closed my eyes and wished I wasn't talking to a woman. They could be so vengeful. As soon as the thought entered my brain, I wondered why I'd discounted the most obvious possibility. 'Aside from Lorna, who did he mix with socially? Did he attend parties with the great and the good?'

Mathilde let out a short, dry laugh. 'Why are you asking these questions?'

'Because I'm trying to find out who killed Lars.'

'That's a heavy allegation,' she said fast as electricity lightning.

'It is,' I said simply. 'Did he mix in playboy circles?'

'*Himmel, Arsch und Zwirn*, how the hell should I know?'

'Is it likely?'

'For the old Lars, no. For the new Lars, perhaps.'

Perhaps was good enough. 'Did he ever mention a French woman by the name of Simone Fabron?'

'Never.'

'You are absolutely certain?'

'What makes you think he'd confide in me?'

'Because he told you that he was being followed. He told you he felt under threat. Mathilde, the man still cared about you despite what you think.'

It wasn't like me to get empathic but I believed Lars had cared. Whether or not Mathilde had once cared for Lars until, emotions trampled, she'd reached the point of no return was up for debate.

'I hope so,' she said in a small voice before hanging up.

Removing a finely tailored suit and a smart pair of shoes from my collection, I took a Tube to the Barbican and booked into a hotel – part of an upmarket chain in Charterhouse Square – for a couple of nights. I needed somewhere to clean up, eat a decent meal, sleep and think. I was frustrated. McCallen's mobile had sprung back to life but McCallen was still missing. Every lead revealed loose associations and, at the dark heart of a murderous campaign of revenge, the ghost of Billy Squeeze hovered. I wasn't exactly running on empty. I still had the party the next evening. Darren was sniffing around on my behalf. In twenty-four hours, China would have got the message, cleared out of his riverside apartment and gone to ground. I hoped Leonid was right about his boss's chosen lair.

The German connection bothered me. Something that struck me in conversation with Mathilde made me view events in a different way. What if there was no link between McCallen's disappearance and Lars Pallenberg's death? What if things had happened simultaneously? In other words, was Mathilde innocent? Had heartbreak morphed into humiliation and then led to violence?

Mathilde came across as level-headed, a good soul, but the more I thought about it, the happenstance of her being in the right place at the right time, outside the Pallenberg's apartment at the moment of my arrival, forced me to wonder whether I'd missed the obvious. Mathilde Brommer had more reason than anyone to want Lars Pallenberg dead. McCallen had smashed the certainty that Mathilde was ever going to marry the man she'd loved and lived with for over a decade. I frowned. I'd never been hired to settle domestic scores. Wasn't my bag. In spite of my lack of experience in such things, it doesn't take a degree in relationship counselling to know that a scorned woman is immensely dangerous. Truth was I had to face the possibility that

Mathilde had ordered the death of her former lover. I cursed my failure to consider this before. How it tied in with McCallen's fate, I was less certain.

I took out my phone and ran through the crime scene shots, attempting to profile the psyche of the killer from the evidence on the ground. The method spoke of cool, calm surgical precision followed by total wipeout. It didn't bode well for McCallen's chances.

Unless I'd got it all wrong about the solitary killer.

Recalibrating my thinking with regard to McCallen's disappearance, I reckoned it needed one person to abduct, another to do the business. An operational phone was no proof of life and yet, inexplicably, I still believed, and in spite of so many days without news, that McCallen was in the land of the living. She might be in poor shape, be close to death or at risk of dying. Mine was not blind optimism. I simply had a strong, almost visceral, sense of her existence. Right now, gut instinct was all I had and, until proved otherwise, I determined to hang on to it.

I bathed, fixed my nose with a strip of plaster and stared at my reflection in the mirror. The skin around my eyes had turned a deep shade of blue, Leonid's calling card stamped all over my face. Not a terrific look for my forthcoming party. Frankly, I was more troubled by what I read in my expression. I saw hunger and thirst there. Hunger for justice, thirst for action. The sight of the dead man lying at the bottom of the quarry had woken old demons. An unarmed householder is no match for a thug with a Magnum. In the ordinary scheme of things, I'd be hailed as a hero for using reasonable force, but my life was not ordinary. It never had been. Aside from the past twelve months, I'd lived it full-throttle and out loud. This raised wider questions.

How long could I hold out without resorting to my wild and wicked ways? How long before I contacted an old supplier, issued the precise specifications of the model of the gun and ammunition I needed? Would it be hours, a day, a week before I caved in? And then what? Would I ditch my newfound career in property development, say goodbye to Dan and the lads, leave the only place I'd ever been able to call home, the place where I'd once, long ago, had a life with a mother I loved? Was I destined to kill and sleep in the arms of strangers until I got too ancient or too slow and someone younger and fitter took me out of the game?

In despair, I turned away from the unbearable prospect, dressed in dark and sober clothes and ordered room service. I had to do everything in my power to avoid a return to the terrible life I'd known and once lived. I'd be a dead man inside if I didn't.

CHAPTER THIRTY-SIX

Early the next morning I called Barry Wall. I didn't know the hours he kept. I suspected that, as a corrupt screw, he fitted the job around four meals a day and snacks.

The phone rang. I waited for an answering facility to kick in, but nothing happened. About to cut the call, there was a click and Barry's wheezy voice came on the line. I imagined him out of breath from the exertion of dragging himself away from the kitchen table at a critical moment. I gave him a few seconds to compose himself. I did not announce who I was; there was no need.

'Can you see that Darren is all right for booze and blow?'

Barry let out an asthmatic noise, midway between a laugh and cry.

'I'll drop by with the cash,' I said, believing this would make a difference.

'No point,' Barry said.

'Don't mess with me. You've had your cut.'

'He's dead.'

'What? How?'

'Someone slashed his throat.'

In the old days, this would not have disturbed me. These were not the old days. I was disturbed. 'You know who?'

'Not yet, but we will.'

'Barry, I —'

'Spare me the apologies. This is your fault. What did you ask him to do?'

'It hardly matters now.' I wasn't about to confide in a man like Wall.

'I don't like my boat being rocked. I've got a nice little number going and I don't need the spotlight of an enquiry shining in my direction.'

Typically, Wall was covering his sizable rear. Not that I was in any position to take the moral high ground. Wall was right. In spite of my good intentions, it was my fault that Darren had been killed. Following my visit and revelation about Konstantin, Hayes must have got word to one of his men inside to shut Darren up for ever.

'If you want to find the man who killed him, check out anyone from China Hayes's firm,' I said, my final words before I hung up.

Guilt clung to me. I have done many bad things in my life, especially to cruel and vicious men, who thought nothing of torture and depravity. But I have never liked collateral damage. You do the job right and there shouldn't be any. Doesn't mean to say I haven't cocked up on occasion, this being was one of them. Riled by Darren's death, I decided on a change of plan.

If China knew that Leonid had failed, he would expect me to come looking for him. With up to two men down, he'd call in favours and max out on security. This meant his new guys would be hastily assembled and probably third rate. Nevertheless, it wasn't a reassuring prospect. Third rate with a gun is better than first rate without one. I wished I'd pocketed the Makarov – not to use, but to prove I'd lost none of my edge and still meant business.

Undeterred, I returned to the lock-up and picked out false ID, and a stack of cash. My first call was to the barber's in the Caledonian Road where Hayes hung out. The only people there were the barber with his cutthroat razor, a guy in the chair and another reading a tabloid. Next, I returned to the Kingston apartment. No concierge at the desk. Nobody manning the lift. It was as quiet as an abandoned town in a nuclear disaster zone. Sensing trouble, I took the stairs. Straightaway, I could see that the door to China's apartment was open. I imagined a booby-trap or some fat, unfit guy on the other side of the door waiting to do his thing. Only one way to find out.

I sneaked in, alert for sound and movement. No trap and nobody, only a very fine view over the river. A quick search told me that computers and phones had already been shipped out. It seemed unlikely that China would conceal or leave anything behind. Just to be sure, I systematically tore the place apart, ripping up carpet and furnishings, checking for signs of redecoration, areas where the skirting might have been repainted, hunting for clues, for information, for weapons, anything that might join the dots and create a comprehensible picture. I was clean out of luck.

The morning lost to me, I retraced my journey to Waterloo, paid for another ticket and took a ten-minute walk across a covered walkway and down an escalator to Waterloo East. From here I took a train to New Cross Gate, changing at London Bridge. It should have taken me around twenty-five minutes, but the connecting train was late. I didn't arrive in Deptford until almost forty minutes later. I couldn't say why, but I had a bad feeling, stronger than before. The eyes of my fellow travellers didn't tell me anything out of the ordinary. Even so, I wondered whether someone was watching and monitoring my every move. It made me think back to the lights going off in the rental at Montpellier, the crypt and Titus, the red wig over the dead man's hair, the unwritten message that came attached to it, a message addressed to me.

On arrival, I stepped out of the overly warm train and onto the platform and, following the exit, headed for the taxi rank. A couple of minutes later, I was staring out of the rear window of a cab. I had no idea whether the driver was ripping me off by taking me on a roundabout route, but we drove through some depressing-looking streets crammed with too many people, with litter in the gutter and imaginative graffiti on the walls. If these were the lungs of the borough, they had emphysema. I settled back and briefly closed my eyes to ease the tension in my head and the sensation of the walls closing in. When I opened them again the urban landscape had cheered up and I told the driver to pull over, that I'd walk the rest of the way. Stepping out of the cab, I paid the fare. A chill, bitter easterly wind gusted into my eyes, making them smart. I set my face against it and passed rows of tidy terraced houses and neatly tended allotments that spoke of hope and dreams – or maybe they simply whispered them.

The trading estate was off a main road, a collection of terraced industrial and warehouse units built in brick and concrete. Ground floor and two-storey elevations stood side by side, with metal doors and grilles at the windows. To me, it brought to mind a place with sheds and old buildings housing helicopter parts, bad men chasing me, fire and devastation, carnage and death. I shut down the memory. It wasn't wise to seek similarities with another place and time.

Not wanting to be boxed in, Hayes had sensibly taken an end unit. I imagined his men, ready and possibly with a bead on me now. It would take a person with strong guts to shoot a defence-less man out in the open in the middle of the day – or a weak, frightened one. Putting myself in China's shoes, I reckoned he'd have the small fry in the downstairs section, guys pretending to run a legal enterprise, the hard-core loyalists upstairs to protect their boss once the alarm was raised. My strategy was to get inside, one way or another, and 'borrow' a firearm for the rest of the afternoon.

Rating my chances as seventy/thirty in China's favour, I crossed the generous car park, walked up to the door with a purposeful stride, tapped on the glass in the door of the open-plan office and, armed with nothing more than a smile, entered.

CHAPTER THIRTY-SEVEN

Two lads in jeans and hoodies, around nineteen years of age, turned their cold, stony gaze in my direction. One lounged in an office chair, his size tens resting on the desk in front of him. He had a bad case of acne and his peroxide hair did little to improve his pizza-face appearance. Everything about him spoke runt of the litter. The other, skinny like his mate, moved straight towards a filing cabinet the moment I tapped on the door. He stood, one leg twitching, not because he was nervous, but, I suspected, having observed these scenarios dozens of time before, because he was juiced up. Unpredictable as hell, he was the guy I had to watch. As he rested his back against the cold steel cabinet, I had no doubt that, if I presented a problem, a weapon lay within easy reach inside one of the drawers and he wouldn't hesitate to use it.

I flashed another smile and put one hand up in a rough approximation of 'parley'.

'Wondered if you guys can help me.'

They remained expressionless. I got it. These were the kind of kids who wouldn't help their own mothers if on fire.

'There's been a break-in at one of the units further up. Wondered if you'd seen anything or clocked anyone unusual hanging around?'

'You a copper, or what?' Pizza-face either had a south London accent or he was faking it to make himself sound hard.

I put my hand inside my jacket and fished out my fake warrant card. 'DI Benson,' I said. This could go either way. It might make them co-operative, might make them resistant. I watched the shutters descend over their faces. The card had the effect of non-surgically wiring their jaws shut.

I smiled some more. 'I'm guessing you haven't seen anything untoward.'

They both blinked. Maybe they didn't understand *untoward*. 'Who's the boss around here?'

The guy by the filing cabinet twitched and shrugged his bony shoulders. He had a concave chest. I had him down for being bullied as a child. Guys like him either sank or swam. This one was a swimmer.

'You don't know who you work for?' There was grain in my voice.

Pizza-face looked across at his mate. A form of communication took place along the lines of: *Let me take care of this tosser.*

'The boss is out.' He pronounced it 'owt'.

'Anyone else I can talk to? Someone upstairs, maybe.' I angled my gaze towards the staircase at the back of the office.

'They're out too, man,' he said.

I hate being called 'man' by people I don't know. In the great scheme of things, it was a minor irritation. More importantly, I had no idea if he was telling the truth. It seemed highly unlikely that China was somewhere else when he should be lying low. Unless of course Leonid had lied to me or had made a mistake. I needed to be certain.

'So, nobody at home,' I said without expression, my eyes fixed on Mr Unpredictable. 'All right if I take a look around?'

'No, it is not fucking all right, man,' Pizza-face said. 'You got a search warrant?'

'I'm not looking to turn the place over.'

'You're not even peeking inside an envelope. Know what?' he said, with venom, 'you're bang out of order, pig.'

There was absolutely no point debating the issue, or openly taking offence, although I was seriously pissed off with dancing a two-step with these low-grade, talentless sidekicks. 'What would you say to a little incentive?'

For a second the leg stopped twitching and Skinny man's eyes glazed. It would be fair to say that he looked like he was going to come.

'Money for information?' Pizza-face said.

I nodded and withdrew my wallet.

'How much?'

'Depends on the level of information.'

'Nah,' he said, waggling a bony finger. 'Doesn't fuckin' work like that, man. We decide what we're prepared to accept.' He stared at me with feral eyes. The freak show over in the corner let out a laugh, his grin splitting his miserable face in half. Aren't you just the hard man? I thought.

'£250 buys me the answer to three questions. Another £250 buys me a walk upstairs.'

'Two questions and a walk upstairs, £700 in all.'

'£650,' I said. 'If I find out you're lying, I'll have you set up and banged up before you can say China.'

They issued a collective 'whatever' but I had them. Greed glinted in their eyes. They carried out another wordless exchange. Two-bit nobodies, they had no idea of the world they inhabited. I'd give them each a couple of years before they either got rubbed out or wound up in prison. I'm ashamed to say it, but I hoped it was the former.

'You have a deal.'

Very generous of you and thank you very fucking much, I thought. 'All right if I take a step forward?' I held my wallet high in the same way a dog owner brandishes a ball.

177

''Course,' Pizza-face scowled.

I counted out £250 in fifties. Skinny man peeled himself off the filing cabinet and came to see for himself. As his hand shot out to pocket the cash, I clamped mine over his. We had five seconds of deadlock.

'Protocol,' I spat.

Skinny man looked at his friend for a translation. It occurred to me then that if words were weapons, I could wipe them out with a finely turned sentence. Whether or not he understood, Pizza-face had his eye to the main chance, told his friend to back off and said, 'Let the cop do his thing.' So I did.

'When did China leave?'

'A couple of hours ago.'

'Did he go alone?'

'Yes.'

Strange behaviour for a frightened man, and it wasn't what I wanted to hear. If he went alone, someone was upstairs holding the fort, except that, in all the time I'd been there, I hadn't heard a squeak of activity. Judging from the fabric of the building, it would be hard to disguise movement. Perhaps his bodyguards had deserted their posts.

'Who did he go to meet?'

'That's three fucking questions.'

The only words to pass his lips, I turned and stared at Skinny man, surprised by his numeracy. He stared back, dead-eyed. I slapped down another couple of fifties and repeated the question. Both lads grinned. Pizza-face answered. 'We don't know.'

Hoodwinked, I let out a sigh and motioned that I wanted to check out the upper storey.

'Money first,' Pizza-face said.

'Not until I return in one piece.'

'There's nobody up there,' Skinny man burst out, copping a furious look from his friend.

'Cool.' I banged down the rest of the money.

On a scale of one to ten in the mess stakes, upstairs scored a six. Among the remnants of office furniture, there were several sleeping bags, a wall of sealed packing boxes similar to those I'd seen in the backroom of the barber's and, in the far corner, a pile of clothes, including a tropical shirt, a pair of jeans and sneakers. An aerosol of inexpensive, branded deodorant, its top off, also lay on the floor. It looked like China had dressed for an important occasion, or he was worried and sweating with fear, or both. Lunch somewhere? I glanced at my watch. He might be back at any moment.

I went over to inspect the boxes and found two open. Expecting to find guns, I discovered a portable makeshift wardrobe containing underwear, more patterned shirts and soft-soled shoes. The second was more interesting. Underneath a layer of clothing and books, a laptop. My spoils of war, I took it and went downstairs. The kids had other ideas.

Alarmed, Pizza-face leapt to his feet. 'You can't take that. It belongs to Mr Hayes.'

Skinny man broke off from examining their recent windfall and fell into line next to him. I estimated it would take him seven steps to get to the filing cabinet and a couple of seconds to wrench open a drawer and pull out a gun. Wrong place, wrong time, man, I thought.

'It belongs to me now,' I said, crossing the floor.

A flash of steel pulled me up short.

Skinny didn't need a gun. He had a blade.

Contorted and ugly, Pizza-face snarled, 'Shank him, Skins.'

Skins came at me with all the flair of a carbon-fibre racing car. Strong, light on his feet and very fast, he sliced the blade within a millimetre of my face, missing me only because I took a step back. Instead of freezing, he came at me a second time, this time feinting with his free arm. He didn't want to frighten me. He wanted to kill me. With the next thrust, he caught my good arm, carving through leather. Pain seared through my

179

nerve endings and I let out a gasp. Scenting victory, Skins lunged, connecting again, this time with the lower part of my body. The pocket of my jacket split but my mobile phone took the brunt of the impact. I'm fit but my breathing felt laboured, my limbs slow. Blood rushed through my heart so quickly it was pounding against my ribcage as if it wanted to explode. Everything about the situation told me the best thing I could do was run, but I couldn't leave without the laptop. The laptop was my only piece of hard evidence, a connection that might lead me to McCallen. It was also a shield, a battering ram and weapon.

His blood up, Skinny launched a third time, cheered on by his co-partner in attempted murder. As he struck, I raised the laptop, deflecting his blow, steel striking aluminium. He grinned, unfazed and cocky, and danced lightly on his feet. Another vicious jab and he sliced through the leather in my other sleeve. I didn't know whether or not the gash was deep but now my adrenal glands were on full pump, dulling the pain. Triumphant, Skins faced me front on. Bad move. Always stay side-on to protect vital organs. Jabbing the blade at my face, his other hand balled in a fist, intent on landing a blow, his eyes signalling the belief that his knife gave him a clear advantage. Ordinarily, I'd agree with him.

Powering forward and using all of my body weight, I swung the laptop across his jaw in one choreographed move. It connected with bone-shattering intensity and did the equivalent of shoving his brain in a tumble dryer. On impact, the blade flew out of his hand as he hit the deck, unconscious. One man down, I turned my attention to Pizza-face who, stunned into action, scrabbled to wrench open the drawer in his desk. Before he had a chance to withdraw whatever was inside, I kicked it closed, trapping his hand, possibly breaking fingers, his scream rebounding off the walls. Yanking the drawer back open, I withdrew the weapon, an old-style Beretta that no sane and self-respecting gunman would ever think of using. I released the catch at the left side of the butt behind the trigger, removed the magazine and pulled back the slide to eject a round in the chamber and pocket the ammo.

'You've broken my fucking hand,' he yowled, bloodied fingers tucked up underneath an armpit.

I slow-glanced over my shoulder at Skins. 'Think yourself lucky.'

'You're dead, motherfucker.'

I breathed a big, indulgent sigh – so young and so much to learn. 'The slide often fails on a model as old as this,' I said dropping the Beretta at his feet. 'Can prove dangerous to the user.' Then I scooped up my money and, point made, strode out.

CHAPTER THIRTY-EIGHT

My leather was in tatters. Blood ran down my arms. Adrenalin is a wonderful natural anaesthetic and I knew that the damage might be worse than it felt. I didn't have time for another visit to Mace and I didn't fancy my chances trying to get back to the hotel on public transport to assess my wounds. My fellow travellers might not pay me the least attention. I couldn't expect the same indifference from London Underground staff. For all I knew MI5 could be tailing me, although my gut told me that the action was back in Cheltenham, not here in London. Fortunately, I now had all my cash back in my possession. For the right price, I was sure a minicab driver would be more than happy to pick up a few necessaries from a chemist and ferry me back to the hotel. Violent crime in the borough wasn't exactly an unknown and ferrying the wounded was almost part of the job description. Sure enough, Zap Cabs were happy to oblige and I was soon on my way.

After two brief stops, one at a chemist, the other to pick up a purple dress shirt, collar size 16, I crossed the moody, darkened foyer of the hotel and returned to my room loaded with antiseptic, painkillers, the all-important steri-strips, and enough bandages to embalm a mummy.

Peeling off my leather jacket and sweater exposed the extent of the damage. Experienced in the art of patching myself up, I wasn't certain this time that I was up to the job without medical attention. The first slice to my arm wasn't as bad as I'd feared; the second, close to the previous injury and Mace's handiwork, would have been deeper had the arm not already been dressed. In spite of this, a nasty gash outside the hurt zone probably needed stitches. Throwing painkillers down my throat first, I washed my wounds and treated them with antiseptic. Then I bandaged the first and applied steristrips to the second, before again bandaging it. This, together with the multi-coloured skin around my eyes and the strip across the bridge of my nose, was not quite the image I'd hoped to convey at a sex party for the seriously wealthy. Nevertheless, I shaved, changed, ordered dinner from room service, kicked back with a beer from the minibar and opened up the laptop. It got me nowhere.

My computer skills had improved immeasurably during the past year, but I was no hacker. Password protected, probably encrypted, the laptop stared sullenly back at me. It freaked me out a little to know that China Hayes's bloodied fingers had travelled all over it. Wishing it wasn't necessary, I phoned a contact I'd used when I was in the game. A computer analyst by day, Jat broke through all types of firewall by night. Previously, I'd used him to check out potential clients so that I had some idea of exactly what I was getting into. Jat spent his life communicating either by phone or online. He answered as soon as the line connected.

'Yup.'

I pictured his toffee-coloured eyes, slightly too close together, looking into the screen next to him. 'Got a job for you.'

A sharp intake of breath signalled his surprise. 'Thought you were –'

'No, I'm not dead,' I said, beating him to it and feeling like I'd been resurrected. 'I'm very much alive and I need your expertise.'

It was my turn to hold my breath. I wasn't at all sure whether Jat's little brother had survived my last escapade. He'd fallen in with a bunch of fundamentalists who, coincidentally, I happened to be hunting down. I couldn't be certain that I hadn't killed him. I thought Jat might make some reference to it.

'I'm listening,' he said.

Seemed we were all good. 'Meet me tomorrow at ten.' I mentioned the name of a café in Kensington and that was that.

Mid-way through *confit* of duck, my phone rang. Simone.

'You haven't forgotten this evening's arrangements?'

I glanced at my watch. I had plenty of time. 'I'm looking forward to it.'

'Work has been good?'

It seemed an odd thing to say. I guess if your man allegedly works for the security services, you can hardly ask *What kind of a day did you have at the office, sweetheart?*

'Busy.' Which was true. 'I should warn you I'm slightly battered and bruised.'

'You are all right?' Her voice pinched with concern.

'Nothing that won't mend.' In the background, a phone rang at her end of the line.

'*Merde*, I have to go – a client. I will see you at ten. Stay safe.'

Nobody has ever said this to me. Most have wanted me dead. It made me smile inside. Then I realised I was mistaken. McCallen had never wanted me dead either.

* * *

The address was in Eaton Square. Stucco, with grand elevations, worth around a cool £40 million at a guess, the house was instantly identifiable because Frederick was posted outside the impressive entrance. Attentive as ever, Frederick wished me good evening, opened the door, and informed me that Miss Fabron was waiting 'in the basement area, sir.'

Handed a glass of pink champagne by a classically good-looking young male with oiled limbs and dressed in a purple loincloth, I headed inside to a vast room that resembled the set for the court of the Sun King. The buzzwords were lavish, hedonistic and exotic. If the building was worth a packet, the baroque interior doubled it. Most of the invited men were foreign, from parts of Asia as well as the almost obligatory Middle Eastern contingent, an aura of wealth enveloping every guest. Every item of clothing and accessory was designer, the jewellery on show alone ran into hundreds of thousands. This crew might be a very different crowd to the Cheltenham clientele but, on cursory observation, they fucked the same.

I made my way down a walnut polished staircase to an excavated basement area. Here, the vibe was ultra-modern and cool. A wall-mounted screen played an art house movie – or pornographic, depending upon one's point of view. A snooker game on a full-size table was in full swing with two teams of players, the women seductively leaning over the baize to better display their assets. At my arrival Simone rushed towards me.

'You are late. I thought you were not coming.'

She looked fabulous as ever in a striking green muslin see-through blouse, her naked breasts hugging the fabric beneath, and a magenta lace skirt in which tiny jewelled fragments sparkled when she moved.

'*Cherie*,' she whispered, slipping her small hand through mine, drawing me close and kissing me in a way that said to everyone, *He's mine.* I wasn't complaining.

She drew back and studied my face, her soft dark eyes etched with anxiety. 'You need to take care, Joe.'

'Simone.' We both turned towards a stunning-looking redhead called Dido. Chic, with a vampish in-and-out figure, she smiled an apology. I didn't mind. Purple was definitely her colour. 'Might I drag you away from this gorgeous man for a moment, darling?'

Simone tipped up on the toes of her high heels and muttered that she would come and find me.

I drifted upstairs where the noise was louder, the action more intense. Conversation among the cognoscenti ranged from property prices to independent schools and fantasy sex. Casting around for Zara, I spotted a couple of minders – big-boned men with shaved heads and upper arms the size of gammons. Refreshing my drink, I followed a winding staircase to a vast landing with doors off, some open, some closed. Inner sanctums for pleasure, from which came the unmistakable sounds of people lustily having sex. As I wondered what to do next, two women bowled past me, the taller of the two pushing the other woman up against the nearest wall, her hand darting up the woman's skirt. Bored, wondering where the hell Simone was, I ran straight into Zara.

'Hi.' The lascivious expression in her baby-blue eyes indicated that she was immensely pleased to see me. 'I hoped you'd be back.'

To be fair to the woman, she'd upped her game in the sophistication stakes. Her hair was swept up, revealing perfect skin, and the neckline of her silk sequin dress was demure. Only the racy gunmetal cuff on her right arm hinted at something more risqué.

'What the hell happened to your beautiful face?'

'Got into a scrap.'

She ran a manicured nail down my arm, turned on, apparently, by the thought of violence. I flinched and glanced over her shoulder. 'No husband?'

'He couldn't make it. He's in Dubai.' In other words, come and get me. I fully intended to, but not in the way she thought. Observing the rules of the game, I let her make the first move.

'Want to come out to play?' Her voice a low seductive growl, she ran the tip of her tongue along her top lip.

I hesitated. I didn't want Simone getting the wrong idea.

Zara appeared to read my mind. 'Simone is a very liberated woman and I am exceptionally discreet.'

Discreet was good. 'Show me the way,' I said.

She took my hand and led me into a room where a naked couple were wrapped around each other in a way that defied physiology. I dragged her back.

'You're shy.' She smiled as though she found it an endearing quality.

'Here,' I said, toeing open the door to another room, which, although it housed a huge bed that bore the hallmarks of someone having made full use of it, was empty. As soon as we were inside, I kicked the door shut, and turned the key. Zara instantly threw herself against the wall, arched her back, and revealed that she wasn't wearing underwear. Next, she reached out and grabbed my hair, forcing my head down between her legs. Amazed by her strength, I pulled away, straightened up and captured both her wrists, pinioning them above her swept back hair. Expecting this to be the entrée, she let out an animal sound from the back of her throat.

'I want answers,' I said.

'You'll have to beat them out of me.'

'Lars Pallenberg. Tell me about him.'

Mistakenly thinking we were role-playing she pretended to struggle. 'I don't know who you're talking about.'

'Yes, you do.'

'I've never heard of him.'

'You have. He's German, an artist.' I didn't say that he was also dead. 'Blond, good-looking, sensitive.'

'I don't like sensitive men,' she said breathily, and through half-closed eyes. 'I like cruel men like you.'

'He was an invited guest maybe a year ago.'

Her eyelids flickered. Unsure where we were heading, she thrashed about in a doomed attempt to spice things up.

'Stop that.'

187

Pressing her breasts against my chest, she pushed herself into my crotch and tried to kiss me. I recoiled enough to miss her lips, not enough to loosen my grip. 'Fuck me,' she moaned, squirming in my grasp.

'Answer the damn question.'

The edge in my voice finally hit home. Shock gave way to fear, her blue eyes popped open and she caught a glimpse of the darkness contained inside me. Her skin turned pale and pallid. 'You're serious.'

'Deadly.'

'Who are you?'

'Simone's friend, remember.'

'But –'

'Do not play me. Pallenberg, who invited him?'

'I don't know. I've never heard of him.' Her eyes glistened with tears. I hated doing this to her, but McCallen was my big priority and, if any light could be shed on her whereabouts, I'd pretty much do anything to get it.

'Wait,' she said, 'He might have signed in under a different name.'

I'd already considered this. 'Simone has the guest lists?'

'On her computer, yes.'

'And Simone, tell me about her.'

'What do you want to know?' It came out as a wail.

'Who she hangs out with, what she does, who she sees.'

'I don't know. I –'

'Ever heard the name China Hayes?'

Zara narrowed her eyes in recollection. I got the impression that she was desperate to help me so that she could leave and never come back. I loosened my grip slightly. 'I've never heard the name. I honestly don't know if she has close friends. She never strikes me that way. She's a party animal, but you know that already. She's a good-time girl, sporty. She skis, scuba dives, fences, likes big events.'

'What kind of big events?'

'Music gigs, horseracing, polo. I can't tell you any more. I don't really know her that well, nobody does. This,'she said, glancing at the door, 'it's superficial, for kicks, for fun. Nobody gets hurt.'

'What about the drugs?'

'What drugs?'

'Heard any rumours about her dealing?'

'Never.' She looked at me with such bewildered, haunted eyes I released my grasp. Her entire body shivered.

'I'm sorry.'

'It's fine,' she said, relieved, her tone clipped and reproachful. 'I don't want to know what this is about. I won't say a word to Simone, I promise,' she added quickly.

'Zara, I'm not going to hurt you.'

'No?' she said. 'Can I go now?'

I nodded and unlocked the door. Feeling shitty about what I'd done, I wondered whether she'd set her husband on me. She made a move to go then stopped in the doorway, as though she'd remembered something.

'We don't get a lot of Germans, but there was a guy around the time you mentioned.' She had my full and undivided attention. 'Fucked like a bull. He wasn't an artist. He had a name like the German car.'

'Benz?'

'Yes,' she said with a sudden, glacial smile. 'Dieter Benz. I hope he screws you over.'

CHAPTER THIRTY-NINE

Simone was coming upstairs as I was going down. 'I've been all over looking for you.'

'Sorry, I'm not feeling well. I've spent most of the last hour in the bathroom.' I gestured vaguely towards a door.

She let out a sigh and rested the palm of her hand against my brow. 'Darling, you look terrible.' I felt terrible but not in the way she imagined. 'Do you want to take a lie down?'

I shook my head. 'I think it's better I leave.'

She fished in her clutch bag for a room card. 'Here, take this. We are booked in up the road. Get some rest and I'll see you later.'

'Are you sure?'

She inclined her head, almost coquettish. 'I am positive. Don't worry, I'll be good,' she added with a sudden fabulous smile. Then she looked anxious again. 'Will you be all right?'

'Yes,' I said. I had to be.

In the heart of Belgravia, the hotel was a short walk away in Ebury Street and close to Victoria Underground station. As ever, I admired Simone's choice. Boutique style, it exuded class and luxury. Our room on the second floor was a picture of calm and elegance.

Simone's laptop sat on a small desk underneath the only window. It was still plugged in. I flipped it open. One touch and it sprang into life. I took off my jacket, loosened my tie and sat down. Without thinking, I punched in 'Bagatelle' as the password. Immediately, I was launched into another world, Simone's universe. I scrolled through files on lifestyle, fashion and design, dipped into emails, mostly to and from women seeking Simone's services in one form or another. Some in French, most in English. There were screeds of stuff that I could collectively classify as female. Eager not to miss my opportunity, I opened the 'Party' file and ran through hundreds of names in random order, and then a separate folder marked 'Venues'. Finding a sub-file marked 'Berlin', I opened it, hoping either Pallenberg or Benz would appear, only to remember that Bagatelle had a women-only membership. I ran through names and locations and flipped to another file marked 'Guest Lists'. Sure enough, Benz appeared, although his name stood alone and it was impossible to match him with whoever he'd accompanied. Not one to give up, I returned to the female membership. I had at least four hours before Simone returned. An hour later, I stumbled across something that spun me out.

Shaken, I poured myself a glass of water and wondered why Mathilde Brommer, Lars's former girlfriend, had lied to me and why her name was in the file. I looked at my watch. It was two in the morning. She'd be asleep. If I spoke to her now, she'd be confused. I smiled. Disorientated people make mistakes and say things they shouldn't. I called.

She picked up with what sounded like a full-throttle curse.

'You didn't tell me about the sex parties.' My tone was blatantly accusing.

There was a long silence. When she eventually spoke she was cold, controlled and exceptionally angry. 'You phone me at this time in the morning to lecture me about my private life?'

'You don't deny it?'

'What is there to deny, Mr Porter? Are you looking for an invite?'

'You know Simone Fabron?'

'Not intimately.'

'You told me that you'd never heard of her.'

'I told you that I'd never heard of her in connection with Lars.'

I wasn't going to get into an argument with her over semantics because I never fight battles I can't win. 'How do you know her?'

'Isn't it obvious? Through her website and services. It's a professional relationship,' she said smartly.

I rubbed my eyes. I was going wrong somewhere. Things were shifting in ways I couldn't pin down. It was akin to walking through a wild Arabian desert riddled with quicksand.

'Did you ever take Dieter Benz with you?'

She swore in German. I got the message.

'Did you ever take Lars with you?'

'Never. He was already with your Miss Spencer by then. How is she, by the way?'

Her nasty question broke over me like a huge wave running at high tide. 'What the hell is it to you?' I said.

'Excuse me?'

'What do you know about her disappearance?'

'She has disappeared?' She sounded triumphant. I repeated the question.

'I know nothing. It's the first I've heard of it.'

'You'll have to do better than that, Mathilde. You had the motive. I've already caught you in one lie. How many more?'

'You think I am responsible?' Her voice roared down the line.

'Why not?'

She gave a short, incredulous laugh. 'Because it is ridiculous. I wouldn't have the first clue how to go about it.'

'You don't need to. You could have given the order to someone else.'

192

'Sure, of course,' she said, the tone as dramatic as it was ugly. 'Send in the cops. They can check my passport. I have only one thing to say about your lovely Miss Spencer.' I waited for the punchline. 'She was a bitch.' The line went dead.

Mathilde's denial weighed heavy. Dispirited, I resumed checking the laptop but nothing leapt out at me. It was all business stuff; there was no link to China, no link to either Pallenberg or Benz. Again, I was stalked by a memory from the previous job – people often operated from more than one computer.

Opening a personal file, I unearthed more email correspondence written in French to people I assumed were friends, with names like Anaïs, Guillaume, Nicole, Jacques and Davide. Details of hotel bookings in all parts of Europe revealed no startling surprises. Using the camera on my phone, I captured as much varied and random data as I could so that I could study it at a later date, match it to other information or, if necessary, send it to Jat.

Next, I checked out the room, opened drawers – mostly empty aside from a set of expensive underwear and a hotel hairdryer – and ran my hand over the few clothes hanging in the wardrobe. Simone had one pair of boots and a tan brown leather shoulder bag, tear-shaped. I picked up and shook out the contents, which included a large purse with a hundred pounds in cash, credit cards in her name, a passport, a travel toothbrush and toothpaste, moisturiser, tampons and a blister pack of contraceptive pills with twelve days' use. Pushing everything back inside, I returned the bag to the bottom of the wardrobe, took off my clothes, crawled into bed and lay there, too wired to sleep.

China Hayes had colluded in the murder of his rivals, but now he had disappeared. He'd had a connection with a German – maybe Pallenberg, maybe Benz. Why would a London crime lord be doing business with a neo-Nazi? Mathilde Brommer had attended the same parties as Benz, either at the same time, or on a separate occasion. Too much of a coincidence? Mathilde had the motive for murder and yet her outrage down the line had been strong and convincing. Titus was dead. McCallen was missing. Billy Squeeze lay at the heart of it, or at least, someone was using his name to invoke terror. However I tried to assemble the pieces, I couldn't make the picture fit, couldn't make it work. I seriously hoped that where I'd failed to locate McCallen the security services or the police would succeed. After that I drifted off. Clear, dreamless unconsciousness eluded me.

When Simone returned a little after five, I pretended to be out for the count. Shoes slipped off, a rustle of clothing and then the mattress yielding as Simone's cool, naked body climbed in beside mine. She fell asleep instantly and, some time later, I must have dozed off. Around eight, the light in the room leaden, she hooked one leg over my body and rolled me underneath her. Skin on skin.

'Morning,' she said, languidly.

'Nice wake-up call.'

She smiled, studying my arms, her brow creased. Blood had seeped through one of the bandages. 'What happened?'

'Someone came at me with a knife.'

'Have you seen a doctor?'

'No, it's fine.' I didn't want her fussing over me.

'I worry about you.'

'You shouldn't.'

She ran an index finger over my lips and pressed it into my mouth. 'I don't expect you to tell me about your work.'

'Good.'

'But you can trust me. Sometimes it helps to talk, not about specific details but –'

'You know Mathilde Brommer.'

Simone frowned at my sudden, serious tone.

'She attended one of your parties in Berlin.'

Her face lit up and she threw her head back and laughed. 'Joe, have you any idea the number of women on my mailing list?' As it happened, I did. She had a point, but I wasn't smiling. All her mirth vanished. She slipped off me and grabbed a robe. 'Why do you want to know?'

'I can't tell you that.'

'So you get to ask the questions but I am not allowed?' Her small nostrils flared. The pretty features instantly became a collection of sharp edges.

'What about Dieter Benz?'

At once, her face darkened. She rounded on me. 'Dieter Benz?'

'You remember him?' I propped myself up on one elbow, felt the tingle of excitement that accompanies the thrill of the chase.

'For all the wrong reasons. He's a vile anti-Semitic thug who practically raped one of our guests.'

She crossed the room in a theatrical fashion, swiped at her handbag and produced a pack of expensive-looking cigarettes. I didn't know she smoked and I bet the hotel wouldn't like it. Not that I was going to stand in the way of an angry, highly strung woman and her chosen drug. Immediately, my mind flipped back to the graveyard, the discarded pack I'd found in the grass.

She shook out a cigarette, placed it between her lips and lit up. Plumes of thin grey smoke seeped into the atmosphere and curled up towards the ceiling. She stood erect and taut, arms crossed as though she were holding herself together in case she might shatter and fall. 'He is blacklisted,' she added, as if that concluded the conversation.

'Who invited him?'

'I don't remember.'

I looked her straight in the eye. If Benz had behaved so badly, why didn't she remember who'd invited him? Zara had said that he 'fucked like a bull'. She had not said that he'd almost raped a guest.

'Why are you looking at me like that?'

'Things don't add up.' I slipped out of bed, reached for my clothes.

'The guy in the gold mask.'

She rolled her eyes at the ceiling and let out a terse sigh. 'We have already been over this.'

'I want to go over it again.'

'Why?'

'Because he's dead.'

She looked astonished. 'And you think this is connected to –'

'You.'

She stared at me as if I'd punched her hard in the stomach and winded her. When she finally composed herself, her eyes were black with rage. 'I am not one of your spies,' she spat, 'or informers.'

'I don't understand why you are so defensive.'

'Because you are accusing me of things I haven't done. You are using me – first my body and now my mind.' She glanced sideways, her gaze alighting on the laptop, making the connection. Her mouth fell open. She turned back, took several paces at speed and slapped my face so hard my fillings shifted. I reached out and grabbed her. The robe slipped off her shoulders.

'You vile shit, let go of me.'

'No,' I said. 'Calm down.'

'I will not calm down,'she bellowed. 'You've been snooping. You have no right.'

'I have every right,' I shouted over her. 'A friend of mine is missing and I'm busting my guts to find her.'

I stood, utterly shaken by my lack of discretion. Seconds rolled by like days. To my surprise, a tear rolled down her cheek. I let her go. She wiped her face with the back of her hand and drew me towards her, kissed my forehead, my cheeks, like a mother kissing a child better, then she kissed my mouth, softly at first, the rest a blur of desire, angry sex and passion.

CHAPTER FORTY

I arrived at the café late. I'd had to travel back to the hotel, grab China's laptop and then trek back to Kensington. Fortunately, the hotel extended my checkout time so that was one less thing to concern me.

Jat was already seated. He still had his trademark dark hair and sideburns. He did a double take when he saw me.

'I apologise for my clothes,' I said, getting in first.

'Don't tell me – an all-nighter and you got mugged on the way home?'

'Something like that.' I ordered a double espresso and handed him the laptop.

'Want me to open it now?'

I looked around the café. Mums with young kids, teenagers, a couple of old folk. 'Can you do that?'

'I can do anything,' he flashed.

'Cocky sod.'

As it turned out, he couldn't. He tapped keys, chased from one window to another, muttered something about lockdowns and case-sensitive passwords and a host of other stuff I didn't understand.

'With time, could you open it?'

'Sure.'

'How long do you need?'

'Days, a week, who knows?'

This was not the answer I wanted. 'Are you busy right now?'

Jat's face lit up. 'Got quite a workload.'

'It pays well?'

'Sure does.'

'I'll triple it if you put my job ahead of everything else.'

He let out a big 'whoa' and then a 'yay'. I have never understood the popularity of these phrases, which translated mean 'goodness' and 'yes', but it was a welcome response.

Jat didn't need a sign of good faith. He knew I was all right for the money. I drained my espresso and stood up. 'I'll phone you in a few days.' Before I left I asked a question that had been nagging me for the past year.

'Your little brother, is he behaving himself?'

A smile sprang to Jat's lips, warmth in his eyes. 'Found himself a nice girl with a wicked sense of humour.'

I was glad. 'He's seen the light then.'

The edges of his smile faded a little. 'Yeah. It was touch and go for a while. You know he never talks about it but something bad happened, something really freaked him.' He looked at me with a questioning expression.

People got killed, including the men he was mixing with. I shook my head in a 'don't ask' gesture. 'He's fine, that's all that matters.'

* * *

I walked to the nearest Tube station. The sky was dull and the perishing east wind made me shiver in my party gear. I wished I'd kept my mouth shut in my exchange with Simone. My momentary loss of control was a bad sign. I guess I was taken aback that a woman, who seemed so self-possessed and cool, had cared enough to want to comfort me. It had been a long time since that had happened.

About to cross into the Underground, I spotted a newspaper hoarding: 'MAN'S BODY FOUND IN THAMES NEAR LUXURY DEVELOPMENT'. I stopped, picked up a *Metro* and read it while crushed between an Italian guy talking non-stop on a phone and an Eastern European woman with a small, unsettled baby. The piece was patchy, not particularly informative, but the time frame matched China's missing status. It did not say how the man died but death by drowning was the clear inference. In a population of millions, it could have been anyone in the drink. In my bones, I knew it was Hayes. You reap what you sow. Whatever China had intended for me was lying dead on the mortuary slab with him. It didn't mean I was out of danger. Now China's killer, whoever *he* was, would be gunning for me.

I returned to the hotel, showered and changed, packed and checked out. I didn't return to the lock-up. I went straight to Paddington to catch the train back to Cheltenham. Before heading for the main station, I stayed on the Underground, tracing the route of my last journey over a year before on the day that Billy died. I stood on the same platform in roughly the same position, imagined him standing up ahead and close to the tracks, unaware of my presence. Closing my eyes, I remembered how I'd moved forward, the way he'd turned, the frozen shock on his face at the grim realisation that what goes around comes around.

I visualised the faces of those nearby, mouths open in horror at the tumbling man, women screaming, men reaching for mobile phones, some standing mute, fists pressed into their mouths. Not one had stood out from the crowd. On that fateful day, my single purpose had been to get away, to escape. I had – yet I had not.

I returned to the main concourse from where I boarded my train. Going back would be tough. My hometown now the focus of the enquiry, the place would be thick with police and security services. Most would be on the lookout for McCallen, the rest, if they could be spared, on the hunt for me. They were not my greatest fear. Someone was jerking my chain and I had a sense that in the game that lay ahead there were only two players.

Him and me.

CHAPTER FORTY-ONE

My mobile rang as I walked through the front door. It was unlikely to be Simone. She'd mentioned that she had to meet with her accountant and visit her solicitor about an inheritance from an elderly aunt, and would try and sort out a time to meet soon afterwards. I squinted at the unknown number and pressed receive. An electronically distorted voice came on the line, electronic, low and alien. It said my name – not Joshua Thane, not Joe Nathan, but my criminal soubriquet, 'Hex'.

I killed the surprise in my reaction. Mentally, I was in a good place. The call meant we were in play. 'Yes,' I said.

'I have your girl.'

Which girl? Shock made me dull-witted. 'Simone?'

The voice laughed. 'Simone? I thought you'd taken care of her. Looks like I'll have to deal with it myself.'

China, I thought, wrong-footed – had to be. He must have faked his own death. 'Who is this?'

'Irrelevant.'

I wanted to punch holes in the walls. I wanted to call him a scheming, double-dealing bastard. Losing my temper would not extend her life, however, so I said, 'You have McCallen?'

'I do.'

'She's alive?' Blood pumped through my temple until I thought my brain would burst.

'You didn't really think she was dead, did you?'

'Where is she?'

'All in good time.'

'What do you want?'

'To make you suffer.' The mocking tone vanished.

I didn't go into why he was doing it, no point. 'This has nothing to do with McCallen.'

'It has everything to do with McCallen. You were quite a duo.'

'It was nothing more than a straight business transaction. I did her a favour. She helped me out. As did you, if you remember, or have you forgotten how you helped me to nail Billy Squeeze?' China's precise motivation now eluded me.

'I have not forgotten.'

'Why Titus?' I said.

'Collateral damage, and he had blood on his hands.'

Seemed I was wrong about the extent of China's knowledge. He'd obviously done his homework.

Then another thought occurred to me.

'What's with the special effects? Why aren't you talking directly to me?'

He let out a laugh. 'All part of the plan, Hex. China Hayes is dead. I faked my own death.'

'How do I know that McCallen is alive, that this isn't a trick?'

'You want proof of life?'

'I do.'

'You'd like me to send a picture?'

'Whatever.'

'How about a scream?'

Before I could answer, I heard a woman's voice shouting no, followed by such an agonising cry of pain I almost dropped the phone. Was it McCallen's voice? Anguished, I couldn't tell. I wasn't prepared to take the gamble. I wanted to tell him to stop hurting her, yet I knew that it would imply an emotional connection, which would make me weak. Uber-cool, I didn't react.

'Convinced?'

'Yes. Take me and let her go.'

'I'd hoped you might say that.'

'Do we have a deal?' I knew that there would be no trade, that this psycho wanted us both dead. He was simply having fun with me.

'I think we might.'

'Might isn't good enough. Tell me where she is now.'

Silence.

It was as if the clocks had stopped turning and time had come to a shuddering halt. She was alive, I kept telling myself, which was good. What state she was in as China's prisoner I dreaded to consider. China was a heartless man. In common with his kind, he enjoyed abusing women. He liked hearing them scream. The sound of her pain ripped through me with such exquisite intensity I had to exert every effort to concentrate.

'I won't contact the police or security services,' I assured him.

'Of course you won't. They'll ask too many uncomfortable questions about the man you killed and dumped in the quarry.'

I clamped my teeth together to prevent a response. I hadn't disclosed that level of detail. How did he know? Was I seen? Did he have others watching me? Automatically, my eyes flicked to the window. An empty street apart from a stray cat. I was in danger of allowing paranoia to make my thinking sloppy.

With a first-class honours degree in cunning, China knew my methods. He had an approximate grasp on how I ticked. I felt a partial sense of relief because now I was dealing with a known quantity even if it meant doing business with a vicious and ruthless bastard. The whole Billy Squeeze story had been nothing more than a ruse to destabilise me. It wasn't working. I had to keep him talking. The fact I had his laptop provided no consolation. I wondered if he knew I'd stolen it.

'What do you want me to do?'

'I'll let you know.'

'When? Tell me now.'

'You're in no position to call the shots, Hex.'

He was right. I swallowed hard.

'You'll hear from me in twenty-four hours.'

'Twenty-four hours and then what?'

He hung up.

CHAPTER FORTY-TWO

I phoned Simone.

'Where are you?'

'I told you, with my solicitor. Excuse me,' I heard her say to someone, 'I have to take this call.' Next, the sound of high heels on wood in a hollow, empty space. 'What is it?' Her voice sounded low and a little tetchy.

'Where are you going afterwards?'

'Why?' she brightened. 'Are you still here in London?'

'No. Look, there's no easy way to put this, China Hayes is gunning for you.'

'What?'

'He wants you dead. I'm serious. Your life is in danger, Simone.'

'But you said it would be all right.'

I didn't remember saying this. 'It's has nothing to do with the drug mules. It's a complicated story and I don't have time to explain.'

'Shall I come to you?' I heard the catch in her voice.

'You must stay away.'

'But I don't understand.'

'Listen to me. Don't go to a friend. Don't visit favourite haunts. Book yourself into a cheap hotel and stay there. You don't surface for anything. Keep your phone switched on but only answer if I call. I'll come to you as soon as I can. It might take a couple of days.'

Her voice soared. 'Forty-eight hours, why?'

'I need to take care of something here first. Trust me. Can you do that?' It was a big ask for a woman whose trust was as limited as my own.

'I have no choice?'

'None whatsoever.'

'*D'accord*. I will do as you say.'

Relieved, I phoned Jat. 'Have you made a start?'

'I have a day job, remember?'

I'd forgotten. 'Look, things have changed. I really need as much information as you can pull off as soon as possible and as quickly as possible.'

Jat let out a patient sigh. I felt like a writer who's accidentally deleted a novel he's been working on for a year and Jat, my computer geek, was my only hope of salvation.

'I'm looking for a location.'

'Anywhere in particular?'

'Cheltenham.' I didn't know this. She could be held in London, or anywhere, but as McCallen had disappeared from Cheltenham, it was a fair bet. 'Look for any links, addresses, references to a remote spot – warehouses, basements, lock-ups, somewhere you might hold a kidnap victim.'

'A what?'

Jat was accustomed to my more arcane questions. He knew what my line of work had been, although it was never mentioned. My remark obviously struck him as unusual and outside my usual sphere. 'I'm one of the good guys,' I said in an effort to convince him that he was batting on the side of the angels, albeit fallen.

'Right,' he said, uncertainly. 'I'll get on it.'

Next, working to China rules, I made plans. Nine times out

of ten, Hayes would keep his victims chained or manacled. A set of bolt cutters was top of my shopping list. I sped down the street and around the corner to the hardware store and shot in before they closed. On the way, I drummed my fingers lightly on the window of the watchmaker's, nodded thanks. He nodded back – no smile, no light in his eyes, nothing more to report.

The choice was limited to very cheap and very expensive. I picked out an industrial strength heavy-duty pair of bolt cutters with high carbon steel blades that cost me almost two hundred pounds. It was a risk because monumental strength was needed to open the blades and I was at a disadvantage because the wounds to my arms had weakened the muscles. However anything less powerful wouldn't work. I added nylon high-tensile rope, strong enough to strap McCallen to me if she was too weak to walk. After paying in cash, I nipped into the butcher's, the counter already cleared for the day. I must have looked hungry because they sorted out a rump steak in no time. Next door I paid for two high-energy drinks with enough glucose to bring back a diabetic from a hypo. Back home I raided the medicine chest for an illicit brand of painkiller, which, if used in the right quantity, would knock out a donkey.

I'd done as much as I could for the day so I cooked and ate and pushed McCallen as far from my mind as possible, somewhere indistinct and on the edge. China's motivation, however, continued to baffle me. He'd never been a pal of Billy's and was happy to do his best to help me nail him. I offered no threat to China – I never had done – and only a foolish man takes out others without a damn good reason. China could be inconsistent and unpredictable, yet he'd always ticked to an internal logic. The way he was acting now suggested he'd had a brainstorm, the use of the electronically disguised voice a particularly unusual move. Maybe the guy was ill, I really didn't know. What I did know was that I was up against a formidable enemy, the equivalent of Cheltenham Town FC versus Bayern-Munich. In one way it played to my strength. Against impossible odds, I became motivated and aggressive.

I itched for a gun in my hand. I knew how to get hold of one, even at short notice. In the circumstances, it was desirable. To do so would cross the line. There would be no going back.

That was my big dilemma.

CHAPTER FORTY-THREE

I checked up on Simone before I hit the sack.

'I'm freezing,' she complained.

'I said cheap, not bargain basement.' My joke fell flat. She had no idea what I meant and by the time I explained, it had lost impact. 'Where are you exactly?'

'In a boarding house between Hackney and Lower Clapton.'

'Have you eaten?'

'I bought food and ate it here. I'm so bored.'

'Watch TV or surf the net.'

'No Wi-Fi.' She sounded miserable as hell.

'I'm sure you can amuse yourself for a day or so. Read a book, catch up on your beauty sleep.'

'No fun without you.'

I smiled, flattered.

'I could as easily book into a cheap hotel in Cheltenham.'

'It's not safe.'

'You can protect me.'

'Stay where you are – please.'

'As you wish.' She sounded put out. I imagined her exhaling a big petulant sigh and regretting the day she'd met me.

'It's not as I wish. It's how it is. I'm not prepared to jeopardise

your safety. Stay calm and I'll be with you before you know it.'
The thought that I might not succeed, that I might fail both the
women in my life didn't bear thinking about. I wished her good
night and fell asleep. Three hours later, I was wide awake. Unable
to settle, I ventured downstairs, padded about, restless. I asked
myself why the security services weren't knocking on my door.
Answer: they had no knowledge that I was back in the picture.
McCallen had stayed true to her word; Titus's involvement was
based on what he'd seen over twelve months before and whatever
he'd got himself into before he died. Feeling reasonably secure,
in spite of having GCHQ on my doorstep, I reckoned I could
take a calculated risk. My false identity, backed up by false credit
cards, together with my false digital footprint ensured my
anonymity, if only in the short term.

Pouring myself two fingers of whisky, I fired up the laptop
and checked out the latest news. The dead Russian in the quarry
remained unidentified although, according to the news report, a
tattoo on his back suggested links with Russian organised crime.
Good luck with that, I thought. There were so many gangs it
would take the police several months to track and identify him.
Apparently the cause of death was regarded as unexplained rather
than suspicious, the break in his neck pre-fall not yet established.
It was simply a matter of time.

The body in the crypt was more revealing. Initially hitting the
news in glorious colour – bondage gone wrong the favoured
theory – it had dropped from the headlines as though Titus had
never existed. As for the 'missing civil servant', the trail hadn't
gone cold – it was in the freezer. I didn't know whether the lack
of coverage was smart or stupid. It seemed to be the way the
services operated. It didn't mean they weren't chasing leads, only
that they were chasing them in secret. Gritty-eyed, I went back
to bed and, against the odds, fell into the deep.

I resurfaced around ten. First up, I phoned Jat.

'Nothing doing,' he said. 'It's like trying to hack into the

Pentagon.'

'Are you saying you can't crack it?'

'No,' he said, chippy. 'There's no such thing as an unbreakable code.'

'Then what are you saying?'

'I need more time.'

Something I didn't have. 'What are you like at tracing phone calls?'

He let out a groan. 'Is this extra?'

'It is.'

'Not my field. I could maybe have a go but I'm not GCHQ.'

And I was hardly going to take a trip down the road to the doughnut, as it was known, to ask them to do me a favour.

'No, forget it. Just crack on with the computer.'

'I will, but phoning me constantly isn't helping.'

I got the message, apologised and backed off. Next, I phoned Simone. It went straight to voicemail. I glanced at my watch. Maybe she was taking a bath. I made coffee, showered, shaved. I dressed from head to toe in black, then phoned her again. Still no reply. A little concerned, I sent an email to the contact on her website: 'Checking in. Can you answer your phone?'

Examining the car and finding it clean of any hidden devices, incendiary or otherwise, I drove it down to the nearest garage, filled the tank and drove back. All through breakfast I had the gnawing sensation that Simone might disregard my orders, that, headstrong as she was, she'd turn up without warning, expecting my undivided attention when it was already divided. I didn't know her well, but I was familiar with the reckless, risk-taking side of her nature. If she wanted to do her own thing, she'd cut off, cut loose and to hell with the consequences. There was invincibility about her that I found as worrying as it was intoxicating.

The afternoon plodded along in a fog of silence and frustration. I covered around six miles on foot in sleety rain, checking warehouse locations, rented lock-ups, places where a person could be held. The lock-up situation in Cheltenham is peculiar to the area. They rarely come up for sale because it's more lucrative to rent, the perennial parking problem and lack of garages creating a ready supply of clientele. It was like looking for a coin in the Treasury.

On my return, I left a 'tell' on the front step close to the front door, a delicately placed potato crisp that anyone entering the house would crunch if they broke inside. I did the same with the back door then spent most of my time at the window, watching people slipping by, waiting for the phone call, wondering if China, enjoying domination, would send me halfway across the country, or, changing his mind, leave me and McCallen to fester for another twenty-four hours for no other reason than that he could.

Light faded. Workers came home. Darkness fell. This used to be my time and my terrain. No more.

Patience runs through my DNA but I needed the patience of angels. Every time I checked my watch, it seemed that only a minute had passed. A grim thought struck me that this was only a single instalment on the price I had to pay for all the acts of violence I'd committed.

Wired with coffee, I nearly dropped the phone when it finally rang.

'Hello, it's me.'

'Fuck's sake, why didn't you answer my call?'

'Because I knew you would be angry with me.'

I closed my eyes in an agony of frustration. Simone had broken loose, as predicted, and now she was blocking the line. 'Where are you?'

'Somewhere more comfortable, the Chapter.'

Crazy woman. 'Were you followed?'

'I don't think so.'

'Think' wasn't good enough. 'Stay there. Don't answer the door to anyone.'

'Apart from you.'

She sounded immensely pleased with herself.

'I have to go.'

'*À bientôt.*'

See you soon. Maybe, maybe not.

An hour later the call I'd waited all day for came through. Same electronic voice, same anonymity. It didn't bother with niceties, for which I was grateful. I muted my surprise when told the address.

'And Hex,' the voice said. 'Remember – no cops, no backup. One stupid move and she's dead.'

CHAPTER FORTY-FOUR

The address was on an industrial estate in Alstone, a suburb of Cheltenham, the type of area where nice streets with tended homes and gardens co-existed with not so nice streets with boarded-up houses and broken-down cars outside. As soon as I reached the no-through road, I realised the hopelessness of the situation. China's men would be everywhere, waiting to pick me off. More than ever, I wished I'd procured a gun. Martyrdom is never a good look.

I pulled up, cut the engine and, grabbing the bolt cutters, stepped quietly out of the car. Immediately, I was flooded in light. An image of another site, lit up like Wembley Stadium and crawling with men out to get me, rattled through my brain. Smashing the thought, I darted for the shadowy cover of a low, blocky concrete building with metal shutters in the doorway. Hunkered down inside, I worked out the immediate layout. At my back a front door made from toughened glass; beyond, a set of shallow stone steps; and, to the right, a reinforced door. I looked above my head for cameras and signs of an alarm. I couldn't see anything but that didn't mean they weren't there. As soon as I made a move, the whole place could go off. However, if I were China and wanted to get rid of a couple of people, I'd hardly want an alarm to sound and grab the attention of the local police. I was only grateful there were no dogs. To date, I've never killed one, not even in self-defence. I wasn't about to change the habit of a lifetime.

I tried the door, which was locked. At any moment I expected a figure to explode in front of me, a gun shoved up against my temple, but aside from me, there seemed nobody around. Actually it was quiet – too quiet.

I bent low and, scuttling on the balls of my feet, covered the perimeter, meticulously checking entrances and exits, by touch and by sight. It must have taken twenty long minutes. Each one I believed might be my last.

About to turn the final corner, a chink of light ghosted into the night from between a metal grille set low down and into the wall of the building. I squatted, resting on my heels, and put my eye to the slit. It was difficult to make out anything very much, but there was definitely an empty space, a single forlorn bulb swinging from the ceiling the only source of light. Realising my vulnerability, I glanced back over my shoulder, watching out for a puff of warm breath in the chill night air and the specific sound of a hard man's footsteps. The only noise was the frantic beat of my heart. I was alone. It made no sense. It had to be a trap.

Putting my mouth against the metal, I called McCallen's name softly. Getting no response, I called again, louder. Frustrated, I took out the bolt cutters and started on the grille when, suddenly, my phone vibrated. Ripping it from my pocket, I pressed it close to my ear.

'Managed to break in?'

I said nothing.

'I'll take that as a no.'

'Where is she?'

'Who?'

'You know damn well who. Stop fucking me about.'

And then it hit me. The call, my drive here, my fruitless search was nothing more than a smokescreen. Simone. He had Simone.

I stood up, tore back across the yard to the car, China's disembodied voice blaring in my ear. 'You've slipped up, Hex, might have cost you your girl's life. Careless.'

In spite of everything, I stopped dead and spoke with the utmost clarity and cold determination. I did not want China to be in any doubt what I would do to him. I also had to openly kill any emotional attachment to Simone. He had to believe the women were straight business. 'If you've damaged either set of goods, I'm going to hunt you down and make you scream until you beg me to put a bullet in your brain.'

'Threaten all you like, I had enormous fun, by the way. I'll call you tomorrow night about the intelligence officer.'

'So you can play another of your games? I don't think so.'

'If you care anything for McCallen, be ready.'

CHAPTER FORTY-FIVE

I ran two red lights and nearly took out a group of late-night revellers. China's men might have abducted Simone, or done what they needed to and abandoned her down a dirt track on the outskirts. You didn't have to travel far to go from urban landscape to rural with the Cotswolds on the town's doorstep.

The hotel was my starting point. As to what I'd find, I gave no thought. I did not dwell on what he might have done or the lengths to which he'd gone. The time for analysis would come later.

I threw the car into the closest parking bay and flew through reception and upstairs to the penthouse. I heard the sound of crying before I'd even knocked on the door. My legs felt weak with relief. Tears meant that she was in one piece.

'Simone, darling, it's me, Joe.'

The door opened a chink, the safety chain restricting entry. Simone's tear-stained, swollen face emerged as she hovered on the other side. Two thin stream of mucus travelled from her nose to her mouth. I had never seen a woman look so dishevelled.

'It's all right now,' I said, 'let me in.'

She took the chain off, opened the door and collapsed onto

me. Glancing over her head, I saw an overturned chair, the glass in the mirror above the desk smashed. In between furious tears, she gabbled so fast in French I couldn't follow a word. To my untrained ears, it sounded angry and accusing, as though it was my fault. It was, I guess. All I could do was hold her tight. The front of my shirt, where her face had burrowed, quickly became sodden.

Gently, I inched her towards the bed, unpeeled her from me and got her to sit down. Shivering, she perched on the edge, bent forward, arms crossed tight, hands clutching her elbows. Her hair was down, a mess, strands sticking to her face. I put my jacket around her shoulders and took a spare blanket from the wardrobe and wrapped that around her too. Next, I raided the minibar, poured brandy for her, whisky for me. I pushed the glass into her hands. Two nails, I noticed, were broken. She cupped the glass tight as though huddling over a campfire.

'Drink,' I said, 'it will help with the shock.'

She did, cautiously, and pulled a face at the sudden heat and warmth.

Pushing aside her hair, I examined the extent of the damage. Her bottom lip was split, her right cheek shiny and swollen. It could have been worse.

'Tell me exactly what happened.'

She snatched at her drink and feasted on me with dark, cold-as-night eyes. She blames me, I thought, for not being there to protect her.

'He raped me,' she said, leaden.

My stomach lurched. I reached out to touch her.

She recoiled. 'Don't.'

My hand dropped. I was out of my depth. How do you pump a woman for information when she's been violated? 'I'm so sorry. I –'

'Should have been here.' She screamed at me, spit flicking

across my face. Now was not the time to tell her that, if she'd only done as I suggested, she would probably have stayed safe. I waited for her anger to abate.

'Who was the man?'

She regarded me with slow, cynical eyes. 'Funnily, he didn't tell me his name.'

'Okay,' I said evenly, 'can you describe him?'

'He was a big guy, white, I don't remember.'

'It's important you try.'

'Why?' she snapped. 'All I want to do is forget.'

'I know,' I said. 'But I need to know who did this.'

'So that you can catch him?' She arched an eyebrow contemptuously and took another swallow of brandy. 'He smelt of cheap cologne. He wore a brightly coloured shirt.'

I briefly closed my eyes. China. Christ, what had he done to McCallen?

She got up suddenly. 'I am going to take a bath.'

'You can't. You should report it.' I didn't actually mean this. It would draw all sorts of unwelcome attention, but I knew it was something that had to be said.

'Forget it,' she said. 'The police are not interested in a woman who runs sex parties for a living and it's hardly a threat to national security,' she added, the pained look in her expression spearing my conscience. 'I would make juicy headlines in the newspapers, nothing more.'

She was right. A defence team would rip her to pieces. In any case, my form of justice entailed more than a long prison sentence.

She disappeared into the bathroom, locking the door in defiance, the sound of rushing water loud and clear.

I took a long deep swallow of booze. I don't like surprises and surprises were coming thick and fast. China a rapist, China a mental torturer, China who consorted with neo-Nazis and crossed up intelligence services, China who'd used the name Billy Squeeze

219

to incite terror and fear, and for what? To punish me for an unknown transgression?

No, none of this tallied with the man I knew.

CHAPTER FORTY-SIX

I slept what was left of the night on the sofa, Simone taking the bed and falling into a deep state of unconsciousness. The next morning I woke, used the bathroom, and called Dan at the student let. The fact he answered so swiftly, with a grunt, indicated that he had just got in, not that he was up early.

'I want the place tidied up, the spare bedroom sorted, the bathroom and kitchen cleaned.'

'Aw, today's not good, Joe.'

'Not my problem.'

'We've all got essays to write.'

A popular excuse for inactivity, I was not persuaded and said so.

'As our landlord, you're supposed to give us notice of a visit.'

Smart-mouth. 'This is not a visit. This is you preparing for a guest.'

'What guest?'

'Mine.'

'There's no room.'

'Yes, there is, and she's picky.'

'She?' I could practically hear Dan put his brakes on and screech to a halt.

'Don't get any ideas. I need it ready in two hours.'

'What?' You'd think I'd asked him to run for the US presidency.

'She's not been well and needs a place to stay undisturbed. You'll hardly know she's there.'

The mutinous tone returned. 'I'd like to help – honest, Joe – but no can do.'

'This is not a request. This is an order. Under the terms of the tenancy agreement, you're due for a rent increase. I might play nice. I might be a total bastard. Maybe you'd like to think about that while you get the place cleaned up.' I cut the call. Dan was the easy part. Persuading Simone posed the real problem.

I let her sleep on, made myself coffee from the tray and, as she was stirring, ordered room service for both of us. I sat on the bed at a respectable distance and watched as she became properly awake. She peered at me for a moment like she didn't recognise me.

'Hey,' I said.

'Hey,' she said on autopilot, cool and distant.

'I've found you somewhere to stay, somewhere safe.'

She stirred, rearranged the bedding, punching the pillows hard. I think she imagined they were me.

She sat up straight, her expression impenetrable. I told myself her irrational behaviour was symptomatic of what had happened to her. Wild at heart, she would have put up a fight, a fight she'd ultimately lost.

'Where?' she said. 'A safe house?'

'Sort of.' I badly regretted my snap intelligence officer cover. I hoped the attack on Simone had dulled her sharp thinking. 'I have a student let. There are three young guys there.'

Her face fell. Couldn't say I blamed her.

'Nobody will think of looking for you there. It's only for a short time.'

'How short?'

'A couple of days, tops.'

222

She thought about it. I could see she was looking for reasons to decline. 'And this house,' she said, 'is there somewhere I can park my car?'

It was an odd question. Understandably, she was in a strange mood. 'One space and it's yours.'

I'd clearly supplied the right answer because she softened.

'Where exactly?'

'Near the university, St Pauls.'

She glanced away, let out a sigh. I could see she was wavering. This was not the time to weigh up personal comfort against security but if I said another word I'd blow it.

'All right.' She stretched out, feline, and covered my hand with hers. I looked into her eyes, read the smile inside. Truce, I thought.

'Good,' I said.

She smiled properly. In spite of the bruising to her face, she looked ravishing to me. I leant towards her and this time she didn't recoil as I kissed her cheek. As she drew away a little, a serious note entered her voice.

'What are you going to do, Joe?'

'Sort things out once and for all.'

'How?'

'I know the man who attacked you.'

'You do?'

'China Hayes, the guy I told you about.'

Her laugh was thin. 'Absurd, ridiculous, *incroyable*. I am no threat –'

'I already told you. It isn't about you.'

Her brow creased. 'I do not understand. You told me about him. You told me …' Her voice became small then disappeared over the horizon.

'He attacked you to get to me. It's my fault, Simone. I should have protected you.'

She looked down. I was millimetres away. It might as well have been a mile. She looked up at me with sad eyes. When

223

she spoke her voice was soft. 'You cannot be in all places at all times.'

'No, and I'm sorry.'

* * *

Simone didn't rush. We ate breakfast together. She bathed, dressed, packed her minimalist gear into her minimalist luggage, settled her bill, including a hefty payment for the damage to the room, and we drove in convoy to the other side of town. I let Simone park her car, told her to stay where she was while I left mine close to a skip three streets away.

Sprinting back to join her, we went inside the house together. No bicycle in the hallway, no skateboard, the familiar odour of late teenage unwashed males replaced by an altogether cleaner smell of fresh air and cleaning fluid. I was impressed. It was nowhere near hotel standard, but it was a hell of an improvement on the usual 'sweep the floor with a glance' school of house-keeping.

Dan popped out first, duster in hand, the others sidling next to him like Fagin's pickpockets. Simone was obviously the draw in spite of her wounded looks. I ran through the introductions and said that I'd show Simone to her room.

'Would you like coffee, Simone?' Dan said. I did a double take. Nobody had ever offered me so much as a glass of water.

'Thank you, that would be lovely,' Simone said graciously.

Maybe this was going to go a whole lot better than I thought possible. Almost immediately, the memory of McCallen's tortured scream ripped through my mind, blackening my thoughts, dragging me kicking and screaming back to reality.

Simone followed me upstairs and across the narrow landing to a back bedroom. 'A single bed,' she said, arching an eyebrow. 'I haven't slept in one of those for years.'

I put her bags down and showed her the bathroom next door.

224

The boys had done a good job, and there were clean towels and the sanitary ware was clean. The floor left a little to be desired, but I'd seen worse.

We went back to her room. She swung the strap of her bag off her shoulder and placed it carefully on the bed and sat down. Something dinged in my mental database.

'What?' she said.

'Nothing.'

'I don't believe you.'

'Don't be arch with me.'

A tap at the door signalled the end of our spat and the arrival of coffee, which came on a tray with a plate of ginger biscuits.

'There's sugar in the bowl,' Dan said – obsequiously, I thought.

'Don't I get a drink?' I said.

'You didn't ask,' he replied, shooting out of the room.

Amused, Simone lifted the cup to her lips and looked over the rim through dark eyelashes.

'I'm coming back as a girl,' I said, raising a smile. She opened her mouth to respond when my phone beat her to it. It was Jat.

'I'll call you back later, yeah?'

'I thought it was urgent. I've bust my balls on this.'

'It will keep.' I switched off my phone.

'Problem?'

'No.' I smiled. She smiled back.

'Want a biscuit?'

'I'm good.' Glad that the cloud between us had passed, I said, 'Seriously, will you be all right?'

'Yes.'

I held her gaze. '*Are* you all right?'

She swallowed, looked away. It seemed to take an eternity for her to wrench out an answer. 'I will be,' she said eventually.

It was the most I could hope for. I glanced at my watch. 'I have to go.'

'You have plans to make?' A rhetorical question, but I

225

answered anyway. I wanted her to know.

'I do.'

'When will I see you?'

I had no idea. If China contacted me when he said and everything went to plan, it could be as early as the following day. If things went badly, I'd never be coming back. I forced a smile, brushed her lips with mine and said, 'Maybe tomorrow.'

CHAPTER FORTY-SEVEN

I had six hours to prepare mentally and get into the zone. I was taking no chances. Recent events had forced me to make a mental leap. I likened it to driving a fast car. Responsive, swift movers got you out of trouble better than slower models. A weapon would make me feel confident. I didn't have to use it, but if I was in a hole it would probably save my life and McCallen's. I still had my contacts, some abroad, some in London, but they were absolutely no use to me now. I'd used a guy once for a job in the south-west. He hung out in Bristol. As soon as I reached home, I planned to call him and make the necessary arrangements for drop-off and collection. This was not the type of conversation to have in a street.

I was almost at the car when I remembered Jat's call. As I was about to phone him back, a Volvo pulled up with two guys inside. The back of my brain processed 'problem'. I quickened my stride when, without warning, another two men rushed out from behind the skip, aerosols in their hands. Instinctively, I took a step back, but the spray connected with my face. My vision blurred, my eyes poured tears, the skin around them on fire. Confused, disorientated, wheezing, I raised my hands. Someone slapped them away and threw a hood over my head. Three car doors opened and I was bundled, blind, inside. It was a classic out, grab, shove inside movement. If I'd been watching, I'd have said they'd got it down to a fine art. Nine seconds is enough to take a guy off the street in broad daylight. China's men, if that's who they were, were good, and I was now out of the loop; my skills and thinking were so rusty I'd drawn all the wrong calculations, made all the wrong calls. It spelt the end of the road for me, disaster for McCallen.

Sandwiched between two bodies, I couldn't breathe and sneezed ferociously. At any moment I expected either to pass out or die. Someone handcuffed my wrists.

'Don't touch the hood,' one of them said. 'It will only spread it around and cause further irritation.'

English accent, I registered. Made no difference. Whoever had done this to me were bastards. The longer we drove, the tighter my chest became. Breath rattled painfully through the narrowed airways, the hood sodden as my eyes went into overdrive.

'Jesus, how long?' I moaned.

Nobody answered. I must have blacked out because the next thing I remembered I was being bundled out and frogmarched across a short stretch of turf and into a building. The hood came off and I peered out through half-closed and swollen eyes. I was standing in a kitchen. Blinds drawn, light artificial. Someone gripped hold of my elbow and propelled me through a corridor and manhandled me up a flight of carpeted stairs and into a bathroom. I struggled but I was so out of it I made little impact. All at once, my body was pushed back over the bath and my face plunged into ice-cold water. I struggled and bucked, desperate for oxygen. Dragged up by my hair, cool water from a showerhead sprayed directly into my eyes. I gulped and swore. Paradoxically, the relief to my vision was instant and I stopped fighting.

After a few minutes of the water treatment, a voice said: 'Okay, he's good to go.'

I caught sight of myself in the bathroom mirror. My eyes were like slits. At least I could see.

Hauled back downstairs, I was pushed into a spartanly kitted out sitting room. Chairs, no sofa, no television, and books, mainly thrillers, on the shelves. Two mugs of hot drink, tea, at a guess, sat on a low table. It wasn't what I expected. As in the kitchen, the blinds were drawn. The man who'd pushed me into the room I now recognised as the same man I'd hit in the gut when Titus had bagged me. It was not an encouraging start, but it was a whole lot better than a one on one with China's crew. The fact was I'd half-expected a visit from MI5 and, in the absence of a formal call, I'd become complacent and assumed I was off the hook. My fault.

My thought processes up to speed, I had a good idea what the security services were now thinking. With Titus dead, they had me pinned down as his murderer. The reality of my situation sucked every bit of air out of me. It wasn't so much as out of the pan and into the fire as into another pan. Rescuing McCallen suddenly appeared a remote possibility.

'Sit down,' he said.

I sat, compliant.

Footsteps rattled down the hall. The door swished open and another man entered. Shorter than me, he wore tailored trousers, a casual, open-neck shirt and soft-soled shoes typical of men with indoor occupations.

A silent exchange took place and the guy who'd brought me down removed my cuffs and left. His colleague drew up a chair and sat. Older than the others, he had dark wavy hair streaked with grey, wide features, the set of his mouth slightly curved up as though he'd been told a good joke and it still amused him. His brown eyes studied me as I studied him. They didn't seem particularly penetrating. There was something almost lazy in his expression, as if he couldn't give a damn whether I talked to him or not. He had a tremendous aura of stillness and calm. I do not take to people easily, yet I took to him. I also realised that his benign appearance was a front cultivated over many years with a view to interrogating people like me.

He leant forward, pushed a mug of tea towards me and, picking up his own, held it to his full lips and took a sip.

'Quite flavoursome,' he said in the way someone might comment on a bottle of wine. 'I'd drink yours while it's still hot.'

I wondered how many times beverages had been thrown in his face. Strange to say, I didn't think that often. I took a drink, placed the mug back on the table. I wondered what he was called. He looked like a Casper or a Dominic. Actually, I thought Casper suited him better.

'I apologise for dragging you here so unceremoniously. CS gas,' he said with a sympathetic sigh, 'nasty stuff.'

I gave a silent nod of agreement.

'Do you know why you are here?'

My normal response would be to lie but, as one of Titus's men had help spirit me away on the last occasion, I could hardly plead absolute ignorance. 'No, not really.'

Casper, as I thought of him, nodded as though he understood my position.

'You see, we have a problem, Hex. May I call you Hex?'

'Sure.' My mind raced back to the last job a lifetime ago. Someone in MI5 had sanctioned the order for McCallen to bring me in back then. I wondered if it had been him.

His smile was wide, yet there was a sudden hardness in his eyes.

'Or would you prefer me to call you Stephen, Mr Porter?'

CHAPTER FORTY-EIGHT

My skin must have turned the colour of greaseproof paper. Either McCallen had briefed 'Casper' on my trip to Berlin, or more likely Mathilde Brommer, Lars Pallenberg's ex-girl, had shopped me to the British security services. While my mind reeled, he fired his next salvo.

'You had dealings with one of our colleagues last year, Inger McCallen.'

So he had been involved. 'Yes.'

'You did good work and we were grateful.'

That was something. I sensed a 'but' coming.

'You have been in touch with McCallen more recently.'

'She contacted me.'

'About?'

Either he didn't know, or was testing the water. 'A guy on your watch list.'

'Why would she do that?'

'You'd have to ask her.'

'I would if I could, but we both know that isn't possible so I am reliant on you.'

'I can't help. Sorry.'

'Really? How long do you wish to stay here?'

Give him something useless, something he already knows, I thought. 'She mentioned someone,' I said.

'Go on.'

'A German woman, Mathilde Brommer.'

He didn't skip a beat. Physically, he didn't give anything away. 'Anyone else?'

'Dieter Benz.'

'You know who he is?'

'A radical with strong links to neo-Nazi groups in the UK.'

'Which is why you flew to Berlin?'

'Correct.'

I watched his expression and saw the pieces dropping into place for him. I hoped I came out on the bright side of the picture.

'What were you asked to do?'

I shrugged. 'Watch him.'

'You didn't think it an odd request?'

I flashed an easy smile. 'I'm accustomed to those.'

This raised a brief laugh. 'Yes, I see that.' He waited several beats, continued the heavy eye contact. He had the sort of stare from which escape was impossible. 'Your relationship with McCallen, how would you describe it?'

'I'm sorry. I don't understand the nature of your question.' There was truth in my lie. I knew what 'Casper' meant. However, my relationship with McCallen was impossible to describe.

'You're an extremely intelligent man,' he said. 'I find it difficult to believe that you cannot answer a simple question.'

'There is nothing simple about it. I'm not emotionally literate.'

'And yet you risk your life for a woman you barely know.'

'My way of giving something back to society,' I said, knowing he wouldn't buy it.

He observed me for a few moments, as if giving serious consideration to what I'd said.

'Benz,' he said, bringing the conversation back to where he wanted it to be. 'She didn't ask you to kill him?'

'Certainly not.'

'You seem emphatic.'

'Because it's the truth. Has something happened to Benz?'

'I have absolutely no idea.'

He got up, walked to the window and, as if remembering that the shutters were closed and there was no view to admire, returned to his seat and sat back down. He gave me a square look.

'Titus.'

'What of him?'

'He's dead.'

I feigned shock.

'Didn't you know?'

'Why would I?'

'Your patch.'

'I don't have a patch.'

'I think you do and it's here.'

'I had no reason to kill him.'

'Casper' said nothing. His penetrating gaze continued to lock onto my eyes. A glance at my watch told me that they'd consumed two of my precious hours. 'You have somewhere you need to be?' he asked.

'Not especially.'

'That's good, because this could take time to resolve.'

'There is nothing to resolve. McCallen came to see me. I did her a favour –'

'You travelled to Berlin.'

'We've already established that,' I said, indicating there was no point wasting both our time with meaningless and repeated diversions designed to trip me up. 'And then I came back.'

'And met with Titus.'

'Only because he invited me.' I said it with a smile that 'Casper' returned as if we were two old mates sharing an amusing anecdote.

'Where?'

'In London.'

'What did he ask you to do?'

'I don't remember.'

'Try.' His voice raised a semitone.

I leant forward. 'You already know. You sanctioned it.'

He hesitated. A smile glanced across his lips. No, he didn't know. Titus had been working his own number. 'Casper' repeated his original question and I obliged with an honest answer. Push-pull.

'He asked me to find McCallen.'

'Unorthodox.'

We were in agreement. I didn't think he knew about Titus's more unconventional methods of gleaning information and I didn't enlighten him. His next question slayed me.

'Who do you think killed them?'

'Them?'

'Titus and McCallen.'

I felt as if someone had taken an ice pick to my guts. A bitter taste was on my tongue, crackling interference in my head. 'You've found a body?'

'We generally don't in our line of work, do we?'

I didn't care for the 'we'. 'I don't know what you mean.' To my ears, my voice sounded thin and tinny and unconvincing.

His expression was one of undiluted scepticism. 'Missing for over two weeks? No kidnap demand? It's a given.'

I was in a dilemma. Was this the moment I told him what he wanted to hear? Was this my chance to request backup? But China didn't want backup. He wanted me. One whisper to the security services and McCallen would be dead. For all I knew, China and his team had seen me getting picked up. They seemed to have eyes and ears everywhere.

I spoke with a slow, weary delivery that only faintly replicated what I truly felt. 'I suppose you must be right.'

'Which is where you come in, only we don't understand why.'

'Why what?'

'Why you murdered them.'

'I didn't.'

'Forgive me, Hex, but you kill for money, right?'

'Not any more.'

'Who gave the order?'

'I don't know.'

'You deny it?'

'Categorically.'

'Was there a middle man?'

'How many times do I have to tell you? I did not kill either of your intelligence officers. I don't know who did and I have no information about who is responsible.' And every second you spend chasing the wrong lead is a nail in McCallen's coffin.

'There is also the small matter of a dead Russian.'

I muted my natural physical response and looked him straight in the eye.

'You know nothing about it?' His voice was soft, melodious.

'No.'

'Are you comfortable?'

'What?'

'It's a little cool in here. Would you like us to turn up the heating?' His expression was solicitous. He thought he was going to drag out the truth with kindness. It overturned my previously long-held beliefs about MI5 involving dingy basements, beatings and water-boarding.

'Did you accede to Titus's request?'

'Yes. I wanted to help.'

My interrogator stretched his legs. 'So what did you do?'

'I asked around.'

'Who?'

'People.'

'Would you care to elaborate?'

'I would not.'

He inclined his head to one side as though I were a rare species in danger of extinction. Maybe I was. 'You listened to the grapevine, kept your ear to the ground, on the lookout for chatter, is that right?'

'Exactly as you do,' I said. 'We simply have a different clientele.'

Again, the amused expression. 'You talk a good talk.'

'It's not talk. It's the truth.'

'And you discovered nothing of interest?'

'No.'

'And yet you seem to have suffered for your trouble,' he said, surveying the bruising on my face.

'A common response when you ask too many questions.'

'Only if one strays too closely to the truth. Did you press a nerve, Hex?'

I fell silent. He was certainly pressing my nerves and my anger was on the rise.

'Why do you think you met with a wall of silence?'

'Because there was nothing to tell. Whoever killed your people most likely had a political axe to grind, unconnected to those I used to serve.'

'Ah, *used to*.' Again the slow, droll smile.

'In the past, yes,' I said.

'Someone like Dieter Benz, for example?'

I agreed with my eyes. 'It's a fair bet that if you're after him he will be after you. Maybe you should pay him a visit.'

'We may well do that. Thanks for the advice.'

'You're welcome.' I changed position, as if I were about to stand up and leave.

'Until we do, you will stay here.'

'Why? You have nothing on me.'

'We have nothing on a lot of people. It doesn't mean that they don't have blood on their hands, which is why you will remain.'

I flinched. I didn't like to be reminded of my many crimes.

236

'What happened to innocent before proven guilty?'

The man I'd christened Casper leant towards me. 'That's for the hoi polloi and lesser mortals. Men like you,' he said with a slow conspiratorial smile, 'are in a different league altogether.'

CHAPTER FORTY-NINE

'I want a lawyer.'

'Later.'

'Casper', or whoever he was, had slipped into another room, and I was left with the guy who'd brought me in.

'I have a right to make a call,' I insisted.

'This isn't a game show. You don't get to phone a friend.'

I protested loudly. When they took my phone I told them in the strongest possible terms that they had no right to keep me and promised to sue the arse off them. Inevitably, my voice ran out of road and I was bundled back upstairs.

Locked in a back room with boarded up windows, all I could do was count the second hand on my watch as it ticked by. In a couple of hours, my phone would ring and I would not be able to take the call. Nothing I could do about it. Even if I escaped there was no time to source a gun. Without a gun the rescue mission and McCallen were doomed.

I kicked the walls and the door with frustration and yelled. It didn't raise a flicker of interest. They seemed to have so little on me and yet, in the absence of a more obvious lead, the security services had elected me for the role of public enemy number one. There was a weird irony that I was indeed guilty of murder, but not those of which I was now standing accused. Perhaps it was divine justice.

Noise penetrated the film of silence, the sound of three car doors opening and shutting followed by the throaty growl of an engine turning over and, next, the change of engine note, followed by the spit and crunch of tyres on gravel. It meant that some of them had more important matters to deal with than me. My mind simmered with possibility. How many men would they leave behind? Based on experience, I estimated that there was one man between freedom and me. And that one man, in all probability, had a gun, something I needed. Envisaging a 'kill two birds with one stone' scenario, I smiled.

Desperate measures.

I ripped off my jacket and, tearing off my shirt, unwound the bandage from my left arm. The wound was still a mess and the simple act of removing the dressing reopened it. Bracing myself, I messed with it and squeezed until the blood flowed freely. Smearing this around my neck, I let several large drops drip directly onto the wooden floor. Every nerve ending screamed in tortured protest. Sucking as much air into my lungs as possible, I let out a terrific, unholy scream and dropped deadweight onto the floor, making as much racket as I could.

Within seconds, a set of footsteps pounded up the stairs, the key plunged into the lock and the door flew open.

'Fuck, fuck, fuck,' the guy let out, squatting down, thinking I'd slashed my own throat.

I kept my eyes wide open, staring up to the ceiling.

As he bent over to put a finger to the pulse in my neck, I struck.

Shooting up, I grabbed his windpipe and squeezed the larynx hard and fast. Clamping both hands over mine, he clawed, eyes popping, throat choking, pain exploding through every pore in his body. I clung on and rolled him, pinning him to the floor, my knee on his chest. Still, he resisted, jerking and twisting in an attempt to dislodge my hold. Any increase in pressure could prove fatal and I had no desire to kill him, only to knock him out. It wasn't easy. Needed balance. Tricky when someone is trying to rip the skin off the back of your hands. Maintaining my grip, I held on, vice-like, until I felt his body sag and the fight leave him. Finally, eyes rolled, he lost consciousness and keeled over.

After a quick check to make sure he was still breathing, which he was, I put him in the recovery position. Removing a Glock from his waistband, I ran my fingers through his pockets, removing first his phone and then my own. I assumed they'd trawled my phone history, yet Caspar's line of questioning seemed to indicate that it was of minimal importance. Perhaps they hadn't had time to decode it or, more likely, failed to fully grasp the significance of the contents.

Desperate, I tore downstairs, found a set of wrist-cuffs, probably the same he'd used on me, and returned to cuff him. Throwing my jacket back on, leaving the shirt in a bloodied heap, I locked the door and tore down the stairs and out under a baleful sky. A quick glance around me revealed that I was somewhere in a residential suburb, over a mile from where I lived and two and half from the car.

Would my place be staked out? I didn't know. But I had to get back home.

CHAPTER FIFTY

Lungs bursting, heart racing, I'd hammered along for the best part of two miles in pouring rain when the spook's phone in my pocket went off. I stopped, doubled over, sucked up enough air from my diaphragm to speak and answered.

'Yep.'

'All quiet?'

'Yep.'

'Good, Flynn wants to sweat him for the next twenty-four hours.'

''kay.' Flynn (Casper in my book) wasn't wrong in that regard. Perspiration was dripping off my nose.

The caller checked out. I checked out. That was it.

My car was exactly as I'd left it and I jumped inside, glad for shelter, and floored the accelerator. I didn't go straight home, but left it in a car slot in a bay of spaces in front of a short parade of shops minutes from my door.

The watchmaker usually closed up around seven in the evening and we had a prearranged signal that acted as an early warning system. If someone had been at mine, he would leave a teddy bear alone in the window. To sound the all clear, a pocket watch was planted in the teddy's lap. Sure enough, the pocket watch was in place. Pushing eight, it left an hour unaccounted for. In theory, someone could be waiting, or on stakeout.

I went around the back first, the 'tell' I'd left still there. It was the same around the street side, the crisp on the step, close to the front door, unbroken. I burst into my own home a shade after eight.

Peeling off my leather jacket and slinging it across the banister, I rushed upstairs to the bathroom. Redressing my wounds took longer than expected. I now had badly lacerated hands to add to the gouges on my arms. Everything hurt. I felt sick. Adrenalin dump made my legs feel like concrete and my heart rate soar and had given me a nasty dose of the shakes. My only consolation was the loaded pistol. I couldn't have chosen better. Extremely accurate and, with minimum recoil, there was no bullet drift on repeat shots. I only hoped my injured hands would be steady enough to fire and hit a target with accuracy.

With no word from China, I packed a torch, rope, bolt cutters and bandages into a holdall and dashed back to the car, dumping the tools on the passenger seat. Driving the Z4 around the rear and into the carport, I reversed it in, prepared for a fast getaway. Back inside, I made myself a brew of strong tea with little milk and plenty of sugar, and washed it down with a cocktail of pain-killers and B vitamins recommended by the gym. Once I felt stable enough, I beat up four raw eggs and downed them. I had no idea if it would work, but I began to feel better.

When my phone rang I didn't snatch it up. I waited, breathed deep, took my time, ice cool.

It was Jat. Excited, he rattled off a load of techno-stuff concerning web-based email accounts, usernames, passwords and draft folders.

'I get it. What did you find?' I said.

'It's cryptic but it appears to be a list of times and jobs that stretch back eighteen months, including six shipments that never made their destinations.' Drugs deals gone bad. 'Airports are mentioned in three countries, including Heathrow.'

'Let me guess, Berlin and Paris.'

'Got it. There's also a list of names.'

'Read them out, Jat.'

He did. They included Chester Phipps, Faustino Testa, Daragh Dwyer and Simone Fabron. 'There's an asterisk after Fabron's name with a note that says "pending".'

'Any Germans mentioned?'

'Erm …'

'Mathilde Brommer, Lars Pallenberg, Dieter Benz?'

'Benz is mentioned.'

'On the list with the others?'

'No.'

'Where does he figure?'

'In contacts.'

I scratched my head. 'And where do I figure?'

'You don't.'

'What? Not at all?'

'Nowhere.'

'Is Joe Nathan included?'

'No.'

'Joshua Thane.'

'Who?'

I repeated the name.

'Nope.'

'Any mention of locations as we discussed?'

'*Nada.*'

'Keep looking.'

I cut the call, stretched, flexing the muscles in my calves. Why wasn't I on the list? What was China's connection to Benz? I had no time to think about it because, for a second time that evening, my phone rang. But it wasn't the call I expected.

'Hey.'

'Simone, I'm sorry, I can't talk.' I needed this like I needed

243

root canal work without anaesthetic.

'No?'

'I'm on my way out.'

'But I'm afraid.'

'Why?' I sparked. 'Has something happened?'

'No.' She sounded plaintive and lost.

'Are the boys treating you all right?'

'Sure. They are very sweet.'

'Good. Stick with them.'

'You really cannot talk?'

'I'm sorry. I can't. Now I really must go.'

'We will speak tomorrow?'

'Yes.'

'*Au revoir.*'

By midnight, I'd heard nothing, the silent phone at my side goading me. Every time I checked, I was reminded that McCallen's life lay on a knife-edge – if she wasn't dead already.

Flynn's question about our relationship whistled through my head. He had unwittingly probed my heart and it had deeply unsettled me. McCallen was a force of nature. The first time I'd clapped eyes on her I knew in a flash that our paths were inextricably linked, and sensed that she'd be important to me, although not in the way I first thought. The fact is, anything unattainable – whether things or people – I'd conditioned myself not to want. I could never envisage a relationship with her because it wasn't possible. She was way out of my league. She'd pretty much said so herself. If I were brutally honest, it was why I'd gone for Simone. Lust is a good substitute for love.

And yet …

I must have fallen asleep in the chair. I woke with a start. Three in the morning, I was muddy-eyed with fatigue and my phone was blaring.

It could only mean one thing. Time to roll.

CHAPTER FIFTY-ONE

Astounded by the address given to me, I ran out of the back door, through the garden and, throwing myself into the driver's seat, gunned the engine and tore onto the road. McCallen was being held prisoner two or three streets from where I lived. I could hardly take it in.

Doubling back and cutting onto an adjacent road, I slung the car illegally near Suffolk Court and grabbed the bag. As soon as I stepped out, I heard the sound of fire engines and frantic human activity. Across towards Montpellier, dozens of blue lights flashed into the night sky. Bomb or natural disaster, or, more likely, an accident of some kind? Perplexed, I killed the idea of a connection to McCallen, and veered towards a long, narrow service street with cars parked nose to tail. On one side was a sprawl of broken-down student flats and serviced apartments. On the other, a scramble of houses, some more dilapidated than others. Further down, at the more salubrious end, were family homes and a popular pub, The Beehive. Beyond, classy Montpellier Terrace.

Under sporadic illumination from Victorian lamp posts I slipped from one pool of darkness to another and past a house subject to a recent brothel bust, a garage with folding doors, and a pair of wooden gates with steps beyond that led down to a basement. This was not my destination.

Following China's precise directions, I clocked an iron gate with no spikes on top; three metres of brick wall and a parking area; and a couple of painted and locked doors. Here, I was to cross over to the right-hand 'student' side and a row of tatty buildings that looked as bad by night as they did by day. Flashing the torch around, I picked up a grey four-storey edifice with an entire wall of sash windows with frames that were chipped and broken down and in imminent danger of collapse. Next to this was an open space of rough ground piled high with bricks and rubble, old tyres and an ancient washing line. Plastic garden chairs lay upended, legs pointing aimlessly at the stars. Journey's end.

Slipping out the Glock, I negotiated an obstacle course of detritus, my boots squelching on rotting garden cuttings and general crap until I came to a set of stone steps, the metal railings broken and twisted out of shape. At the bottom was a heavy wooden door, which was padlocked.

I took out the bolt cutters and cut through without making a sound. Swinging open the door, I slid inside and ran my fingers along the damp brick walls for a light switch and came up empty. Stepping further in, pitch darkness enveloped me, closing off my escape route. I stood for a moment, blood drumming through my temples, ears pricked, eyes adjusting, trying to get my bearings.

My gun hand stretched ahead, I inched forward and plotted a slow route through what I believed was the centre of the room, from one wall to another. As I hit brick, I felt around again, my fingers connecting with metal. It was another door. To my surprise, this cranked open. Immediately there was an odour of stale, damp air laced with mould and a more pungent smell of urine and excrement. Again, I felt around for a light switch and, this time, struck lucky.

A brick wall faced me. To my right, a staircase descended. Instinct has served me well and I followed it and entered another dark, all-consuming space. Here, the heady atmosphere was charged with silence, the type you encounter when someone is there but doesn't want you to know it. Instantly, I was transported to another time, another place, with tunnels and caverns and bad men desperate to kill me. I thought of Billy Squeeze and his evil plans and how everything had gone rotten since then.

I put down the bag and clung to the shadows. If China's men struck, I knew I'd cross the line and fire back.

Noise, faint at first, no more than a breath. If I opened my mouth, I'd give my position away and it would be their cue to turn their guns on me first and then her. Unless …

'McCallen, is that you?'

A sound of rattling chains, then: 'Go away. Leave me alone. Fuck off.'

I hardly recognised the voice. It sounded scratchy and old, but the bite in it confirmed it was my girl. 'Are you alone?'

Silence.

I tried to work it out. Was she sending me a coded message? Was she telling me to get lost because she had company? Had someone rigged her so that, as soon I drew near, we'd both be blown to hell?

Suddenly, screams shattered the silence.

I jumped into the unknown and in six long strides collided with a body. She paused for breath, whispered urgently in my ear. 'Light switch at the bottom of the stairs on the far wall, audio device on the underside of the table.'

'Video capability?'

'No.'

She screamed again, providing cover, and I backtracked to the staircase, found and hit the switch. Light careered through the basement and, momentarily, I stood blinking like a newborn, the sight before me scored into my brain. In chains, held fast to the wall, her head sunk low on her chest, McCallen looked like an ancient victim of medieval torture. She had two black eyes, one so badly swollen the green shone out of a slit. There were cuts and grazes to her face, some fresh, some healing. Her hair was dirty and matted. The rest of her was in poor shape too. Shivering and barefoot, blood oozed from her wrists and ankles where she'd tried to wrench herself free of the restraints. She wore a sweater, but the bottom half of her was naked apart from a pair of torn knickers. Her legs were covered in cigarette burns. When she raised her head and smiled, I believed my heart would shatter. The emotion was fleeting, swept away in a torrent of rage.

I advanced towards a table littered with cigarette butts, empty plastic bottles, sandwich cartons, and uneaten and rotting food. Just as McCallen said, a cheap transmitter, held in place by magnet, clung to the underside. It explained how her screams had been relayed to me. I ripped it off and crushed it into the concrete.

'I knew you'd come,' she blurted out, her voice stronger now that she could speak freely.

I touched her face, smoothed the hair from out of her eyes. 'Are you hurt?' Of course she was. I wondered how she would fare mentally later, wondered if her spirit would fall apart and shatter.

She looked at me with soulful eyes. 'Nothing broken.'

I kissed the top of her head and grabbed the bag.

She eyed the bolt cutters. 'You came prepared.'

'Always.' I took out an energy drink, peeled back the ring-pull from the can and pressed the opening to her cracked lips. 'Not too fast,' I warned as she gulped it down. 'Here, take this, it's a painkiller.' I broke one in half and pressed it into her mouth, letting her wash it down with another swallow. 'You do realise, don't you, that you now owe me dinner?'

She pulled away. Drink dribbled down her chin and she forced a smile. 'Let's hope I brush up okay.' Her voice shook and a tear ran down her cheek. I wanted to put my arms around her, tell her that nobody would hurt her ever, that I'd got her back and I'd never lose her again. Instead I got to work with the bolt cutters.

Throughout, and ever the spook, she kept up a running commentary.

'I was stupid,' she said with feeling. 'I made the classic mistake of working a lead alone. I thought I was following him when all the time he was following me.'

'Him?'

'Dieter Benz.' The heavy way she said it confused me.

'He did this?'

'Oh yes,' she said, meeting my eye.

Zara's words tumbled through my head. *Fucked like a bull.*

CHAPTER FIFTY-TWO

I let out a grunt, strained hard against the steel and wished it were Benz's balls in the vice. Breaking off for a second, I reattached the short blades to the same stress point and, a few seconds later the chain attached to her right wrist snapped. McCallen's arm dropped like a game bird shot in flight. It had taken me around twenty-five seconds all told.

'One down, three to go,' I told her. 'I can do something about the cuffs once we're out of here.' I had absolutely no idea how I'd go about this. It looked like an oxyacetylene job to me and I wasn't confident I could do it without further injuring her. Maybe Flynn and his pals would prove useful, but I didn't know how long it would take for them to come to the rescue. Benz could return at any moment. 'Did Benz mention a guy called China Hayes?'

'Never.'

Then how the hell did China connect to Benz? Jat had said Benz was on China's list of contacts and Simone's description fitted China Hayes. Had she made a mistake? Or had I made too many assumptions? Then I got it. Benz wouldn't be the first political agitator to involve himself in drugs operations. I put this to McCallen. The chain attached to her left wrist snapped.

'He did a neat line in smuggling cocaine,' she confirmed.

So Hayes and Benz were working a number together. It didn't altogether compute with the man I knew, but neither was this an impossible alliance. It certainly explained their desire to get rid of Simone, who they perceived to be a threat to trade. I looked around, anxiously wondering what was taking them so long to strike. They hadn't lured me here to see if I could rescue their captive. There would be a price to pay.

'How many men are working with Benz?'

'You mean here?'

'Yes.'

'None.'

'What? He's working alone?'

'Not exactly.'

'He doesn't have a gang on standby to take us out?' I was mystified.

'Benz is my captor. His only desire is to punish me.'

Confusion descended for a second time. The more I found out, the less I knew. It seemed that Benz, not China, had made the calls to me. 'What exactly happened?' I crouched down and manoeuvred the blades around the lower restraints.

'The morning I was meant to meet you I spotted Benz in a café in town and followed him.'

'There's reckless and then there's plain dumb.'

'I don't need a lecture.' Still sparky, traces of the old McCallen shone through – thank God. 'I've had a considerable amount of time to contemplate my own stupidity.'

I glanced up and grinned. The third chain snapped and she almost keeled over. I reached up to steady her. 'Fuck, my leg hurts.'

'Pins and needles. Work your leg up and down, get the blood flowing properly.'

She did as I said. 'Christ, I stink.'

I couldn't contradict her. Changing position, taking a deep breath, I strained to reopen the blades again and clamped the cutters for the final time.

'How did Benz nab you?'

'Led me down an alley and Tasered me. 50,000 volts is no joke. I might have been all right, but he followed up with a heavy-duty tranquilliser injected straight into my neck. I blacked out after that.'

'Audacious,' I said.

'Like I said, he wasn't exactly working alone. He had a woman in tow.'

Crack – the last chain separated. She all but collapsed. I reached out, put both arms around to support her. 'Who?'

'I don't know. I heard him talking on his phone once.

'Once? He called me several times.'

'Not in front of me. Not from here.'

'Okay, sorry, go on,' I said.

'He spoke in German and I could only pick up the odd word.'

'Then how the hell do you know it was a woman?'

'Body language. Clear as these.' She looked down at the cuffs on her wrists.

I had a reasonably good idea who it was. Now I thought about it, lots of other pieces slotted into place. Mathilde Brommer had, most likely, shopped me to Flynn. She had tipped me off about Benz and his demonstration so that someone could eliminate me. Plus she had links to Simone through the sex parties. Maybe Brommer's man was Benz. Perhaps she had set Pallenberg up to be shot. I ran my theory past McCallen.

'Exactly my take,' she smiled through crusted lips. 'Mathilde Brommer, the scheming evil bitch.'

I took off my jacket and wrapped it around her shoulders. She was freezing cold and her skin had a bluish tinge so that it was impossible to tell where the bruising stopped. I wanted to ask so many questions but our main priority was to get out fast. 'Can you walk?'

Fire flared in her eyes. 'Oh, yes.'

We shuffled across the floor together, my arm around her waist, the Glock in my free hand. My tools would only slow us down and could stay where they were, a memento of our escape.

As we were about to ascend the steps, a loud bang thundered through the cellar. For a second, I feared it was a gas leak or, worse, an explosion, confirmation that McCallen was bait and I'd walked into a carefully laid trap.

'What the hell was that?' she said.

Next came the sound of rushing water. A burst water main, a river in flood, something engineered? My God, I remembered the fire engines. The Chelt had broken its banks twice in the last ten years, flooding basements over large areas of town, trapping drivers in vehicles and cutting people off. With the River Severn being tidal, water often backed up into the Chelt, the real problem that there was nowhere for fire crews to pump it to. When I looked back it was pouring through the walls and bubbling up through the foundations.

CHAPTER FIFTY-THREE

'Hurry!'

I held McCallen tight, pushed her up to the top of the stairs, squeezed past, and, grabbing the handle, shouldered hard against the door. Nothing happened. I glanced up and lunged again, putting all my weight behind it.

'It's jammed.'

'Or locked.' We both looked at each other. Another glance over McCallen's head revealed we were in serious trouble. The water wasn't draining. This meant that, unlike most tanked basements and cellars, there was no pump in operation.

'Think the room on the other side is flooded?' she said.

In which case, pressure against the door would make it impossible to open. At the rate it was pouring in, it was possible. I took out my phone with the intention of diverting the fire service, but couldn't get a signal. Back to plan B.

'Most dead-bolt locks have a five-pin cylinder. If I had a drill, I could probably shift it.'

'Have you got a knife?' McCallen said.

'A knife against a reinforced metal door is like a peashooter against a charging elephant.'

'Fuck's sake, if you've got one, give it to me.'

I reached inside my jacket and pulled out a Swiss Army tool and handed it to her. I hoped she was thinking smart while I was thinking hard, a combined effort of brawn and brain our best chance of survival. Meantime, I went to retrieve the bolt cutters.

With no sign of abating, water had already poured over the three lowest steps and was dangerously close to skimming the bottom of the fourth. I jumped down with a splash and plunged through the icy stagnant filth, the smell of raw sewage strong and overpowering. This presented us with another problem: hydrogen sulphide, or sewage gas. I was already feeling queasy. At high exposure, it can kill. I wanted to take action, to do something, anything, to make things right. Instead, I stopped and focused.

Water is like electricity – it takes the path of least resistance. We'd had a lot of rain, which could have a dramatic effect on water tables. Somehow, I didn't think the jammed door was a natural disaster. But there might be a natural solution to the flood.

'There has to be a floor drain,' I said. Beneath it a P-trap, I remembered, thinking of the times I'd unblocked the lavatory at the student house. If I could find it, I might be able to buy us time. I reached into the murk, felt around for the cutters and found them about a metre from where I'd left them. Closing my eyes, I navigated the filth a step at a time, sloshing across the cellar floor, trying to locate the natural slope, digging around for the round plate that covered the drain. Sure I was in the right spot, I plunged the blades into the floor again and again and each time hit solid concrete.

'It's been cemented over,' I yelled to her. 'How are you doing?'

'It's useless. I need you to smash the metal to loosen it.'

Without warning, the little light we had extinguished. The water had blown all power.

Plunged into darkness, thigh-high water lapped around me. Numb and cold, I could feel the energy draining out of my body. Blindly, I waded through and, hitting the staircase with the toe of my boot, climbed back up and past the fourth step, now submerged. We changed places and McCallen retreated a little so that I could get a good swing, hopelessly tricky in the narrow space.

'Aim for where the lock sits,' she said, wheezing painfully.

I gave it four shots of my best. Pain shot through my arms. McCallen crept closer to escape the rising scum and the noxious smell. Hefting the cutters, I gave the lock another two strikes.

'Okay, let's hope this pays off,' she said, shuffling in front.

I watched as she inserted a blade between the lock and the wall. She jiggled it right and left and pushed down. Desperation made her stronger than was possible. It might have been my imagination and yet it appeared as if our island of dry land as represented by the staircase had rapidly diminished.

'Can you grab the handle and pull the door tight against the frame so that the lock tongue doesn't spring back?' Calm under pressure, she failed to disguise the urgent note in her voice.

I did as she said. She wiggled it again. The locks shifted. The door stayed shut.

CHAPTER FIFTY-FOUR

I was certain we'd hit the end of the road. Water was now no more than a foot from the ceiling. At the rate it was gushing in, I reckoned we had fifteen minutes before it completely flooded the cellar. Every brick and piece of wall seemed to shake and roil with the force of the torrent.

'What was that?' I said.

'What?'

'You didn't feel anything?'

'Tricky when you're numb.'

It was difficult to describe, but it felt like a sonic boom travelling through water. I had one last idea and I should have thought of it before.

'Is there a window?'

She shook her head. 'I've been here weeks, I'd have noticed.'

'The top part of some cellars is often above ground.'

Her eyes widened with excitement. 'Could the wall be boarded, like a stud wall, and painted over?'

'That figures, but even if it is, any opening between the ceiling and the wall will be hellishly narrow.'

'We've got to give it a try.'

'Stay put,' I said.

'Do I have a choice?'

'If I don't come back, here.' I reached down into my jacket, withdrew the Glock, and pressed it into her hand. 'As long as it's fully submerged, it will fire. The velocity will be slower, but it will still do the job.' She took it, her eyes meeting mine. There was no need for words.

With the bolt cutters in one hand, I swam out to what I hoped was the facing wall. Hitting brick, I felt along the edge, my fingers connecting with the jagged remains of plywood and glass, shattered with the force of water bursting through. Swimming through the narrow gap, I felt air on my face, light from a full moon shining down onto a padlocked metal grille that blocked the escape route. Treading water, I drew on every reserve and hoisted the cutters for the last time and cracked open the lock. Next, I jammed the cutters in between the bars and, with a monumental effort born of desperation, pushed up and out, sliding the grille aside.

'Don't shoot,' I yelled, as I grabbed a lungful of air and went back for McCallen.

Half-dragging McCallen through the water, I pushed her up through the open space and clambered out after her. Legs giving way, shock took its toll and every part of her trembled. Scooping her up, I held her tight to my chest, carried her in my arms, triumphant. We were free.

For now.

I wasn't complacent. I no longer had my gun but, juiced up, it would take little for me kill anyone who got in my way.

I retraced my steps and stumbled through the dark, moving as quickly as I could while holding on to McCallen. My soaking, stinking jeans clung to my legs. McCallen was quiet, body spent and mind numb. We got back to the car and I laid her on the passenger seat. She looked up at me, grateful, unable to speak, teeth chattering.

I rushed around to the driver's side and climbed in beside her.

The clock told me that it was 4.50 a.m.

'I'm taking you straight to A&E.' I turned the ignition.

'A fire station might be a better option.' She attempted a laugh, not easy when your body is racked with the shakes. 'They can cut these off.' She looked down at the metal attached to her wrists and ankles.

'You need medical attention first. I'm not sure how I'm going to account for the state we're in without someone notifying the cops.'

'Just drop me off.'

'No, I'm coming with you.'

'There's no need.'

'I want to.'

'Then I'll explain to them, don't worry.'

'Maybe you can also explain to Flynn.'

'You know Flynn?'

'Our paths crossed. You may need to put in a good word for me. I almost killed one of your colleagues.'

She let out a dry, throaty laugh.

I glanced across. Normally, she'd be rattling my cage, wanting to be first with the information. The fact she hadn't pressed me told me that, now she was free, the impact of what had taken place had hit her. I suspected that the road ahead was going to be tough. I put the heater on full blast and floored the accelerator. Three minutes later, we arrived at Cheltenham General's accident and emergency department. The department had been cut back but, in my book, a hospital was a hospital and the best place for McCallen.

* * *

I kept a spare phone in the car. McCallen used it to call HQ. She told them about Benz and ordered an alert on ports, airports and Eurostar. As soon as her release reached the right ears, I imagined the security service equivalent of a SWAT team putting in an appearance and carting me away. Made me wonder why Benz had led me straight to McCallen. There could only be one explanation: Benz intended to kill us, probably with a bullet to our heads, but the sudden, if anticipated, flood had played right into his hands and he'd decided to let us drown instead. It's why the door was jammed tight.

The early hour of the morning, combined with McCallen's status and condition, did the equivalent of 'Open Sesame' when we got to A&E. Avoiding triage, we were whisked straight in to see a duty registrar and, once McCallen explained the circumstances and insisted that she was taken care of in Cheltenham and not in Gloucester, I decided a low profile the best option.

'You'll be okay?' I took her hand and stroked it. She looked so small and fragile against the white hospital pillows. I really didn't want to leave her.

'I'll be fine.'

I nodded, awkwardly patted her arm, and made to go.

'Hex,' she said.

'Yeah?'

'I wouldn't have made it on my own. Thank you.'

A soft glow of pleasure enveloped me. I smiled.

'Something else,' she said, her voice stern.

'What?'

'Don't do anything stupid, will you?'

''Course not. I'm going home.'

'You'll come back later?'

I beamed. 'Promise.' I had a slew of questions. 'Hang onto the phone,' I said. 'If you need me, give me a call on the usual number.'

'Talk soon,' she said, warmth in her expression. 'Keep safe.'

'And you.'

'All I want to do is sleep.'

'Fat chance,' I winked. 'Flynn and his crew will be after one hell of a debrief.'

The sound of sirens greeted my exit. I must have cut a strange figure with my battered appearance and smelly clothing. Head down, I hurried on, eager to clear out before someone in law enforcement flexed their muscles.

Dawn broke reluctantly, grey and drab. I stepped into it with something close to joy. McCallen was safe. Together, we'd pulled off the impossible. I was euphoric. Despite my body screaming for rest, my mind was sharp and alert. I had scores to settle – that evil sod Benz first in my sights. Even if I had to travel to Berlin to do him, I was going to take him out of the game. Next up, China Hayes. Brommer I'd leave to McCallen.

Reaching the car, I climbed inside and worked out my next move. Secure in the assumption that we were both dead, Benz was either far away, intending to catch a flight back to Germany, or lying low nearby to check on his handiwork. Without any knowledge of the man, it was difficult to fathom which action he'd take.

And this was where I suddenly lost the plot. Filed under all's fair in love and espionage, Benz's hatred of McCallen made sense. She'd used Lars Pallenberg to penetrate his nasty little neo-Nazi group. But why me? Was Benz working for China, or the other way around?

Puzzling this, I started the engine, pulled out of the car park and returned to the Backway. Crossing the rugged ground for a third time, this time I was looking at it with daylight eyes, searching for clues, something that would answer the unanswerable and fill in the gaps. I didn't know Benz, bar the bare strap lines of a security profile. A champagne terrorist, he married radical, repellent and anti-Semitic views with a wealthy playboy lifestyle. Prone to violence, especially against women, he was like so many others I'd known: vengeful, stubborn and vicious. Still, I didn't know how this particular guy ticked.

Retracing my steps into the building, it was much bigger inside than I'd imagined. The area I'd originally stepped into fed into another warren of rooms, the metal door to the basement one of four other doors, the remainder of wooden construction. Rust-coloured and filthy water lay mute and belligerent half a metre deep. Had we been trapped inside, we would have drowned. I gave an involuntary shiver and beat it. Knackered, I needed to recharge, catch some sleep.

Back in the car, I stuck the gear into a lazy reverse with the intention of rejoining the main route when, out of nowhere, an unmistakable flash of colour, vivid against the spectral light, whipped past, almost clipping my rear. Startled, I shook myself awake, my gaze fixed on a Lamborghini Aventador, two cars up ahead. My mind zipped back to the rectory, the party night.

Keeping pace, I followed at a discreet distance, conscious that, if the Lambo floored it, I'd be left behind. The Z4 was quick, but no match for a top speed of 217 miles per hour, not that it was likely to reach such dizzying speed in the middle of town.

One car turned off and I moved up the line, only a car between us. I caught a glimpse of foreign plates, German.

We were heading towards the hospital. It would be an audacious man who attempted to finish what he'd started. It didn't mean he wouldn't try. Sure enough, the Lambo slowed as we drew near. Flashing lights and a battalion of unmarked police cars posted at each entrance and exit had the desired effect. The driver changed his mind and sped up.

We travelled south-east. On the approach to a roundabout, the flare of the Lambo's lights indicated a left turn. I followed suit. The sculpted outline of the Aventador snaked across the first exit. A silhouette in the passenger seat, just visible through the tinted glass, caught my eye. So fleeting, so obscured by the low narrow triangle of a window, it would be easy to make a mistake, yet I couldn't rule out that the driver had company, and that company was female. Brommer, I thought.

Straight over the next roundabout, marking time, I watched the Aventador turn right onto the London Road and A40. Next thing, it pulled out and, with minimal effort, overtook three cars. I guessed the capital was the possible final destination. It didn't matter. With the driver's window down, I got a good look at him. I'd recognise those blond dreads anywhere.

CHAPTER FIFTY-FIVE

I pulled over and called McCallen. When she answered her voice was low, as though she was speaking from underneath the blankets.

'I've just seen Benz.'

'Where?'

'Heading for London. He's driving a sapphire coloured Aventador.' I reeled off the registration. 'And he has a woman with him.'

'Brommer?'

'That's my guess.'

I heard her relay the information to someone else. 'We're going to pick them up.'

'Pity,' I said, wishing I hadn't. McCallen would know what I meant. 'Everything all right?'

'Yes.'

'Want me to come back sooner or later?'

'Later would be good.'

I got it. The monosyllabic replies were code for 'I'm still trying to save your skin'.

I drove against a tide of morning traffic. My endorphins had bunked off. I was filthy, in pain, and exhaustion was killing me.

It took every effort to stay awake long enough to limp back home.

The house was fine. No nasty surprises. The clamour from neighbouring streets suggested that the remains of the constabulary of Gloucestershire were in the process of decamping from the Lansdown Road HQ to Cheltenham General. Suited me.

I showered, took a couple of painkillers washed down with strong tea and crashed out. I must have slept for around three hours. Stirring, and in time to catch the one o'clock news, I switched on Radio 4, not my usual choice, but good for serious coverage. Unsurprisingly, and in spite of the commotion, McCallen's reappearance on the planet didn't feature. Swinging my legs out of bed, I stood up and reached for a clean pair of jeans when an item, two below a shout line on more promising economic news, punched me full in the face.

'A man found dead in the Thames last week has been identified as Horace Hayes. It's suspected that rivals deliberately targeted Hayes, a former gangland boss, in a dispute over a cocaine deal.'

I sat back down. Simone had said that the guy who raped her wore a tropical shirt, not exactly the sartorial equivalent of a smoking gun and, no doubt, a wily defence lawyer would demolish any prosecution argument if suggested that it was, but it seemed a peculiar coincidence. It also left me with a can of maggots. Benz had no beef with me as far as I could tell. With Horace, aka China, out of the picture, who was out to crucify me?

I closed my eyes, went right back to the beginning, to Billy Squeeze. I'd come to believe that Billy was nothing more than a tool to wind me up, a noose in which to hang me, a raw nerve to press. Crazy thoughts crawled at the edges of my brain. What if, by some miracle, he'd survived? Failing this, what if, during those months of life on the run, he'd appointed a secret successor?

It's said that when people die they take their secrets with them. Invariably, this isn't so. Truth – a threatened, submissive commodity in life – has a habit of coming out fighting in death. The long-time mistress is revealed; the debts exposed; the faithful wife a serial adulterer; the kindly husband a cruel paedophile. Death doesn't just level the dead. It levels the living. Rumour had it that Billy's wife and daughters had been well provided for. Rumours, like Chinese whispers, can get lost in translation. I'd accepted at face value that Billy's widow and family were left in the lolly because China had told me so. Either way, it was inconceivable that the Frankes didn't now realise where the money had originated from, and it was a given that they knew more than me about other aspects of Billy's life. I had to find out what it was.

First, I kept my word to Simone and, walking to the end of the street, flagged down a cab to take me to St Paul's. I'm not superstitious, I'm target aware. If the security services were on the lookout for my car and me, I didn't want to dish us up to them with all the trimmings. Hopefully, they were focused on Benz and Brommer. Even the security services had limited budgets and restricted objectives.

My taxi driver was chatty. 'Don't know what on earth is going on here today. The place is swarming with coppers.'

'Probably a rugby match or something,' I said, dismissively.

'You'd think the doughnut was under attack.'

The driver dropped me off and I paid up. Angling myself past Simone's car, I let myself in and, as a courtesy, called to the others that I was about. My voice bounced off the walls, hollow. There was no TV blaring, no music pounding, not even a snore.

Walking down the corridor and past the downstairs rooms, I tipped open the doors. Same old mess. Same idiosyncratic odour. Weirdly, I found the familiarity comforting. From the bottom of the stairs I called up and asked if anyone was home. No response. I went upstairs and, thinking Simone might be asleep, knocked softly on her door. Getting no reply, I pressed my ear against it. All quiet. I checked the bathroom, which was empty, and tapped again and called her name. Surely she hadn't gone out? I'd been so specific about her security. Frustrated and angry that she'd disregarded my advice, I pushed open the door and felt the world shift beneath my shoes.

Every piece of furniture in the small room was smashed up and ransacked in a way that defied possibility. The bed was overturned, the mattress slit open, its innards spread across the torn up carpet; the shattered blind dangled from the window; one wardrobe door was wrenched from its hinges and upended; and these were the edited highlights. Anything that could be broken lay in pieces. A quick check told me that her limited luggage remained although the laptop had vanished. Most disturbing of all, so had Simone.

I thought back to the mystery woman in the car. Had Benz taken Simone against her will, possibly drugging her? Or had Benz taken and killed Simone, dumping her body, before making off with Brommer? Or …

I looked at my watch. Benz could be miles away. An agonising thought hit me. If the security services caught up with him, full firearms team in tow, there might be a shoot first, ask questions later policy. My mobile bleeped in my pocket. I took it out, recognised the number, and answered with dread in my heart.

CHAPTER FIFTY-SIX

'We've traced the Aventador,' McCallen said. 'Pulled over near Witney.'

'And …'

'We found Benz.'

Relief seeped out of me. 'And the woman?'

'No sign of Brommer.'

'No, not Brommer, a French woman, Simone Fabron. I believe Benz may have abducted her. You need to question him immediately.' I didn't yet articulate the alternative thought whipping through my mind.

'That's going to be difficult. He's dead.'

'Jesus, do you never take prisoners?'

'My line, surely?'

A pulse ticked in my neck. McCallen's cynicism and smart mouth signalled a remarkable feat of recovery. 'What are you suggesting exactly?'

'You called it in.'

'You think I killed him?' I could hardly contain my anger. 'How was he killed, incidentally?'

'Bullet to the brain. Close-up, with a pistol. Your speciality.'

'I'm not even going to comment.' It was meant to sound

dignified. It didn't come off, mainly because I'd have been more than happy to whack him myself had I been given the opportunity.

'You stole a gun from one of my colleagues.'

'Borrowed. You seemed fairly happy when I showed up with it in the cellar.'

'It doesn't look good.'

'Appearances are deceiving.' This mimicked the alternative film score currently playing through my head. I was the one who'd been deceived by appearances.

'Have you fired it?'

'Tell me something, is this Flynn's working theory, or yours?'

'I'm simply looking at the facts.' She sounded maddeningly superior. God, she'd only returned to the fold a few hours ago and she was reverting to type. 'They told me about Titus.'

'And your point?'

'Anyone who crosses your path has a habit of winding up dead.'

'My postman and the guy I buy meat from looked okay this morning.'

She did not find me funny. 'You know damn well what I mean.'

'Did Flynn tell you how Titus died?'

'Dead is dead.'

'Wrong. Remember when Billy got his dirty little hands on me?'

'Yeah,' she said uncertainly.

'Trussed me up like the traditional Christmas turkey?' I added, so that there was no mistake and we were speaking exactly the same lingo. 'Well, that's how Titus died. And if you think me capable of that level of cruelty then I suggest you hang up right now.'

The line went quiet. I took a deep breath and exhaled slowly. Getting angry never solved anything.

'Think Brommer killed Titus?' So she did believe me, sort of.

'Maybe, I don't know.' Which was not exactly the truth.

'The French woman you mentioned. How does she fit?'

I gave an edited potted history and told her about the Titus connection. For reasons I didn't want to admit, I left out the nature of my relationship with Simone.

'Titus and sex parties?' She sounded surprised.

'Is it so much of a stretch? All kinds of guys attend those gigs. Benz, for example.'

'I didn't know that.'

'No?' This took me by surprise. 'Don't you spooks share information?'

'Only when there's something relevant to say.'

'It *is* relevant.'

She ignored me. 'The fact is, with Benz dead and Brommer on the loose, it's going to be difficult to locate the French girl.'

'I found you.'

McCallen let out a laugh. 'You were practically given an A–Z. We were supposed to die together, remember?'

I remembered. I also remembered something else. 'I have to go.' McCallen was abouy to say something, but I cut her off. I had my own ideas and I'd always worked better solo.

CHAPTER FIFTY-SEVEN

I headed up Tommy Taylor's Lane, past the swimming pool and, turning right, cut across the Evesham Road and into Western Approach. On one side, a tennis court and skate park, Pittville Pump Room on the other side. Dan was easy enough to pick out from the other long-limbed youth. So this was how he studied for a degree.

I hollered, my voice competing with the screech and grind of metal on tarmac. Dan looked up and gave me a 'what the fuck is he doing here' look? Undeterred, I marched towards him. He cast his eyes to the ground, walked with a low lope, shoulders rounded. Not happy to associate with me, it seemed. In his eyes, I was the opposite of cool.

'Yep?' he said.

'Simone. Where is she?'

'How should I know?'

I bit down hard to stop myself from giving him a slap. 'Let me rephrase. Where did you last see her?'

'At home.'

'When was that?'

'Dunno, a couple of hours ago, maybe more, can't remember.'

'What about Jack and Gonzo?'

Dan shrugged. 'You'll have to ask them.'

'I would if they were there.'

'Must be in bed.'

'They're not. I checked.'

Dan scratched his ear. 'What day is it?'

I pulled a face. 'Wednesday.'

'Explains it. They've got lectures, solid.'

'Does anyone else have keys to the house?'

'No.'

'Are you sure?'

'What's with the interrogation?'

I flung him a look that startled him. He took a smart step back. 'Someone trashed Simone's room,' I said darkly, 'and she isn't there.'

'Fuck.'

'Fuck, indeed.'

'Was she there last night?'

'As far as I know.'

'Did you see her this morning?'

'Nope.'

'You didn't take her a cup of tea?' I said, in a facetious tone.

Dan scowled, his look the equivalent of giving me the finger. 'Did someone rearrange your face?'

Tempted to rearrange his, I stalked off.

Skirting the perimeter of the tennis court, I noticed a young girl, around fourteen years of age. Reaching up and over, she thwacked balls with immense style and precision over the net, her coach throwing one after another to improve her swing. Dark-featured, she could have been a young Simone. *I ski when I can. I enjoy tennis and polo.*

Shaken by the way my mind was working, I sat down on a low wall and pulled out my phone. I checked through the information I'd captured from Simone's laptop and the list of hotel bookings she'd made in the past twelve months. It took me several minutes to find what I was looking for. Thinking it had to be a blind, I decided to corroborate the information before springing to hasty conclusions. Closing the picture, I logged onto the internet and punched in 'New Forest Polo Club'. A website popped up with a list of fixtures. I compared it with the date Lars Pallenberg died – 20 May – and discovered that the Dunlop Cup was played on the same day. Scrolling down revealed that a high-class hotel sponsored the club, presumably in some kind of reciprocal deal whereby polo teams and social members could take advantage of hotel facilities. I called the club first and spoke to the polo manager.

'Hi, I wonder if you can help me.'

'I'll do my best.' So it was true what the website said. They really were friendly. Frankly, I was banking on it.

'My girlfriend has let her membership lapse and I'd like to renew it, is that possible? She doesn't know a thing about if, of course,' I wittered on.

'A surprise – what a nice idea. You say she's a member, would that be social or player membership?'

I hesitated. 'Social.' I recalled Simone had told me she liked to watch. 'The name's Fabron.'

'Simone Fabron?' the manager asked.

I closed my eyes, cut the call and followed up the hotel connection, the same hotel that had appeared in Simone's personal file. I started off the same way with a subtle variation.

'Hi, I want to book a double room for next weekend.'

'I'll see what I can do, sir. May I ask how you found out about us?'

'My girlfriend has stayed with you before and she recommended it.'

'That's always good to know.'

'Would it be possible to have the same room? She stayed around 20 May last year, maybe the night before. The name's Fabron.'

'One moment, please.' I waited, looked at the ground, made a pattern with the sole of my shoe, thinking about connections and lies, those we tell to ourselves and those told to us by others.

'Yes, Miss Fabron stayed in room 10 on the 19th. Would you like –'

Moving fast, I hung up.

CHAPTER FIFTY-EIGHT

I jumped on the first bus heading back to the centre of town. Staring out of the window, I went over all the little things that had snagged in my mind, that like a fool I'd discounted. My mind reeled back to the hotel room in London. I'd believed that Simone's laptop, left deliberately open with an easy-to-crack password, was a sign of her trust in me, rather than a deliberate ruse to put Mathilde Brommer in the frame for murder. Then there had been the alleged rape.

When people wake up and bad things have happened to them, their initial reaction is one of optimism. It lasts usually for no more than seconds, half a minute at most, before reality kicks in, and with it a terrible sense of unhappiness. After Simone's rape, this never happened. I was there. I watched her face. I thought it odd at the time, yet I didn't know why.

I'd expected bruising on her body as she'd struggled with her rapist. There was none. The brand of cigarettes she smoked matched the Gauloises I'd found in the grass in the graveyard, close to the crypt where Titus had met his death. In matching the timing of key events, I saw that she had plenty of time to be involved in abduction and murder. Whether she carried out every killing herself was debatable. It would take a level of skill that I found tricky to credit. What was certain was that she had killed Lars Pallenberg. Her leather shoulder bag had given her secret away. I knew because I'd used a similar trick myself once. Front opening, purpose-built, a bag like that could easily conceal a weapon like an MP5. I imagined her stopping Lars for directions, her fabulous looks turning his head and halting him in his tracks. It was so simple to empty three bullets into his head, and to spray the rest of the magazine at the unfortunate couple who happened to stumble upon the scene. I understood how Phipps had met his end; China, too. A hapless pawn who initially believed it would save him, China had helped Simone to wipe out his enemies. I could almost hear her stringing him along, carrot and stick, seductively assuring him that it would suit his best interests, and threatening if he didn't comply. As for Titus, God only knew what happened, but I suspected she'd suckered him like she'd suckered me, his crime to pillow-talk in the dead of night and give away priceless information about McCallen. Right up until the last moment, I bet Benz thought they were in it together – until she put a bullet through his brain.

I called McCallen. 'Brommer's clean.'

'How do you know?'

'I know.'

'Well, she's definitely not in the country and from our latest information she never left Berlin. The BfV are giving her the once-over.' Internal German security, I registered. 'This French woman …'

I sharpened. 'What of her?'

'She's not coming up on our system.'

'She has to. She runs businesses. She pays taxes. She works here, for Chrissakes.'

'No, you don't understand. Simone Fabron is a fabrication, as Hex is yours. She's a ghost.'

Modelled on me, of course. 'Like Billy.'

'Shit!'

'Fabron has been jerking our strings from the beginning.'

'The other half of the Benz duo. Right, I need to get out of here.' I had visions of McCallen throwing back the covers, grabbing her clothes and heading out of the hospital.

'No way.'

'Fuck's sake, I'm part of this. It was my mission.'

'It's *always* your blasted mission.'

'I'm serious.'

'So am I. For once in your life, do as you're told.'

'You might need backup.'

'You're in no state and you need rest.'

'Sweet of you to care.'

She was sarcastic and I was vexed. McCallen was thinking of targets and results and promotion. Give me revenge any day. It was more honest. Picking up on my anger, she tried a more conciliatory approach.

'It was a joke.'

'I know.'

'Hex, you sound strange.' I felt strange, as if all the demons I'd locked inside were throwing a party. 'Reminds me of when we worked together before.'

'That's good.' I rallied. 'We won.'

She fell silent. 'But that was then. You're out of that business now. I'll alert Flynn. He can take care of it.'

'Why? This was never about national security. It's personal.'

'But Benz –'

'Is dead, used like all the rest until he exceeded his sell-by date. The security services got the outcome they wanted.'

Seconds ticked by. My stop was coming up. I stood up to exit the bus.

'You can't go after her alone. Kill her and you lose.'

'I'm not going to kill her. I'm going to bring her in.' Did I mean a word of it? The thought of killing a woman made me baulk. The only time I'd ever set out to do so I'd been beaten to it and it had got me into a shitload of mess. I also had a major problem in that I no longer had access to a gun.

I stepped off onto the pavement. 'I have to wrap up the call now.'

'Hex?'

'Yeah?'

'Don't get hurt.'

'I don't intend to.'

'Are you armed?'

'No.'

The line went quiet. I was about to hang up when McCallen suddenly spoke and gave me a location. 'There's a DLB there. Inside is a replacement.' She meant a dead letter box with a gun.

'You're taking one hell of a risk on me,' I said.

'I did that the first day we met.'

I smiled and thanked her.

'Win this time,' she said, 'for both of us.'

CHAPTER FIFTY-NINE

The thirst for revenge does not diminish with time. There is no statute of limitations. For Fabron to go to extremes, to plot and scheme, to play cat and mouse with her primary victims, with all the associated mental torture, she must have had a close association with Billy. Fabron, a ghost in the eyes of GCHQ and MI5, had outwitted us all. So far, her luck had held. That was about to change. Everyone had a weakness. Drugs, debts, an important relationship, whatever – I needed to know what hers was. It wouldn't be easy. I'd been intimately involved with her and yet hadn't known her at all.

But I had a head start.

Knowing the enemy is key to survival. If you know how they think, you can stand tall in the winner's enclosure. I knew that Simone was cunning and clever, a mistress of deception, as cruel as she was patient. She liked the long game and she enjoyed the art of manipulation. I knew all this because I was the same animal. Where we differed was that she enjoyed mental and physical torture. This had never turned me on.

I took my usual cut-through on the way back home. A nursing home overlooked the alley with a wall running alongside its boundary, rising in height after a couple of metres. Shrubbery and dead leaves spilt over the lower section almost covering a chalk mark in the brick. Directly beyond this were a couple of parked cars and a large plane tree, the earth beneath a repository for all kinds of junk, tin cans, discarded plastic water bottles and general detritus. The way ahead clear, I glanced over my shoulder to ensure I was not seen, reached over, my hand touching what appeared to be a food carton half submerged in the undergrowth. I pulled out the reinforced box and tucked it inside my jacket and walked on.

Home again, I opened my treasure trove. A loaded Glock, identical to the gun I'd stolen, nestled inside.

I called Jat once more. Where the combined forces of the security services had failed, Jat might yet succeed. It was worth a punt anyway.

'Forget everything I asked you to do,' I told him, 'and see if you can dig up anything on Simone Fabron. It's not her real name. She's a French national with an English mother, allegedly dead, and has a connection to the late William Franke. She runs a number of businesses.' I gave him the rough spec. 'I also need you to find out who owns a property in Cheltenham.' I gave the address where McCallen had been held.

Jat doesn't curse – it's not his style – he whinges. Two minutes of moaning later, he hung up.

By the time, I finally set off for Chobham, Billy's former family home, it was after four. Due to heavy traffic and a road closure, a journey that should have taken me the best part of two hours took almost double that. It gave me plenty of time to think about the woman I'd willingly allowed to dupe me.

I have never underestimated the female of the species. In my opinion, and based on fifteen years of dealing with horrible people, a ruthless woman has the edge on a ruthless man any day. Their capacity for cruelty is epic. Their ability to discern emotional vulnerability and manipulate it to advantage spellbinding. When women are bad they are very bad: more scheming, more reckless, more creative. When they hate, they make it entirely personal. I had met women like this before: Mafia women, Russian wives who allow their crime lord husbands to believe that their more dastardly plans are their own creation, and Lady Macbeths of the Orient. Simone and her ambitions exceeded anyone's I'd ever met. She was off the scale.

I pulled up outside the wrought iron electronic gates of the Franke residence a little before eight. I'd been working on how I was going to lie to gain access. Should I say I was an old friend of Billy's? How would that play? And if, by whatever means, I blagged my way in, would they read death in my eyes, see the blood on my hands, spot that the man standing in their living room asking questions was the same man who'd pushed a husband and father under a moving train? I needn't have bothered. A sign outside stated that the property was sold.

Dejected, I cut the engine, climbed out, stretched my legs and arched my back. The air temperature had dropped several degrees, a thin rime of frost already on the ground. At the end of a long drive, the black and white farmhouse was impossible to see from the entrance. That was the way Billy liked things. No trace and no connection between Billy landowner and family man and Billy vicious gangland boss. I thought about his widow, the revelations that must have rocked their world.

Unless she'd known all along.

I climbed back into the car and drove to the nearest pub. Old English in style, with lots of brass, highly polished beer pumps and gleaming glasses, it was a decent, honest-to-God local. I bet the beer was good and asked for a pint of the most popular, along with a menu. I couldn't remember the last time I'd eaten. Adrenalin has a deadening effect on my appetite. With the pressure eased off, I was suddenly ravenous.

Tall, lean, bald-headed with a moustache and an authoritative manner, the guy behind the bar wore a tie with a tiepin. I had him figured for the landlord. I also had him down for ex-army.

It's difficult to shake off the vestiges of years serving in the military.

I ordered and paid for local sausages with onion gravy and mash.

'Where do you want to eat?' he said. 'You can either sit here at the bar, or at one of the tables.'

'Here's fine.' I sipped my beer, which was clean and with the right balance of hop and malt, and took a good slow look around the bar. A group of red-eyed regulars were gathered at one end, the rest of the customers were businessmen dining alone and couples out for a few mid-week drinks. It didn't look the type of place where anything kicked off. The military landlord would never allow it.

'Come far?' he said.

'Gloucestershire.'

'Home of my old regiment.' His eyes shone with fond memory.

He went off to serve a customer. My dinner arrived and I ate. Twenty minutes later, I pushed my clean plate away and thanked the waitress who appeared delighted. Maybe people didn't express their gratitude often in this neck of the woods. Small and pretty with bright blue eyes, she had a ballet dancer's walk.

'Is there anywhere around here I could stay for the night?' I asked her.

'We've got a couple of rooms.'

'How much do you charge?'

'£90 with full English. Want me to check to see if one's free?' She spoke well. I reckoned she was a sixth-former, working the odd night to earn a few quid.

'That would be good – thanks.'

My army friend returned. 'Anything else I can get you?'

'That depends on whether you have any accommodation.'

A wide smile cracked his face. 'A Coke if we're full. A pint if we've got room.'

'Yeah, that's about right.'

The girl returned and said something to the landlord. He winked at me. 'I'll pull a pint then. Amy will sort out the paperwork later.'

I smiled thanks, paid for my bed and beer. 'The big house that sold up the road?'

'What of it?'

'Happen to know where the Frankes went?'

'You're a friend of the Frankes?' He did his best to sound casual. The change of light in his eyes gave him away.

'Of Justine's. I heard what happened.'

He looked through me. I didn't blame him. With the story about Billy out, I could be a guy eager to call in an old debt. 'No idea,' he said, shut down.

After that, he avoided me until I picked up the keys to my room.

'Travelling light?' Suspicion etched his voice.

'I am.'

The room was fine. For me, it was too much like the old days: strange beds, strange hotels and strange towns. Consequently, I slept badly, my mind seared with thoughts of Simone. Having seduced me, she'd done an excellent job of maintaining my interest. Had it all been for show, an act designed to distract me while she engaged in a rampage of murder? Had there ever been chemistry between us? Was I that dumb? I guess a part of the attraction for me was that I could identify with her free spirit. Looking back, and though I pretended otherwise, the signs were all there, her actions designed to throw me off the scent, my absences giving her the requisite time she needed to step up her plan. I'd been like an ardent cinemagoer viewing a foreign film. So busy watching the acting, I'd forgotten to read the subtitles. That she'd modelled the vicious part of herself on me did not escape my attention. On the last occasion I'd spoken to Billy, he told me how impressed he was with my killing abilities, that he admired my methods. I hadn't realised he'd been studying them to pass on to someone else.

The next morning it was me and Amy and a plate of bacon, sausage and egg. Not normally one for talk in the morning, I struck up a conversation. 'No school?'

'Half-term.'

'Local?'

'Yes.'

'You're a sixth-former?'

'Studying for my baccalaureate.'

'Smart young lady.'

She smiled shyly. 'I'm not that smart. You should see some of my friends. We have a lot of kids who've lived abroad, kids from China, too. They're the really clever ones.'

'You must know the Franke girls.'

Her sunny face clouded. 'Indie was never a close friend.'

'I know Justine,' I said.

'Really? It's sad what happened. They had to leave school.'

'Leave?'

'Couldn't afford to stay.'

I quickly recalibrated my thinking. 'Do you stay in touch?'

'Indie never went away.' The bridge of Amy's nose creased. 'Her mum and sisters moved – abroad, I think, to Mrs Franke's parents in Spain. I see Indie from time to time. She works at the racing stables down the road, has lodgings there.'

284

CHAPTER SIXTY

Horses with wild eyes, red shiny nostrils and sinuously muscular bodies clattered and skittered across the yard in single file, riders perched, it seemed to me, in defiance of the laws of gravity. They headed off down the road and quickly turned into a field where low winter light trickled behind a ridge of trees. I watched as they took flight, hooves lashing soft ground, soil and stone scattered beneath.

On each side of the yard were ten empty stables, their doors open, a shovel scraping cobbles the only sound. Tracing the source, I leant inside and my mind flashed to blood in straw, equine and human remains, and one of Billy's victims. I blinked the memory away.

A girl around Amy's age had her wiry back to me. She was shovelling manure and dirt and dumping it into a wheelbarrow. Engrossed, she failed to notice she had company. I cleared my throat, hoping not to startle her too much. She wheeled around with terrified eyes.

'It's okay.' I tipped the palms of my hands up. 'Sorry to frighten you.'

'Who are you and what do you want?' I could see Billy in her straight away. She had the same look, the one that could nail a guy to the floor. Fortunately, the rest of her features resembled her mother's. She didn't have Billy's darker colouring.

'Indie, I –'

'How do you know my name?' She drew the shovel towards her, tightened her grip. She looked like she was prepared to wield it. A tiny bird of a girl, I didn't doubt that, if provoked, she was capable.

I smiled. 'Is there somewhere we can talk? It's pretty cold here.'

'What are you suggesting, that we sit in your car?' The suspicious sneer on her face was Billy's too.

'No. Don't you have somewhere to take a break – a tack room or something?'

She sniffed and wiped her nose with the side of her hand, not very ladylike. 'Why would I want to talk to you? I don't even know your name.'

'People call me Joe, Joe Nathan.'

'Are you alone?' Her eyes lifted to a point beyond my right shoulder.

'I am.'

'So, Joe Nathan, why are you here?'

'Because I can help you.' This wasn't strictly true. If pushed, I might say things that would further devastate her.

She didn't soften, although her grip on the shovel appeared less intense. 'I don't want your help and, by the way, the guys will be back soon from the gallops.'

'Then we should press on. Want a hand?' I took a step towards her.

She took a step back and pointed the spade head at me. 'No.'

'Fair enough. If you don't want to hear what I have to say, I'll go.' I turned on my heel. 'Have a nice day.'

'Wait.' I turned back. Her eyes met mine. 'I'll talk to my boss's wife and see if it's all right for us to talk in the house.' I didn't like that idea. The woman might snarl things up. From Indie's point of view it was a good move. 'Meet me in five minutes,' she said.

I did as she asked. Five minutes was all they needed to call the police. In ten, I could be picked up and taken away. Twenty minutes later and, in spite of calling in a favour from McCallen, I'd be cooling my heels while the cops danced through a number of bureaucratic hurdles and, if I were fortunate, signed off the paperwork. I stayed because I had no choice.

My phone rang: Jat.

'If you were a woman, I'd expect sex.'

I let out a laugh, quite something given the mood I was in. 'What have you got?'

'Your man left a coded message. It's taken me all this time to work it out.'

'Spare me the technical stuff, what is it?'

'Simone Fabron is an anagram.'

'Of what?'

'Simon O.N. Faber. That's how your man China corresponded with Simone Fabron. It's all there in the draft folder.'

I didn't understand this, but that wasn't important to me. 'What did they communicate about?'

'Everything. It reads like a criminal Who's Who. Details of drugs deals, including a guy called Dieter Benz who seemed to act like a go-between. Remember the list of names I pulled off?' I told him I did. 'Well, under each name, China supplied information about the subject's address, close relatives, routines, times they went out, the vehicles they drove, you name it. Simone pretty much wore China's balls for earrings.' And when China got sick and tired of it, he tried to hire me to eliminate her. Made sense.

'There's more,' Jat said, in full spate now. 'I did some online detective work and discovered that Simon Faber is a charity. It buys up properties on the cheap, often from councils, does them up and rents them out at reasonable rates to people who'd otherwise find it difficult to find a cheap place to live, what with the economy tits up.'

'All very laudable. There's a "but" coming.'

'Damn right, the charity is a front. Out of a hundred homes bought, only two have gone back into the rental market. The rest have been flogged off for a fat profit. And that's the tip of the iceberg.'

'A method to launder money?'

'That's my guess.'

'And the property in Cheltenham?'

'You got it. It's owned indirectly by Simon Faber.'

'Indirectly?'

'There are a number of holding companies. Simon Faber is buried in the mix.'

'Anything connecting Simone Fabron to Billy Franke?'

'Billy Franke,' he repeated, articulating the syllables.

I held my breath.

'No,' Jat said, 'the name isn't here, sorry.'

'Apology isn't necessary. I owe you.'

'Although Franke Holdings is one of the shroud companies,' Jat said. 'Does that help?'

Five long minutes had passed. Time to move it.

CHAPTER SIXTY-ONE

The trainer's house had seen better days. I guessed every pound went into the stables. Indie let me in through a veranda masquerading as a conservatory and into a quarry-tiled kitchen with an ancient Rayburn that whacked out more heat than looked feasible. She sat down opposite me at a large kitchen table.

Her eyes fastened on mine. 'You said you could help.'

It would be easy to dish out a string of lies, easy to exploit her vulnerability and manipulate her. I decided to play it straight because I sensed she'd had a rough time and deserved better than that. 'I am not here to frighten or cause you grief. It's important you know this,' I began.

''kay,' she said slowly, one finger tracing a line around a gouge in the tabletop.

'I knew your father. I knew what he did and how he made his money.'

'Then you knew him better than me.' Hurt then fear flashed across her features. 'Who are you?'

'I am not a police officer or private detective or one of your father's cronies,' I assured her.

'That doesn't leave too many pleasant alternatives.'

I smiled. 'I'm someone who believes you've had a raw deal and

I want to put it right.'

'Who do you think you are, Superman?' The accompanying laugh was hard-edged for a girl so young.

'I wouldn't blame you if you lied to me, but did your mum know?' I'd always believed that Justine, a pleasant, family-minded woman, was in the dark about Billy's dealings.

'About what? My father's criminality? Of course, we didn't know. We found out when he died. It's so, so unfair. Like, we had this really nice life and now it's all disappeared.'

'That's tough.'

Her eyes were shot through with anger. 'We've had to pay tons of money back to all sorts of people. My mother is practically destitute. You know what, I'm glad he fell under a train. I hope it fucking well hurt and ripped him to pieces.'

She tipped back in the seat, crossed her arms in front of her small breasts, defying me to disagree. Rage came off her in waves.

I paused, hoped she'd calm down a little, knowing I'd yet to deliver the hammer blow. 'When I asked the question, I wasn't referring to what your dad did for a living. I meant your father's lover.'

She practically leapt across the table. 'Holy shit.'

'I'm sorry. You really didn't know?'

She shook her head vigorously. 'But it explains a lot.' A light went on in Indie's eyes. 'So that's why my father split his time, although,' she laughed with black humour, 'I guess running a drugs empire eats into the average day. Who is this fucking woman?'

'A French national.' I didn't know for certain. Simone dealt in half-truths. She had lost her mother like me but I doubted her mother was British. Had she been, she'd have been easy to trace.

'What's her name?'

'Simone Fabron.'

Indie sat back, her clever mind processing the information. I could practically see the electrical connections her brain was making. 'You know he left the house to a charity?'

China had mentioned it, I remembered. 'I'd heard a rumour but how does that work?' I said. 'Surely, the police would have sequestered it?'

Indie shook her head. 'The deeds of the house were transferred seven years earlier.'

'Seven years?' I said, taken aback.

'Yeah,' she said, with a grim expression. 'Imagine how my mum felt.'

Pissed off beyond belief, I thought. Premeditated, and a brilliant move on Billy's part to protect his asset, it displayed a degree of cunning that was entirely in character.

'Simon Faber, by any chance?'

Her jaw went slack. She looked at me in astonishment. 'How did you know?'

CHAPTER SIXTY-TWO

I rolled off a wad of twenties and tried to hand it to Indie. She shook her head.

'I can't.'

'Why not?'

'Because it's your money and I don't know you.' She gave a nervous little laugh.

'Take it.' I stretched across the table and pressed it into her hand. 'You've given me information and I'm paying you for it, a straight business transaction.'

'Well …'

'Didn't your mum contest it?'

'To contest, you need a lawyer. She couldn't afford it.'

'Didn't she have jewellery to sell?'

'Yeah, but it went nowhere. Have you any idea how much money was owed?' She ran a grubby hand through her hair. 'Honestly, it's so hard to remember everything. None of us were thinking straight. Overnight, the money ran out. Everything was tied up in offshore accounts and stuff she couldn't get her hands on. She had to sell what she had to live. All kinds of people, bad people, came knocking at our door.'

I could imagine exactly the type of vultures circling. 'And you say she's in Spain?'

'Yeah.'

'Do you have an address, a contact number for her?'

'Whoa, I'm not sure about that.' Suspicion darkened her eyes. One question too many and in a couple of seconds I'd smashed the fragile trust between us.

'All right, do you have a pen and paper?'

'I guess.' She twisted around, snatched a pad and biro from a work surface and pushed them across to me.

'When you next talk to her, tell her I called and, if she wants to contact me, this is my number. No pressure.' I scraped back the chair and stood up.

'Is that it?' she said.

'What were you expecting, a box of chocolates too?'

She gave me an odd look and smiled. We were friends again. As I walked back across the yard, I felt her gaze scored into my back. She was a smart kid. All the time I was there I hadn't heard a floorboard squeak or the sound of human activity. Thinking fast, Indie had told me a lie to protect herself. The only decent legacy bequeathed by her father.

I climbed back into the car. Next stop: the family seat. If it all panned out, Simone would be hiding out there.

The pub where I'd spent the night was on my way. In the twilight zone between breakfast and morning coffee, the car park would be quiet – a couple of staff vehicles, max. I was wrong. Sharply indicating right, I made a cartoon-like swerve and pitched up immediately outside the entrance. Mystified, my thoughts turbo-charged, I slipped my gun into my jacket and walked inside.

I saw her before she saw me. She sat close to the open fire, hunched over, warming herself. She wore an elegant long coat, jeans and boots. When she looked up she had the strained eyes of a fugitive. It reminded me so much of Billy's last stand.

'Thank God,' she said, throwing herself at me.

I stood, rooted. If Simone was about to hand herself in, it

293

rated as the fastest and easiest takedown in history. 'How did you find me?'

'You are still suspicious.'

Damn right, but I did my best not to show how much. What I said next was a perfectly reasonable statement. 'It's a hell of a coincidence that you pull into a pub in the middle of nowhere when I happen to be driving past.'

'Maybe you followed me.' There was a sour tone to her voice. 'I didn't.'

'Then I followed you. It's true,' she said, exasperated.

'Followed me from where, exactly?'

She led off on a rambling tale of driving back to London, spotting my car and shadowing me. 'I slept overnight in the car park,' she said with feeling. 'I was so cold.'

'Then why not wake me?'

'I thought you would be angry. You were so mad when I left London against your wishes.'

I unclamped her arms from around my neck and pushed her down into the nearest seat. I was gentle, no point in making a bad situation worse. I asked if she wanted something to drink.

'Coffee and, if possible, brandy.' She was the most submissive I'd ever seen her. I thought it an omen.

I went in search of someone to take the order, found Amy and returned to Simone. I made sure I sat opposite where I could see her hands. I didn't ask how she found me. I pitched straight in.

'You have one hell of a lot of explaining to do. Why did you do it, Simone?'

She looked at me with shocked, hurt eyes. 'Do what?'

'Don't,' I spat. 'We both know what we're talking about – abduction, torture of intelligence officers, murder, drugs deals, assassination.' I left myself out of it. I was relatively unscathed.

Her eyes widened and her mouth fell open. 'It's not true, I tell you. You have to believe me.'

The coffee and single brandy arrived. Amy darted a look from

294

Simone to me. An encouraging smile flickered at the corner of her mouth. She clearly thought that Simone was confessing to infidelity. In a sense, Amy was not far from the truth.

Simone took a deep swallow of brandy. I splashed coffee into two cups, dumped two sugars in mine, and sat back. Time to get specific. 'The guy with the tropical shirt, who was he?'

'I told you, I don't know.'

'Who smacked up your face, or did you deliberately walk into a door?'

'Why are you talking like this?'

'What relationship do you have to Benz?'

'None, other than what I already told you.'

'That he attended Bagatelle parties?'

'Yes.'

'Why did you leave Dan's place?'

'I got scared. I thought someone was watching the house.'

'How? It's right on the main road and there are double yellows running down it.'

She frowned with exasperation. 'People on foot, I saw the same two men walking by.'

I wasn't buying. There were too many superfluous men mixed up in this and most remained unconnected to the main event. 'So you fled, right?'

'Yes.'

'With your laptop?'

'Yes.'

'If you were scared, wouldn't you just get out and make a run for it?'

'My laptop contains my life.'

'So where is it?'

'In my car. I will fetch it if you don't believe me.' She spoke with a smile, as if I was entirely unreasonable and she was humouring me.

'Where were you on 19 May last year?'

'Last year?'

'I'll refresh your memory. You stayed in the New Forest, allegedly to watch a polo match.'

'Why ask when you already know the answer? And what of it?'

I was clearly going too easy on her because a feisty note had crept back into her tone. 'A man was shot and killed the following day.'

'This is ridiculous. You can't think –'

'How long have you run Simon Faber?'

'I have never heard of this man. Who is he?'

'It's a company, damn it. Your property company. It owns a building that was used to imprison an intelligence officer. Seven years ago, the deeds from a house, a stone's throw from here, were transferred to you.'

'*Quoi?* I have no idea what you are talking about. My only companies are Bagatelle and the lifestyle businesses.'

'So you deny everything?'

'Absolutely.'

'You deny an association with one very dead China Hayes?'

'I already explained this to you.'

'You deny killing Lars Pallenberg?'

'Me, kill?' Her eyes filled with tears. 'How could you even think it?'

I glanced down, searched for her trademark bag. It wasn't with her. Maybe it was in her car. She carried a smaller bag, in red leather, to match her gloves. I wondered what lay inside.

I looked at her with contempt. I'd saved the best for last. 'For how long had you been Billy Franke's lover?'

'You are talking shit, you know that? I have never been this man's lover. I do not know who he is.'

Looking up into her midnight eyes, fury boiled inside me. 'Tell me one thing, just one thing. No, make it two,' I said, changing my mind, knowing how easy it is to sell a single truth.

'Give me two facts that are genuine and true.'

She bit her lower lip. Her eyes filmed over. She shook – genuinely anguished, it seemed. '*D'accord*, you win.' Her voice was soft. She ran her fingers through her long dark hair. Expecting her to pull out a weapon, I reached inside my jacket.

Looking me dead in the eye she said, 'My mother is alive and she gave me away.'

CHAPTER SIXTY-THREE

As fragile as a dragonfly, a thought flittered in and flittered back out again. It was not the answer I'd sought or expected.

'Sad, but is it relevant?'

'I do not know.' She took a deep swallow of brandy. 'But I know she hates me.'

I changed position. For me, like most men I'd ever dealt with, relationships and families were minefields, alien territory, not the kind of stuff with which to engage. My own set-up was dysfunctional, and I had no real concept of what counted for normal. The mention of emotions gave me the creeps and made me want to run fast in the opposite direction. I guess it would be fair to say that I'm a fully paid up member of the 'failure to commit' club. All this aside, I couldn't see how Simone's difficulty with her mother had any bearing on mayhem and murder. Unless …

'Your mother's name is Justine, isn't it?'

She tipped her head to one side, as if bewildered and impressed and confused. 'Yes.'

'Justine Franke?'

'Justine Smart. But she is married now so who knows?'

I drained my cup. Things were getting properly messy. 'Tell me what happened from the beginning, when you were a kid.'

'My mother gave me away when I was a baby. There were no papers. It was not a legal adoption.'

'How old was Justine?'

'Fifteen. My grandparents organised it, or so she said.'

'And you were given to a French couple, right?'

She nodded.

'Why did they do that?'

She gave a weak smile. 'You'd have to ask her.'

I hiked one shoulder. Maybe I would. 'Go on.'

'The Fabrons were already quite old when they took me on. They brought me up as their own.'

'They loved you?'

'Of course.' She put her glass down and reached for the coffee pot, topped up my cup and poured out some for herself. 'When they died I was still a young woman and, without a family, I decided to look for my blood mother. It took me several years. Life was hard. My adoptive parents were not rich and I was on my own.'

'You had to fend for yourself?'

Her bottom lip trembled. 'Yes.'

'And, eventually, you traced Justine?'

Simone nodded.

'And she agreed to meet?'

'Yes.'

'Where?'

'In London.'

'It's a big place.'

'A café in Richmond,' she said. 'It did not go well.'

'I imagine it must have been hard for her. Not that unusual, I guess.'

She leant forward, fixed me with her dark brown eyes. 'Threatening to kill your firstborn is not unusual?'

I maintained my stare, didn't so much as flicker. I'd met Justine once by accident. This did not square with my impression of her.

But what did I know? 'What did she say, exactly?'

'She said I was a mistake from the past, that she had three daughters and a good life and wanted to forget I ever existed.'

'Hard, but it happens,' I said.

'She told me that she was married to the most powerful criminal in Britain and that he had connections. She threatened me.' Tears sprang to Simone's eyes. Her hand shook a little. She cleared her throat. 'She said that if I came anywhere near her or her family, made any contact, she only had to give the word and I'd be killed.'

'Did you know who she was married to?'

'I found out.'

'But you said that you'd never heard of him.'

'*Non*,' she said, fire in her eyes, 'You asked me if I knew a guy by name and I told you I did not.'

The distinction was so fine I thought it a smokescreen. 'Did you ever meet her husband?'

'Aren't you listening to me?'

'I am, but there are too many gaps.'

'I never met him,' she said emphatically.

'Then how is it that Franke Holdings is inextricably linked to Simon Faber, and Simon Faber owns the old family home? Your home, your company,' I reiterated, in case she didn't get it the first time.

'How many more times? It is not my company. Your information is false, or faked.'

I sat back, thought about it. I'd no reason to doubt Jat's technical proficiency, but I supposed it was possible that we'd fallen prey to misinformation. I took out my phone. The way Simone flinched you'd think I'd pulled a gun.

'It's okay. I'm not turning you in. I need to check something out.' I contacted Jat and outlined my thinking.

'You mean the information is bogus, is that what you're saying?' he said.

300

'Is it possible?'

'Well, yeah, I guess.' He sounded doubtful.

'Could China have been coerced to enter it and leave a false trail?'

'He could, but there's a simpler solution.'

Inspiration struck. 'Someone hijacked the email address and sent phoney information?'

'Backdoor technology,' Jat said. 'It's a means to access information on a computer and bypass the normal security systems. Once in, you can take control.'

'So, for example, an email may look as if it's come from someone, but it hasn't.'

'That's the gist of it.'

'And those emails would go to the recipient, in this case Simone Fabron?'

'Yes. They either went direct to her or they could have gone straight into her spam folder, in which case she wouldn't necessarily receive them.'

'Okay. And the company?'

'Nothing fake about it.'

'I take your point, but is the name the only thing that ties it to Fabron?'

'That's all I have right now.'

'Can you see if there's a connection between Faber and Justine Smart or Justine Franke? Better still, is Justine Franke part of the umbrella organisation, Franke Holdings?'

'Jesus, Hex, I'm not MI5.'

'You're right, scrap it.' I signed off, looked directly at Simone and brightened. 'Looks like I've been *cherchez*-ing the wrong *femme*.'

CHAPTER SIXTY-FOUR

In overdrive, I called McCallen. Never around when I needed her most, her phone went to the answering service. My eyes on Simone, I left a message to the effect that Justine Franke needed to be paid serious attention and an urgent visit in Spain.

A group of walkers came into the bar followed by a woman and a man dressed in business garb. Both wore wedding rings, only the furtive way in which they touched and talked made me think that they were not married to each other. I fleetingly wondered if they had kids. Made me think of Indie. I turned back to Simone.

'Poor Indie,' I said. 'All her illusions will be shattered.'

'Who?'

'Your half-sister. She has no idea that your mother is quite so ruthless.'

'You're well informed.'

I met her eye. 'Yes. Maybe you girls should get together. You can fill in the gaps for each other.'

Simone flicked a tight smile and cast around. 'I need to freshen up.'

I directed her towards the ladies, caught her hand as she made to go. 'I'm sorry for doubting you.'

She shrugged as if it were of no consequence.

'You never said where you went after you left Dan's,' I said.

'To the park.'

'And returned later?'

'Only to collect my car. Can I go now?' she said, brittle.

I let her hand drop. 'Sure.'

I checked my phone for calls – there were none – and warmed myself by the fire, my gaze directed to the window and clear view of the car park. I thought about Justine, the devoted wife and mother, the woman who apparently knew everything there was to know about Billy's nefarious activities, always had. Together they had built a life on lies. I tried out the scenario for size. It went something like this:

In those weeks on the run, Billy had channelled as much of his capital out of the UK as possible, the company already set up as a method to prevent the Financial Intelligence Unit from getting their claws into his assets. With me on his tail, he'd known that his survival was at risk and all through that torrid time Justine had become increasingly unhappy, worried and vengeful. When it came to it, she had his contacts in her pocket, his know-how and years of experience. How easy to send out a false trail and frame the daughter she never wanted. With that kind of cunning and several major competitors dead, Mrs Franke could be back in business within the year.

'Excuse me.'

I looked into the eyes of the female half of the business couple. She held out a woman's red leather glove to me. 'I think your friend dropped this.'

I took it. 'Kind of you to pick it up, thanks.'

'No problem.'

I moved to put it on the table and stopped. A dark stain clung to the fingers. It didn't look like blood. I lifted the leather to my nose, caught the fragrance of expensive French perfume over-laying the unmistakable smoky tang of something else, and pocketed it. Simone emerged a few moments later.

'I need to eat. I'm famished.'

'Suits me.'

We ordered sandwiches and more coffee. Conversation was stilted and unfocused, the magic we once shared gone. Afterwards, I paid and came up with a great idea.

'How would you like to the see the house you apparently own?'

Simone tipped back her head and laughed. 'I want nothing to do with it.'

'Aren't you a little bit curious? Come on, it might be fun.'

Her face clouded. 'It might be dangerous. What if my mother is there?'

'Why would she be? She's in Spain.'

'You have spoken to her?' Did I imagine a catch in her voice?

I shook my head. 'I heard a rumour. Look,' I said, taking her hand. 'You'll be with me. You'll be perfectly safe. We can nail this thing together, once and for all. What do you say?'

She thought for a moment, then spoke loud and firm. 'I say yes.'

CHAPTER SIXTY-FIVE

We travelled in her car. My idea. I wanted her attention fixed on something other than me. I gave her directions and she nodded solemnly, as though taking it all in, and chattered about nothing in particular – unusual for her, a sign of nerves, perhaps. Me, I was silent. I had ten minutes, tops, to plan how to play it. Surprise and superior knowledge had always been my strongest cards, but I was right out of Kings and Queens. The Joker in the pack had never figured in my vocabulary. You get in. You do the job. And off you fuck.

My difficulty was self-restraint. In the old days, I wouldn't have hesitated to remove a problem. True, I had neutralised the Russian in brutal self-defence as recently as a couple of weeks ago. Didn't make it right, but it was an easier position to defend. There was a difference, to my mind, between murdering to survive and murdering for gain. Would I really do it all again? Was I going to undo over a year of living a decent life? Indecision dogged me and indecision was a killer. I had no more than fifteen minutes in which to make up my mind. Whatever I decided would dictate the rest of my life.

I yawned, stretched, leant back into the soft leather.

'You are tired?'

'Bushed.'

I said nothing more. To her credit, she paused at a crossroads, made a pantomime of not knowing which route to take.

'Straight on,' I said. 'Over there.' I pointed at the gated drive. Transferred from Billy Franke, benefactor and philanthropist, to Simon Faber, charity, all above board, I didn't doubt.

'Looks like electronic gates,' she said. 'How do we get in?'

I looked across at her, my grin wolfish. 'We push them. They're open, trust me.'

She hiked an eyebrow and we both climbed out of the car. I took one gate, she the other. She could have taken me then. But I didn't think she would. There was something of the showman in the way she operated. Highly strung, she adored the thrill, the drama and theatre. And she didn't have her special bag.

We climbed back in and Simone drove on. I paid no attention to the familiar rural landmarks, the lake or the dovecot or the green expanse of fields that flanked the long and winding drive. I had other preoccupations. This was no longer about Simone and me. This was about the sort of man I was. Was I still a taker? And if I wasn't, what was the alternative? Where did my future lie? Did I have one?

She pulled up outside the black and white farmhouse, Billy's old lair. We both climbed out. The afternoon weather had taken a turn for the worst – the leaden sky was raw and joyless. I looked out across overgrown lawns to the stable block, the site of so much carnage more than a year ago.

'You have been here before?' She looked playful, with mischief in her eyes.

'I have, many times.'

Simone looked up at the house. 'It looks a little rundown, don't you think?'

She was right. An empty house deteriorates quickly, particularly in northern climates. The paintwork needed attention. Plaster around the front door flaked. Several windows on the upper storey looked rotten and unstable. 'Be good as new with TLC.'

She skipped up the steps across a patio and towards a porch, her long coat wrapped around her.

'Go inside,' I said, close behind. 'It's open.'

'But what about –'

'Justine?' I interjected. 'I already told you. Nothing to worry about.'

'And her heavies?'

'The people who roughed up your room?'

'Exactly. They might be lying in wait.' As soon as the words left her mouth, she realised her mistake. She covered it well enough, but the rare flash of colour that fled across her high cheekbones gave her away. How could she know that her room had been roughed up? She'd only collected her car, or so she'd said.

The heavy oak door emitted a gasp of pain as she pushed it open. I followed on her heels and into a collection of hollow rooms with chequerboard walls of pale and dark colour denoting where dressers and bookcases and other large pieces of furniture had once stood. The air smelt damp and musty and old. I fancied that it was overlaid with gunpowder, smoke and lubricant, the same odour that had emanated from Simone's glove.

'What a fantastic staircase,' she said, eyes alive. Linking her arm tightly through mine, she drew me close. It was a classic move. I imagined the next. Simone taking a gun from her coat, pressing the muzzle next to my ribs, pulling the trigger. Shatter and burn.

'Let's explore.' She propelled me forward and onto a wide run of six stairs, five flights in all, with elaborately carved newel posts and finials, the entire staircase created from a forest of seasoned oak. At one step per second, I calculated that I had thirty seconds to act.

We reached the top and crossed an immense landing, our footsteps loud and ringing in the empty space. Simone let go and darted from one room to another, me trailing along behind. Her mood had changed from one of reserve to exuberance. Eager to give the impression of a woman planning how to restore the house to its former splendour, how she'd arrange the furnishings, choose the colour scheme, she gave it maximum effort. I actually believed she was enjoying herself. Not me – I wanted to get it over with.

'Come and see,' she called. I crossed the floor, staking her every move, her hands clasped together, the way she looked out across the grounds with its walled gardens and pergolas, how her eyes narrowed at the vista of trees and fields visible in the distance. 'It's so terribly English.' She turned to me, her face a picture of little girl excitement.

A flash of hesitation, a moment of doubt, and it came at a price.

CHAPTER SIXTY-SIX

We drew simultaneously. Crack and flare. Her gun had been strapped to her thigh. My shot nicked the top of her left arm, a flesh wound. Hers hit my gun hand, removing the top of my little finger in one clean swipe. I wouldn't bleed out but, with my gun dead on the floor, I was out of action.

'Kick it away.' Her cold-as-night eyes glittered with triumph and hatred. They reminded me of Billy. I got it then. It all locked into place. I did as she ordered.

'Take your jacket off – slowly.'

I peeled it off with difficulty. Rivers of pain coursed through my damaged hand, which I clutched tight to my chest, holding it upright, attempting to staunch the flow of blood.

'Throw it to me.'

I complied.

'You have no reason to smile,' she said.

'I always smile when I learn the truth.'

A picture of swollen pride and arrogance, she viewed me with contempt. 'You think yourself so clever, so superior, the great untouchable Hex, the man who oozes menace.'

'Is that what your father told you?'

'I wish he could see you now.'

'You disappoint me. A daddy's girl at your age is pretty sad.'

She let off another shot. It parted the hair on my head and grazed the top of my scalp. Heat fled over me and warm blood trickled down the back of my neck. She was about to take me apart bit by painful bit. She held a Sig-Sauer P228, favoured by the US intelligence agencies, and she'd fired twice. She had eleven shots left.

'You made him suffer and now it's your turn.'

'Suffer? What about the thousands of innocent people he wanted to annihilate?'

Simone wasn't in listening mode. I doubt she ever was. 'You hounded him for months. He never slept in the same bed more than two nights. You turned his friends against him, everyone he'd ever known. You took everything from him, his family, his reputation –'

'Spare me. This is the monster who personally squeezed a guy's brains from his head because he didn't like the way the man looked at him.'

'To stay on top, you have to be strong. My father was a great man.'

'He really did a number on you, didn't he? Did you take lessons in manipulation from your daddy too?'

Pain flashed, white hot, and shot through the outside edge of my left thigh. Blood bloomed and spread across my jeans in a relentless flow. I gripped the wound tight with my good hand. I wanted to yowl. My heart rate stuttered. Adrenalin flooded my system. I hoped she read in my eyes what I really thought of her, that she was an unhinged, murderous and self-indulgent bitch.

'You're the same as the rest,' she said, cool as chilled plasma. 'I'm going to hunt you down and make you scream until you beg me to put a bullet in your brain, isn't that what you said?' she jeered. 'Now look at you, an amateur. Hayes thought he could outsmart me and Benz was a deluded fool.'

'You killed Hayes, Phipps, Dwyer and Testa and handed

McCallen to Benz?'

She nodded. 'A gift based on mutual self-interest.'

Billy had once told me that he was Jewish. I wondered whether Benz the anti-Semite ever knew that he was doing business with a Jewess.

'What about Pallenberg?'

'Again, it suited Dieter and it suited me. Pallenberg was McCallen's asset and lover.' As she said it, her eyes drilled into mine. 'Lovers make good bait, don't you think?'

'And you acted together with Benz?'

'For as long as it suited.'

'Our escape must have upset your plans.'

'An irritation, nothing more, as you can see.'

Whose idea was it to lock the door to the cellar in the hope that we'd drown?

'You can die thinking about it.'

'I have no intention of giving you that pleasure.'

Her mouth worked into an approximation of a smile. 'Have you any idea the number of times I could have taken you? It was me who pulled the light trick in Montpellier, me who took a pot shot at you in Berlin. I know where you live. I know who you see.'

'Then why didn't you kill me?'

'The clue is in the name.'

'Bagatelle,' I said. 'You play games.'

Her smile was almost proud, as if she admired my electric thinking. 'It's what I do. When and how you die will be when I decide, when I choose.'

Looked like she was close to making that decision. 'You can't win. You know that, don't you?'

She tossed back her hair. 'I've lost count of the times people say such things – always when their situation is hopeless.'

I did my best to shrug. Pain route-marched through my leg and out through my toes, every nerve ending raw and exposed.

Time to change tack. I let out a low moan, vocalised the excruciating pain I was in. I had no need to act it up. 'McCallen and the combined forces of the security services will come for you.'

'Over one dead hit man?'

She might be right. With me dead, it would be easy to pin everything on me. Flynn was halfway there, the film he had scripted already in the can. I shook my head. 'McCallen is persistent,' I gasped. 'You should know that. She won't give up, not after what Benz did to her. She knows where you are. She'll find you.'

Simone pulled a little girl face. Her mouth formed a grotesque pout. 'But McCallen isn't here now. It's simply you and me, my love.'

'Chemistry like ours is hard to find, is it not?'

'True, I've never had a woman like you.'

'I admit we're good together, you and I.' The accompanying smile was slow and seductive.

'We could work things out, Simone. You and me, think about it.'

Silence crawled into the space between us. Her face was a blank canvas, unreadable, her brain tuned out. For a moment I thought I had her. Suddenly, her lips twisted and out of her mouth burst a series of full-throttled French obscenities. Finally, she swore in my native tongue.

'Fuck you. How do you think that would honour my father?'

I would not have put Billy Squeeze and honour in the same sentence, but my opinion was of little interest to her now. The light in her eyes had died as if it had gone out inside. She was getting into the zone, her finger dancing on the trigger. I turned side-on. I didn't feel like humouring her any more.

'How did a nice girl like you become an assassin? Is it a recent career move or have you always dabbled in the dark arts?'

'I'm a quick learner, yes?'

'Exceptional.' Blood oozed through my fingers.

'I modelled myself on the very best.'

'That would be me,' I said, no smile.

'*Was* you.' For a second I thought I read pity in her expression. 'My father held you in high regard. He studied your methods, did you know that?'

In effect, I'd created a ghoul by proxy. Exhaustion swept over me. Maybe shock would get to me quicker than blood loss.

'You didn't really understand him at all,' she said, wistfully. 'I spoke the truth about my adoptive parents. I also spoke the truth about my mother.'

'Justine?'

Her dark eyes hardened. 'Yes.'

'But that would mean –'

'They were both my parents.'

'And your father loved you.'

'Like I always knew he would, as a father should love his daughter. When he found out what my mother had done, that she had given me away, he came to me even after all those years and made provision for me.'

'The house,' I said.

She nodded.

'And he turned to you when he was in trouble?'

'Where else could he go? Together, we worked out a plan, in case things should not work out.'

Hence the fancy financial arrangements. 'Does anyone else know about this?'

'Nobody but you.' Stunned by the disclosure of a long-held secret, a shutdown expression entered her face.

With this moment of dark revelation between us, the dynamics shifted. At the same time, the sound of skidding tyres on gravel rebounded through the room. Simone glanced towards the window. It was the moment I'd been hoping for.

CHAPTER SIXTY-SEVEN

Time slowed.

I lunged forward and powered hard into Simone amid shouts and gunfire. Her gun hand flew up as I connected. Metal stitched the ceiling, kicking up a sandstorm of plaster. Dust and debris half-blinded us. We both hurtled towards the window.

Fearing the drop, I dug in my heels, slowing my flight, while Simone barrelled forward. It was as if some higher force had grabbed my shoulder, fingers digging deep, and wrenched me backwards. I watched as her eyes popped wide on impact, her scream ear-shattering over the sound of breaking glass and splintering rotten wood. The drop had to be at least thirty feet onto paved stone and her car below.

I, meanwhile, lay flat on my back, choking and spluttering, and barely registered as the door exploded from its hinges. There were footsteps on bare wood and then McCallen's eyes stared down at me.

'I've never been more pleased to see you.' I meant it.

'Don't get any funny ideas. This isn't going to turn into one of those parties you enjoy so much.' She peeled off her jacket and shirt, ripped off the sleeves and, with two strips, wrapped one tight around my leg and bandaged my hand. It was the most

I'd ever seen of her in the flesh.

'How did you know I'd be here?'

'Symmetry,' she said, putting her leather back on. 'It's the seat of Billy's lost empire, where it all began.'

'Is Simone dead?'

McCallen cocked an eyebrow. 'Want me to check?'

'Yes.'

She sprang up and crossed to the shattered window, hanging back, looking down. 'Put it this way, her car has an extra spoiler.'

I thought about it. 'Does it count?'

McCallen frowned. 'Does what count?'

'That I killed her?'

'You didn't. She did that all on her own.'

'Artistic licence, surely?'

McCallen shrugged. 'No point stressing. You did what you had to do. End of. Not like you to be introspective.'

She propped me up, rang for an ambulance and called Flynn to give him a status report. From what I could make out, I was to be debriefed. I shook my head at McCallen who put the flat of her hand up to silence me. Very authoritative, I thought.

'It's procedure,' she assured me when she got off the phone. 'First off, you need medical attention.' She eyed the bandage. 'Is that your trigger hand?'

'I've lost the top of my little finger, not that it matters.'

'Of course it matters.'

She gave me a typical McCallen look, as though she had no idea what to do with me. I thought I caught a hint of something else, as though she had plans that I didn't yet know about.

'How come you've bounced back so quickly?' I was genuinely intrigued.

'Revenge,' she said, her green eyes cool and luminous.

* * *

Justine Franke's call came through when I was semi-conscious after theatre. After an initial awkward exchange, I gave her the main headlines and delivered the bad news about her eldest daughter. The line went quiet.

'Hello, Justine?'

'I said no good would come of it.'

'Of Simone?'

Another silence. 'I'm not proud of what I did, but I was only a kid. My parents acted in what they believed were my best interests. They hoped it would kill any relationship with Billy. They'd never liked him. In the end, I defied them and they cut me off.'

'So what happened later? Did Simone track you down?'

'She was only ever interested in Billy. I was the wicked mother who'd abandoned her.'

'It must have caused a few problems for your marriage.'

'It was nothing compared to what happened later.'

'I'm no lawyer, but you might now have a case to get your home back as the charity has been revealed as bogus. Are all the debts cleared?'

'Can anyone clear a debt for multiple murder?'

It struck home and she was right. We talked some more and, depressed and eager to get off the line, I was relieved when she wrapped up the call.

Against doctor's orders, I discharged myself two days later. I had ten stitches in my thigh and I'd undergone surgery on my hand. With most of my fingers and thumb intact, I could function in every respect. The wound to my leg wasn't as bad as it might have been. A few centimetres further across and it would have been a different story. Simone playing a harp and me accompanying her with spoons.

McCallen came to collect me in her souped-up Mini. I detected that it was for no other reason than she wanted something. Some things never changed. From several kilometres, I'd recognise that look in her eye, a combination of ambition and determination. When she told me we were taking a detour I knew exactly what to expect.

She drove me to a hotel out of town, the name of which I was sworn never to mention. Opulent, elegant and classy, the place oozed with calm grandeur and serenity. It was a good call, although peace was something that continued to elude me.

McCallen showed me to a private room tucked away from the main building. Decked out like a mini conference suite, it had a highly polished walnut table and six chairs, including one at each end. The colour scheme was deep red, rust and vermillion. To my eyes, it looked like several different shades of blood: old, dried and fresh.

My welcoming party consisted of Flynn; nobody else. Affable and friendly, he went to give me a firm handshake and I offered my left hand. He indicated a silver tray with cut-glass decanters, ice and glasses, asked me what I'd care to drink. I chose whisky. The softening-up approach was so blatant it made me wonder what the hell they were going to say and what leverage would be used if I refused to cooperate. Maybe they were going to throw me to the tender mercies of Mossad after all.

After handing me a glass, he invited me to sit down. We all did. Flynn at one end, McCallen opposite me. I was the only one drinking.

'How's the leg?' he said, solicitous.

'It will heal.'

'And the hand?'

'It works.'

'I've read McCallen's full report. All right if I touch on a couple of minor issues with you?'

'Feel free.' I tipped the glass to my lips and took a drink and listened.

The issues were so minor they weren't worth the airtime. Having clarified things that were already so transparent you could see through them, Flynn sat back and smiled. I smiled back and glanced across at McCallen.

'If that's it, I'll leave you to it. Wouldn't want to take up any more of your time.' I might as well have been talking to the painting on the wall. They went into collective lockdown.

'This is your second outing with us, isn't it?' Flynn said.

'I wouldn't put it like that.'

'How would you put it?'

I glared at McCallen, who smiled. 'Our paths crossed, nothing more. You do what you have to do. I did what I had to do. End of.' The smile vanished.

'You have unusual skills,' Flynn said.

'Which I no longer choose to use.'

'Pity.'

I took another swallow of booze. 'Do the British public know that the security service outsources work to known assassins?'

'That's a little crude, surely?'

'Is it? In any case, I thought you had your own wet ops team.'

McCallen cleared her throat. 'I think what Flynn means is that we'd appreciate calling upon you for certain specialist assignments.'

'I wouldn't get clearance.'

'Not in an official capacity,' Flynn said with delicacy.

I got it. 'In which case I'd be deniable and expendable.'

To his credit, Flynn made no attempt to dispute my claim or put me at ease. 'You have my personal guarantee that you'd be paid extremely well.'

'I'm not interested in money.'

'What are you interested in?'

'Self-respect. Doing the right thing. Getting up in the morning and being able to look in the mirror without flinching, knowing that I'm going to do an honest day's work that doesn't involve killing someone.' I sounded as agitated as I felt. Justine's simple question, 'Can anyone clear a debt for multiple murder?' had rattled me. I might never be eligible for redemption but if these people undermined my desire to live a better life, I was screwed.

'Is that your final word?'

'It is.'

Flynn got up and stuck out his hand again. I stood and shook, and McCallen, tight-faced, escorted me out. I could tell she was fuming because she didn't look at me, didn't speak. Every traffic light against us, a proliferation of road works and potholes in the tarmac, the mildly uncomfortable drive back took longer than it should have.

'Stop the car,' I said as we hit town. 'You can drop me here.'

McCallen pulled over and slammed on the brakes. I jerked forward. 'Fuck, that hurt,' I growled.

She cut the engine. 'Are you simply stupid, or stubborn? You can't walk back.'

'It's not far.'

'Hex, we're in Prestbury. You live in Tivoli.'

She treated me to a stare that would make a taipan slither away. I know when to give in gracefully. I flashed an easy smile. 'I didn't realise it was a door-to-door service.'

She looked at me for a moment and, against every effort to do otherwise, relaxed. 'Sorry about the leg. Are you okay?'

'If it turns septic I'll know who to blame.'

She let out a laugh. It sounded great. Starting the engine, she checked the rear-view and pulled out. Now that we were back on speaking terms, she finally opened up.

'Why did you turn down Flynn's offer?'

'You know why.'

'I know what you said. I don't know what you meant.'

Nettled, I gave her a sharp look. 'I thought honour and justice were good enough reasons.'

'They are perfect reasons, which is exactly why you should reconsider. Honour and justice lie at the heart of what we do.'

I made a noise, one part cynicism, two parts incredulity.

319

'The real reason you turned us down,' McCallen continued, 'is to save your own skin. I thought you were better than that.'

I opened my mouth to protest, but McCallen was unstoppable. 'Hear me out. You have all the talents needed for a good spy. You can live with secrecy. You understand that sometimes people get hurt who don't deserve it, yet it doesn't turn you into a gibbering heap. Your mental muscles are strong, your instincts sharp. You can still carry on living here, doing what you do. We'd only call on you for the more unusual gigs.'

'The dirty gigs, you mean.'

'The difficult ones, yes. It's an honourable calling.'

'And Mossad?'

'I'm sure we could come to an accommodation with them.'

We had turned into my street and McCallen drove me to my door. She leant across, engine running, and dropped a soft kiss on my mouth. 'Think about it,' she said.

'There's nothing –'

'Do you want to spend the rest of your life in the cheap seats?' She pressed her index finger against my lips to brook all argument. Her smile was pure titanium. I clambered out.

Standing on the pavement, I watched as she tooted her horn and drove away. The sun popped out from behind a cloud, enveloping me in sudden heat and light. I tipped my head briefly to the sky, felt the warmth of its rays on my skin, and then hobbled to the front door. I had plenty to think about.

ESSAY ON FINAL TARGET

The desire for revenge is primeval. It's not considered to have a place in civilised society but, let's face it, we all know what it feels like to want to 'get one's own back' on someone who has hurt us, or those we love, although the extremes to which we're prepared to go probably don't mutate into murder even if we feel murderous. For this reason vengeance is a popular theme in thrillers and crime fiction. It's a gift to a writer simply because it creates the maximum opportunity to slip off those kid gloves and let rip with the action. In 'Final Target,' the old adage 'Hell hath no fury …' is *the* point, hence the creation of sexy Simone Fabron. Women, when they seek retribution, can be very bad indeed.

As much as 'Final Target' is a 'whodunnit,' it's also a 'whydunnit', and this is the aspect of characterisation that interests me most as a writer. In a sense, we're all amateur psychologists and I'm very much in the camp of people aren't born bad, but created, often through a host of complex and converging reasons that don't need to be discussed here. Suffice to say that I don't believe any of us are immune. Given the right circumstances, most of us can be corrupted by life events and, consequently, behave appallingly. It's this motivation, which, for me, holds a certain fascination. Almost more compelling is the horrific chain reaction that can spring from a single malign act. Luckily, this kind of thing is easier to chart in fiction than control in real life.

Any reader familiar with my stories will recognise that I'm a fan of redemptive themes. Having made a pretty good start to redeeming himself towards the end of 'A Deadly Trade,' Hex is still working on his path back to what passes for a decent life in 'Final Target'. But, in addition to a high body count, conflict is the name of the game in thrillers so right from the get-go, Hex struggles with his natural instinct, which is to revert to type. For me, it was an easy sell. Having spent his adult life devoted to the next 'job', the buzz and thrill of the chase, Hex was never going to credibly settle into a 9 to 5, with weekends and Sunday roast lifestyle. He'd find it far too mundane. Fortunately, Inger McCallen, Hex's weak spot – every main protagonist needs at least one – and voice of conscience, turns his new life upside down on the opening page and rescues him from a slow death from boredom.

I love McCallen. Smart, competitive and ambitious, she's a woman who works to her own agenda. Their 'will they, won't they' get it together relationship is a deliberately teasing, fun element in the book. Aside from serving a primary role as joint 'sleuth', McCallen allows Hex to explore that streak of sensitivity that passes for his emotional side and makes him more attractive.

Did I face any difficulties or dilemmas when writing the novel? Yes, there was one. It's virtually impossible to write a contemporary story with more than a passing nod to espionage, without referring to technology in some form or another. This was made doubly difficult because the novel is set in Cheltenham, which is home to the U.K's third intelligence service: GCHQ. In fiction, as in life, there is heavy emphasis on the way we are tracked, watched and studied by unseen powers with the kind of sophisticated technology that can identify, not only the terrorist at a distance, but the brand of cigarette he or she smokes. Technology plays a huge role in all our lives and the UK has possibly more CCTV than any other country in Europe. We all believe that we are under surveillance 24/7 and that the chances of pulling off a crime are zero. And yet, we also know that individuals can and do get away with murder, that crimes remain unsolved, that people evade capture, sometimes for decades, that folk disappear without trace, and that, sadly, airplanes can mysteriously vanish. In the spy world, there are advocates of what's described as 'humint' – intelligence gained from human sources, and 'sigint', which makes up the volume of intelligence, from signals and technical communication. Both systems of obtaining information have advantages and disadvantages, which is why a combination of both is used by security services throughout the world. Some believe that, irrespective of the massive amount of data gleaned from sigint (machines), the gathering of human intelligence from assets provides a closer explanation of why people do what they do. It's also worth remembering that even the most advanced technology is only as a good as the person operating the system. As a writer, this is what interests me and, for that reason, I've concentrated on the human element in the story, sometimes at the expense of the technical. In 'Final Target', the powers that be may well have an inkling of what our main man is up to but, for political considerations, are willing to sit back and let him run his own course and, more importantly, take the flak and the fall for what unfolds. Cutting to the chase, the importance of gadgetry in this work is understated. I hope readers, who are fans of uber-technology, will be forgiving.

Eve Seymour, Cheltenham 2014.

ACKNOWLEDGEMENTS

As ever, my thanks to my agent Broo Doherty at D H H Literary Agency; Martin Hay and Paul Swallow at Cutting Edge Press; to Sean Costello for incisive editorial comment and correction and, last but not least, to Ian Seymour for reading early drafts.

I'm indebted to Paul Barrett, fire officer at Gloucestershire Fire and Rescue Service for providing technical information in the cellar scenes. Immensely patient, he was also generous with creative input. If I have inadvertently made any technical errors, the fault is mine alone.

Again, I'm indebted to the works of two writers who have expert knowledge on matters of national security. These are Gordon Thomas: 'Gideon's Spies' and Christopher Andrew: 'The Defence of the Realm.'

I'm not sure a writer has ever thanked a town before, but I'd like to thank Cheltenham where most of the action takes place. I've taken one or two liberties for dramatic purposes and hope locals will not be offended.